Sign up for our newsletter to hear
about new and upcoming releases.

www.ylva-publishing.com

OTHER BOOKS IN THE SUPERHEROINE COLLECTION

CHASING STARS

ALEX K. THORNE

Ylva
THE
SUPERHEROINE
COLLECTION

DEDICATION

For A, who always makes me feel like a superhero.

(And for N, who made me put her here.)

ACKNOWLEDGMENTS

My thanks go to Lee, whose insights and edits made this story better than I could ever have imagined.

To Astrid, at Ylva, who took a chance on me. Your support has been invaluable.

To Ellen, who constantly inspires me to be a better writer.

To Judd, my techno Yoda.

To the coven for your loving encouragement—Tree, for listening to me read scenes out loud, Syd, for your enthusiasm, Tash, for your artistic contributions, Mum and Nas, for believing in me despite never actually finishing the book, and Gran, who made the best test audience.

And, finally, to my better half, without whom the very first incarnation of this story would have been absent those silly semi-colons and em dashes.

PROLOGUE

THE SHIP CRASHED 200,000 LIGHT-YEARS away from the icy cold spaceport where it had first taken off.

It happened violently and without warning—a meteor storm that pulverized the shell of the ship like a swarm of angry brittawasps. The nine hundred beings on board the broken explorer vessel hurtled toward an unfamiliar blue-green planet that the sonar maps called Earth.

The ship, all sixty-five tons of seloridium and glass, shattered apart in the middle of a hot, sandy expanse they would later discover was the Mojave Desert. The Aquels were the first to go. Their nebulous bodies shriveled under the hot sun, and they died screaming in agony. The Setokyi were next, choked by the planet's air as their four lungs filled with noxious oxygen. They turned a sickly yellow before they collapsed.

Three hundred survived the crash, but only one hundred ninety-seven passengers of the *Andromeda Voyager* were still alive when the tanks and helicopters arrived. One hundred ninety-seven passengers representing two quadrants, six planets, and seventeen races.

Ten-year-old Ava'Kia Vala of the planet Zrix'dhor was among the survivors. Her family was not.

When the men in black suits arrived, she was lost in a panicked crowd of Keelas, Nxases, Amoorties, Sqosdkorlias, Yanagharians, and a host of races whose names she had never learned.

They would become known as the Andromeda Orphans.

CHAPTER 1

"My hero!"

Ava rolled her eyes and tried not to smile at her best friend's dramatics. Nic was batting her eyelashes, with her hand pressed over her heart as though swooning.

"You're an ass, you know that?" Ava moved her arm, yanking the offered box of donuts out of Nic's reach. "You don't deserve a chocolate cruller."

"Okay, no, no! I'm sorry," Nic said, making grabby hands at the box. "Don't take them away from me."

"Just pick one already." Ava shook the box impatiently and Nic wiggled her fingers above it, contemplating. She went with a classic jelly donut and took an impressive bite.

"The OG never fails to disappoint," she mumbled through a mouth covered in powdered sugar, which made Ava grin.

They were on the roof of one of LA's tallest buildings. Nic had discovered the roof-access staircase on her first day as a junior science engineer at RainnTech, almost five years prior. Most of the company's employees stayed hidden away in their cubicles or in one of the building's basement labs. The staff canteen rivaled Google's, and had everything caffeine-deprived, Soylent-chugging employees could ask for, so no one ever considered actually going outside, let alone to the roof. It had quickly become one of their favorite chill spots.

The wind picked up and whipped Ava's flyaway blonde hair across her face, tickling her nose. She rubbed it with the back of her hand and inadvertently got the tip sticky with jelly.

"So, I'm working late tonight, which means you can't watch *Stranger Things* without me." Nic wiped Ava's nose with her thumb and leaned back with her palms spread out behind her as her feet dangled off the edge of the skyscraper. She was sitting hip-to-hip with Ava, whose cape flapped behind them.

"Come on! You've already seen it."

The air was growing warmer, and the morning smell changed from dew to coffee and car fumes. It was almost time for work.

"Yeah, but you know it's not as fun when I'm not there to document your reactions. My Snapchat audience will be so disappointed."

"Oh, gosh! Not the Snapchat audience!" Ava said, but conceded. "Fine, I'll wait."

Nic smiled with triumph and stuffed the last of the donut into her mouth.

Ah, the pros and cons of living with your best friend, Ava thought.

The sky had gone from pink to blue in a second, and the sun was already hot against Ava's skin. A typical Los Angeles morning.

Closing her eyes, Ava tuned into the sounds of the city. Below, cars honked as they inched along congested highways. A door slammed shut, a keypad was being pushed, someone on the 405 turned up their music and Ava winced—it was too early for heavy metal. Her eyes flared open at the sound of the screech. Tires against asphalt and the smell of burning rubber. Ava stood tensely, orientating herself, and trying to find the source of the screech.

She glanced at Nic, who immediately recognized the look on her face and waved Ava off with a flick of her wrist.

Ava shot into the sky like a bullet, a rocket, a bird.

She saw it in slow motion—the rusted pick-up slamming on the brakes but hitting the shiny Porsche in front of it anyway, the Porsche ramming into the SUV ahead of it, the SUV breaking through the barrier and hurtling down the hill.

She took it all in—the screams, the shattered glass, the crack of bone. Ava dove towards the falling car.

The speed at which she flew created what Nic called a wind aura, which acted as both a protective shield and a force that allowed Ava to stop and move large objects without touching them. It had taken her a long time to learn how to regulate her speed, to know how far away she needed to be

3

from an object to avoid crushing it with the intensity of the force. Nic had tried to explain it with equations on a whiteboard, but in the end, it was practice that made perfect. The old car lot on the edge of town was filled with her failed attempts.

She shot around the SUV in an energy burst, the blue, black, and yellow of her suit creating a dizzying blur around the car. Ava's ears hummed as she flew in the wind tunnel of white noise that blocked out all other sound.

She could feel the energy force as if it were a tangible thing. The faster she flew, the warmer it became, and Ava knew that if she got too close to the car, it would crumple like a soda can. Slowly, she moved. Higher and higher, pulling the SUV along in her wind tunnel.

Eventually, she had the car high enough to move it to the road, and she slowed until her form was visible and the car dropped with a gentle thud.

A crowd had formed, as it usually did, and Ava could hear the paramedics on their way. She quickly adjusted her mask. She had always known that she wanted to keep Swiftwing separate from Ava. It was either a mask or a full cowl, and while Ava appreciated anonymity, she also hated the way the full cowl made her look like a small Mexican wrestler. In the end, vanity won out and she went with the mask. Nic had jokingly call her Blue Zorro, before the media dubbed her Swiftwing.

Inside the car, a mother and two children—both, thankfully, strapped in car seats—were crying and shaking, trauma still clinging to them.

Ava opened the door to the front and helped the woman out. She stumbled on shaky legs and wrapped her arms around Ava's neck to steady herself. Cameras flashed from all over, as two dozen onlookers whipped out their phones.

"Bless you, Swiftwing," the woman sobbed, before scrambling to get to her children. The littlest one, who looked to be about two or three, had stopped crying and was sucking on her thumb. Her wide, wet eyes were fixed on Ava. She smiled, and the toddler smiled back.

They were shaken up, but they'd be fine.

Ava, however, was less fine. At the sound of the paramedics, she surreptitiously looked down at her watch.

Shit.

Late for work.

At the security booth of the studio lot, Ava flashed the parking attendant a smile and her badge. She pulled into her regular parking spot, and was in and out of the café on the lot in record time. Being late *and* arriving without caffeine might be grounds for termination.

Ava moved through the backlot with familiarity, past sound stages and exterior sets, past offices and people on bicycles and golf carts, rushing off to get to set or deliver a prop.

The sound of drilling and hammering filled the air. Ava enjoyed being back here. The past few months had been a whirlwind of press tours and hotel rooms, red carpets and plane trips. She had missed being part of this fickle family of crew members.

Weaving her way through trailers, she heard the voices before she saw their speakers.

She'd have recognized the American-British accent and specifically enunciated cadence of Gwen Knight's voice from halfway across the world. The other voice took her a moment to place.

Rounding the corner, she saw Ron Gooding—Gwen's co-star and *People Magazine*'s Sexiest Man Alive for two years running—leaning against Gwen's trailer, his perfectly chiseled face set in a scowl.

"Ron, darling, you were the one who proposed this," Gwen was saying as she pushed her fingers through her hair. It had been colored dark for the movie—almost black. Ava thought it made Gwen look like a classic cinema goddess—like Rita Hayworth or Ava Gardner. It suited her, Ava thought, not for the first time. She knew that Gwen's mother was British and her father Cuban. The dark hair seemed to bring out the olive in her skin and the green of her eyes. Ava was caught between staring at Gwen's face and actually listening to what she and Ron were saying.

"I didn't know that she'd want to be exclusive when I agreed—" Ron stopped as Ava moved closer. He pushed off the trailer and crossed his arms over his chest. The wink he directed at Ava was charming in an obvious sort of way, but she found herself blushing. He was fresh off the latest *Bourne* movie—the first black actor cast in the role. His casting had sent Twitter into a flurry, and even critics all agreed on one thing—the man was charming.

Gwen's expression had changed too. She was looking at Ron with an exasperated frown, and he turned to her before leaning in and whispering something in her ear that made her lips pull tightly together in a sort of smile.

Ava watched the exchange with interest. She hadn't realized they were this close. Gwen was not known for making friends on set.

Ava came toward them and cleared her throat awkwardly. "Your, uh... your coffee, Miss Knight."

Gwen shoved Ron off and turned her attention to Ava. "Eisenberg. Finally. Did you get lost somewhere between falling out of bed and getting to the lot?"

"Sorry." Ava came forward, holding out the coffee, which Gwen took. "Traffic was bad on Melrose. I think there was an accident."

Gwen sighed, taking a sip of her standard almond macadamia milk latte with a smidge of maple syrup. Ava made sure the café stocked a specific Colombian brand exclusively for Gwen's morning caffeine shot.

"I should probably get to make-up," Ron said, looking between them.

"Tonight, then." Gwen gave him a pointed look, and Ava tried to decipher the expression on Ron's face before he walked off.

Gwen watched him go, then turned a sharp gaze to Ava. "What?"

"Nothing." Ava drank her own coffee in quiet contemplation. This was a sort of ritual for them. Ava arrived every morning with two cups. On Fridays, she brought donuts, and Gwen would complain about how they were nothing but sugar and fat, and entirely too sweet. By lunch time, she would have eaten two.

"Come on." Gwen gracefully ascended the steps of her trailer, leaving Ava to follow.

It always surprised Ava how comfortable Gwen's trailer felt. The 46-foot-long on-set home had been featured on *Celebrity Spaces* the year before. It was designed by some French interior decorator whose name Ava wouldn't even try to pronounce. It was light, and open and homey—gray couches with bright throw pillows. There was even a little bookshelf and desk for when Gwen's ten-year-old son came to set after school. Ava had spent countless afternoons helping Luke with his homework while his mom was off dangling in front of green screens.

Gwen settled on that expensive couch and opened the morning's *Washington Post* as Ava retrieved a bottle of LaCroix from the fridge with one hand and pulled up the day's shooting schedule on her tablet with the other.

There was a certain predictability to their mornings that Ava appreciated. Their interplay, born out of years of working together, was like gravity, a universal constant.

Ava could feel Gwen's eyes dart up from the paper a few times, and she tried not to squirm. She always got a bit twitchy when Gwen stared too hard or for too long.

Eventually, Ava lifted her gaze from the bright tablet screen to meet Gwen's stare. It was a weirdly charged moment, with Ava questioning and Gwen looking faintly caught-out. But then Gwen tilted her chin up, just a fraction, and she was all certainty and confidence, and Ava thought she must have been imagining anything different.

"I need you to make me a reservation at the Abortorium for tomorrow tonight." Gwen set the newspaper aside and gave her full attention to Ava, who was already making a note. The Abortorium was impossible to get into without at least a three-month reservation, unless you were Gwen Knight— superstar, philanthropist and *TIME*'s 2014 Person of the Year runner-up (she'd come in behind the vice-president).

"Book it under Ronald Gooding, but mention I'll be accompanying." Gwen's eyes stayed on Ava's face, as if daring her to ask about it, but Ava only nodded, her mind whirring with questions.

"Gooding. Got it."

Gwen went back to reading, while Ava tapped on her tablet, distracted. She knew for a fact that Gwen was not particularly interested in Ron Gooding—or she thought she did.

Production on *Losing Neptune* had gotten off to a rocky start. Gwen had insisted on British theater darling Aziz Kothari as her leading man, but Kothari had had prior commitments. Gooding had been the studio's choice. He wasn't particularly known for his serious roles, and it was no secret that Gwen considered this to be her shot at the Oscars. Six times nominated, but no win.

Gwen was convinced that her politics made her controversial, while Ava had a theory that it was because Gwen made her throw out any projects produced or directed by old white men. There went Scorsese, Spielberg, Cameron, and Weinstein. She'd made an exception for Jean-Pierre Jeunet a few years prior, which had earned Gwen her second César Award. As a general rule, however, she preferred female-helmed projects.

This one was particularly close to her heart, Ava knew. She remembered how hard Gwen had fought for it, finally signing on as a producer. She was playing a defense lawyer whose client was accused of murder. The client in question also happened to be one of the Andromeda Orphans. The film was loosely inspired by a real trial that had occurred a few years back.

Considering Gwen's very vocal feelings about the casting, it surprised Ava that she and Gooding had seemed so cozy earlier, and even more so that they should be having dinner together.

"Oh, and Eisenberg?" Ava jolted, pulled out of her musings at the sound of Gwen's voice.

"Get me the name of the person responsible for Jennifer Aniston's wedding cake. The lime ganache was inspired." Gwen tapped her finger against her lips. "Also, find out if that ginger hobbit, currently top of the charts, is available to play at a private function in two weeks."

"Planning a wedding, Miss Knight?" Ava chuckled. Gwen had been married three times, according to her most recent biography, and swore she'd never do it again.

"Don't be absurd." Gwen turned a page of the newspaper. "I'm paying someone to do it for me."

Ava heard the words, but didn't quite make sense of them for a moment or two. "I'm sorry, what? To whom? I mean, who is..." She frowned, frustrated by her own inarticulate spluttering. "Married?"

Gwen spared her a glance. "Close your mouth, Eisenberg. Before something flies in there."

Ava shut her mouth with a snap as Gwen stood, smoothed down the skirt of her dress, and sauntered past to the kitchen.

"Ronald and I have become...close."

Ava was still frowning. "Ron? Ron Gooding?"

"Of course, Ron Gooding. Keep up, darling."

"So, you're..." Ava squinted in confusion. "You're marrying Ron Gooding?"

"Eventually." Gwen opened the fridge and then closed it again, all restless energy. "The engagement will be announced in a few weeks." She walked back to the couch and sat down. "I'm only telling you this because you'll be helping with the party."

"The party," Ava echoed.

"I'm thinking Swarovski crystals, tear-drop chandeliers. We'll have to have it at Mario's new restaurant, of course."

"Crystal, restaurant, of course." Ava wondered what a stroke felt like. "I, um…" She shook her head. "I didn't know you two were…"

"And why would you?" Gwen raised a perfectly shaped eyebrow. "You arrange my social life. You're not a part of it."

Ava blinked, and cleared her throat. "I-I didn't mean to imply… I'm just surprised."

"Yes, well." Gwen shrugged. "He suits my needs accordingly."

"Your needs? Oh." She floundered. Should she say congratulations? Was that even appropriate? "I wish you all the best, Miss Knight."

Ava wondered if she imagined the little flicker of displeasure on Gwen's face. "Your endorsement is noted. Now…" Ava looked back at her expectantly. "I'm going to need you to call Shayne. I need a dress for tonight. I'm thinking something bold, metallic, whatever. It has to be memorable."

"What's tonight?" Ava planned Gwen's schedule meticulously. She could recite it in her sleep, and she knew for a fact that Gwen was off tonight.

The corners of Gwen's mouth curled up. "I'm accompanying Ronald to the BET Awards."

Ava coughed to mask her choked noise of surprise. "The Black Entertainment Awards?"

"Is there a problem?" Gwen's voice was clipped, and Ava bit down on her lips and shook her head.

"Nope. No. Uh. It's just that you're so…" *White*. "… busy with… stuff."

"Reschedule whatever you need to." Gwen waved her hand. "I want those dresses here by noon." She stood and looked down at Ava, seeming satisfied. "Time for make-up."

As she breezed out, Ava was left shell-shocked and speechless.

Dresses, lime ganache, reservations.

It was going to be a long day.

"It makes absolutely no sense!" Ava landed on the ground with a whump and sprang to her feet to face Horace, the seven-foot tin robot. Horace was programmed to take down anything with a heat signature.

Nic sat behind a glass panel, cackling gleefully over a monitor as she manipulated the robot with a controller that made Ava think of an arcade game joystick.

"I don't know," Nic sang out as she thrust the controller forward, prompting Horace to ram into Ava, who blocked and hovered off the ground, just high enough to kick its head off its shoulders.

"She might be egotistical and narcissistic and possibly a little unstable—" Nic's fingers fluttered over a series of buttons beside the joystick, and Horace's head reattached itself, much to Ava's annoyance.

"She's not unstable." Ava landed a dropkick against Horace's knee and the robot stumbled back.

"But," Nic continued, ignoring her protest, "some people are into that whole whip and smirk thing."

"Whip and smirk?" Ava dodged a punch by levitating backwards with her arms flung out.

"Oh, you know what I mean. She likes the power." Nic pushed her thumb down on the tip of the joystick, and laser beams shot out of Horace's eyes.

"Since when does he do that?!" Ava yelled, patting her head where the laser had almost singed her hair.

"Since I added it this morning." Nic grinned.

She was constantly tweaking Horace according to Ava's progress. In the beginning, when they had first started training, he was barely more than a titanium punching bag. Nic, who seemed to have a knack for finding hidden places, had put him together in the building's supply closet. Of course, supply closet was a bit of an understatement, considering that the "closet" was the size of an Ikea warehouse. Nic had found an area in the back where she could happily and privately work on her projects. It eventually became less of a craft room and more of a superhero training den.

That was almost a year ago, when Ava was learning defense techniques from YouTube videos and taking mixed martial arts at the Y.

"So, you're quick and you can fly," she remembered Nic saying to her one night, when Ava had come home all bruised and bleeding. "That doesn't make you invulnerable."

Ava had wiped her bloody knuckles against her jaw, the bruise already fading. "I heal fast," she had replied, knowing Nic was right. Nic, who had known her since she'd first arrived on Earth, who knew her better than anyone.

"If you're serious about this superhero thing, Ava, then you're going to have to learn how to fight. You can barely throw a punch," Nic had countered.

Ava would have argued then, but Nic had been right. Her Zrix'dhorian biology reacted differently on this planet. After the crash, Ava had found she was capable of impossible things. Flying came first and was the most obvious. Flying to get away from the crash site, to escape the black vans and guns. At first, she had thought it might have been a dream, but then she noticed her enhanced hearing—the way she could detect the mailman's footsteps three houses away, or the engines of a plane 35,000 feet up. Her reflexes had come next. It had taken a summer of catching fireflies between her fingertips for her to realize that she was not just quick, but inhumanly so.

Finally, she'd mastered flying. It wasn't just a fluke, or something triggered by adrenaline, but an intrinsic part of her. By then, Ava had learnt how to control her hearing and hide her reflexes. But flying had made trying to be normal impossible.

She dodged Horace's laser beams by running along the side of the wall, in a move that had Nic whistling. "Been practicing that one?"

Ava laughed. "Shut up. You're impressed."

"So anyway," Nic said, slowing Horace down slightly as Ava leaned over with her hands on her knees, taking a breath. "Maybe Ron Goodlooking will be good for her."

Ava punched Horace in the shoulder, causing the robot to stumble backwards.

"Love might melt the ice queen's heart," Nic continued.

"Love?" Ava looked to the window, where Nic was furiously stabbing at two buttons. She missed the way Horace came at her, and in a second, she was on the ground, looking up at the robot's face. It was as smug as an expressionless face could be. "You think she loves him?" Ava asked, winded and splayed out on the ground.

Nic powered down Horace, and cranked a lever that opened the training room door with a heavy groan.

"Why are you so hung up on this?" Nic gave Horace's head a proud pat.

Ava scoffed and wheezed. "I'm not...hung up."

"I'm just saying," Nic reached out a hand to pull her up, "methinks the lady doth protest too much."

"The lady dothn't do anything, except get fired if she doesn't help plan her boss's perfect engagement party."

Nic laughed. "You know you only talk about yourself in the third-person when you're stressed out."

"Shut up," Ava replied, but she was laughing too.

Nic flung an arm over Ava's shoulders and they walked out of the room. "Does this mean I'm not on the guest list?"

By the time Ava returned home, she was ready for a long shower and a date with the only boys she'd ever really been into—Ben and Jerry. It had been the kind of day that could only be saved if it ended in ice cream. It didn't help that she'd been barely out of RainnTech's basement when her police scanner had reported an incident on the subway. A bomb threat had been called in, but the bomb squad had come up with nothing. They needed Swiftwing's ears to check for anything abnormal, just to be sure. And so, Ava had flown in, closed her eyes, blocked everything out, and *listened*. The scurry of rat paws under tracks, the drip of a pipe somewhere in the tunnel, the bustle of feet overhead, but no tick, no beep, and no bomb.

As usual, the cops seemed both relieved and annoyed to have her there. Some thought she made their jobs redundant, others resented the media attention Swiftwing brought. At the same time, they couldn't deny that LA's resident hero made them all feel safer.

By the time Ava left, her hair smelled of smoke, and her cape was stained with subway dirt.

It had been Ava's adoptive mother Rachel who had come up with the costume idea. Back when Ava was little and the memories of Zrix'dhor were fresh, she would tell stories of her people, and what she remembered of the glass-domed city where she was raised. It was the Zrix'dhorians who had first proposed an interplanetary voyager craft. They were explorers. Star-Chasers, they were called. Rachel would listen, encouraging young Ava to remember. And when Ava had first nervously told Rachel about her plan to become Swiftwing, Rachel had suggested modeling the costume on Zrix'dhorian imperial armor.

Her current suit was the third prototype. It helped that her best friend was a techie-genius.

They had both been seniors—Ava at UCLA and Nic on scholarship at Caltech—when Nic was headhunted. "A black, middle-class, Compton kid at Caltech," Ava remembered Nic saying with a laugh. She'd planned to go into biotechnology, but then RainnTech had offered the freedom to do what she'd always wanted—play with cool shit.

The organization focused its energies on creating security devices (the word "weapon" was never used) that protected against attacks by the less "civilized" Andromeda Orphans.

Andromeda Orphans. Ava had never liked that name. She hadn't been an orphan on the *Andromeda*. She'd had a mother, an older brother, friends—a family.

Ava changed out of her work clothes and the suit underneath. It clung uncomfortably after a day in the LA sun. She didn't feel the heat as intensely as humans, but her sweat glands still worked, and she was grateful for the suit's moisture-wicking material.

By eight-thirty, Ava was spread out on the couch, with an empty Tupperware that once contained carbonara pasta and a half-eaten pint of Cherry Garcia on the coffee table. She was switching between the news on two different channels. Ava wondered how many lives she'd have to save to balance out the heinous crime of watching *Stranger Things* without Nic.

In the end, she decided she'd never be able to make it up, and flipped until she came to a channel that was broadcasting the BET red carpet. Ava sat up quickly, nearly dropping her spoon. She had almost forgotten that Gwen was going to be there—which seemed ridiculous, considering how she'd spent most of her afternoon preoccupied with the thought.

Except, Gwen wasn't there—or if she was, she certainly wasn't on the arm of Ron Gooding, who had turned up with some pop-singer-slash-model who looked barely old enough to be out on a school night. Ava was still wondering where her boss was when her phone buzzed. Darth Vader's "Imperial March" filled the apartment—Gwen was calling.

Ava leapt up to grab her phone from the table, vaguely registering two new texts from Nic.

"Miss Knight. Hi. What's up?"

Ava could hear Gwen breathing on the other end of the line. "I…"

"Miss Knight?"

"I'm out of ice cream," Gwen said in a clipped tone. Calling at this hour was entirely in character; many a time, Ava had been called out of bed to appease one of Gwen's whims. Sometimes it was midnight waffles, sometimes a 5 a.m. green smoothie.

But there was something different about this time. The hesitation in Gwen's voice, the fact that she hadn't shown up at the awards ceremony, and just…a gut feeling.

"Do you…" Ava started. "Would you like some? I can walk to Salt & Straw. It's like, literally a block away." Ava knew that Gwen knew that.

"No." She sounded tired. "It's…forget it."

"Miss Knight, are you sure you're—"

"Good night, Eisenberg," Gwen said and hung up.

For the second time that day, Ava was left feeling confused, a little helpless, and completely distracted by Gwendolyn Knight.

CHAPTER 2

AVA WOKE UP IN A mood that matched the weather. The rain had been intermittent throughout the night, and the morning gave way to dull, muted sunshine.

She was restless and fidgety as she pulled up to the studio lot and made her way to the café. It was an early call morning, and Ava was still yawning when she almost walked into Daniel Cho—Gwen's long-suffering publicist.

"Watch it, Sunshine." Daniel hopped back to avoid a collision. He was perfectly dressed, as usual, in a grey suit, with slicked back hair. Ava had no idea how old Daniel actually was. She knew he'd been working with Gwen since forever, so he couldn't be as young as he looked. "You're here early."

Ava yawned at him. "So are you."

They had, over the years, developed the sort of grudging bond that comes from being together in the trenches. At the same time, they both tended to vie for Gwen's attention, and she guessed that they were both surprised the other had lasted so long. Ava knew that Daniel put up with almost as much crap as she did.

"What are you doing here anyway?" Daniel usually worked out of the Third Planet Production offices across town.

Daniel shrugged. "I'm meeting with another client while Gwen's playing hooky. What's your excuse?"

"Wait," Ava frowned. "I thought they were shooting the courtroom interiors today."

"Change of schedule." Daniel adjusted his satchel and managed to look superior. "You didn't get the alert?"

Ava shook her head and pulled out her phone. "I guess I missed it."

Daniel pointed at Ava's phone. "Oh my God. Is that you?"

Ava had forgotten she'd set her lock screen for the sole purpose of annoying Nic. The picture was one of herself and Nic at twelve, with Rachel in the background. It was one of Ava's favorites. It was also the year that Nic decided to get braids, and the ends of her dark hair were tied with little rainbow hair ties. In the picture, they had their arms around each other, and Ava was grinning. Her honey-blonde hair was pushed under a Six Flags baseball cap, and she was all sun-kissed and freckled. Rachel was making a face in the background. Although already fully gray in the picture, she must have been only about forty-something.

"Early 2000s chic." She shoved her phone pack in her pocket and asked begrudgingly, "Do you know why the schedule changed?"

He offered her a pained expression. "Gwen's licking her wounds after last night's incident. God, if I had a dollar for every time I had to do damage control for—"

"What incident?" Ava asked with some frustration.

"You don't know? Gwendolyn and Ronald had a rather public tiff last night before the BETs. Witnesses overheard Ron going on about how things were different now and yada yada yada. The rest is all rumors clogging up my inbox."

Ava's mind raced. Well, that was clearly why Gwen had skipped the awards. "You know about Gooding?"

Daniel gave her a look suggesting it was a stupid question, but Ava brushed it off.

"What's the deal with them?"

"What has she told you?" Daniel asked cautiously.

"That they're like, engaged?" Ava managed to sound even more appalled by the notion than she had the day before.

"Yeeeah." Daniel looked skeptical. "I'm not buying it. I have spent too many drunken evenings with that woman to believe that she's into that dimwitted beefcake."

"Have you spoken to her?"

"She was less than charming on the phone last night, so..." Daniel grimaced. "Better you than me."

Ava stared at her phone for about twenty seconds after Daniel walked away. She was usually the first to know if anything changed in Gwen's schedule. It was her job to know. The fact that she had no idea where Gwen was, coupled with the weird phone call the night before, had her feeling uneasy and a little bit hurt.

Leaning back against the wall of the fake post office, she called Gwen's number. It rang for so long that Ava was about to hang up, when Gwen answered with an impatient, "Yes?"

"I—" Ava realized, rather belatedly, that she wasn't exactly sure what she wanted to say.

"I'm going to assume you're calling me for a valid reason and not just to waste my time."

"Yes," Ava said quickly. "I guess I wanted to check in. Apparently, the call schedule changed, and I wasn't sure—"

"I had some things to take care of," Gwen interrupted with no further explanation. "But since I have you, call Georgia and tell her I'm on my way. I want to see her immediately."

The last time Gwen had had Ava call her lawyer so early in the day had been almost a year ago, after a lengthy telephone conversation with her ex-husband.

Ava swallowed, waited a beat, and finally asked, "Is everything all right, Miss Knight?"

Gwen was silent for a long moment, and Ava waited, suddenly wishing she could see Gwen's face so she could assess the damage. She was good at that—just looking at Gwen and knowing. She knew every frown, every smile. She knew whether a laugh was born out of humor or spite, whether Gwen was sighing because she was exasperated or because she was just tired. Gwen was made up of expressions, tones, movement—a body of language and code in which Ava had become fluent.

"That will be all, Eisenberg."

Gwen hung up and Ava slumped against the wall. Something was definitely wrong.

The rest of the afternoon played out fairly typically. After Ava called Gwen's lawyer, she decided to get a few errands done before she was summoned again—although she couldn't help but wonder if she was going to be summoned at all. She hated days that went off schedule. They always made her feel a little lost.

Ava was coming out of the drugstore after picking up Gwen's prescriptions when news of a hold-up nearby broke over the police scanner.

Ava hated petty crime. Most criminals were kids trying their luck, or desperate people trying to pay gambling debts or fund a drug habit. Ava hated that she couldn't save them all, that the best she could do was talk them down, or worst-case scenario, stop the bullet they would have regretted firing for the rest of their lives. These usually weren't bad people, just people making bad decisions.

The kid in the little Italian deli couldn't have been older than sixteen. His hand was shaking as he pointed a gun at the young woman behind the counter. Ava could hear the terrified thump of her heart before she even entered the building.

It was over in a second. Ava had the young woman out of the deli and safe on the sidewalk before she went back in and disarmed the boy. He was cursing at her as she walked him out to the police car outside. He called her an alien freak, a fucking abomination, a plague on America. She was impressed with his vocabulary. She hoped they'd let him get his GED in juvie.

The rest of the day was slow. Ava couldn't stop thinking about the kid in the deli. He'd been so angry. Something about the way he'd looked before the cop shoved his head into the back of the car—all surly and scared—reminded Ava of her brother. She didn't think about her brother much. He was fifteen when he died. Fifteen and mad at the world. He had never wanted to be on the ship, he'd made that much clear. She remembered an argument in which her mother had told him that one day he'd feel differently. One day, he'd be proud that he was part of something so important. That day never came.

Around lunch time, she went to visit Nic at work, but her friend was buried in new tech, and distracted by all of the shiny.

"Here." Nic shoved a bag of marshmallows at her, before readjusting her goggles and turning back to her soldering iron. "Stop sulking. It's unhealthy how co-dependent you are with her."

"I am not sulking," Ava retorted, shoving two marshmallows into her mouth so that her cheeks bulged. "And I'm not co-dependent. She's my job." Ava chewed and swallowed.

"You could quit," Nic offered without looking up.

Ava said nothing. She'd never considered quitting. Not even when Gwen had called her two hours after Ava had left work and asked her to go to Beverly Hills and feed Garbo, Gwen's ancient tabby cat, because the housekeeper had gone home early and Gwen was across town getting a facial.

And to an outsider, yeah, she could see how Gwen might be considered a little...mean. But they didn't know her the way Ava did. They didn't see her tackle-hug Luke after he did well on a test, or watch how she cooed over an ill-tempered Garbo. They didn't hear how grateful she'd sounded when Ava flew to Massachusetts to get a box of Gwen's favorite cider donuts (she'd told Gwen that they were from a store in the Arts District) after *US Weekly* had published the gory details of her last divorce.

So by six, after a day of not-sulking, Ava was a little worried when she still hadn't heard from her boss. Of course, it was really none of her business. Gwen could be doing a hundred things which Ava was not entitled to know or care about. And yet she couldn't quite rid herself of the nagging worry.

Ava was still feeling vaguely anxious that night as she and Nic were debating what to watch. It was a toss-up between *Game of Thrones* and *The Great British Bake Off*. She was weighing up the options when she happened to glance at her phone.

Meet me at the house. Don't dawdle.

She practically sprang off the couch, phone in hand. "I, um...I need to..."

"Get Little Tommy out of the well?" Nic finished for her, immediately assuming it was a Swiftwing emergency.

"Yeah." The lie was easier than it should have been. "Something like that."

Nic sighed dramatically. "Fine, go be a hero. Leave me here to eat this ginormous pizza all by myself."

"Don't you dare!" Ava called out as she left the apartment.

If Nic wondered why Ava was leaving through the front door in her normal clothing and not out of the window as Swiftwing, she didn't ask.

Ava pulled up at Gwen's gate ten minutes later—one of the benefits of living in Studio City was how close it was to Gwen's house in the Hills.

She punched in the code and drove up the path to the mansion. Gwen liked things pretty and she liked things expensive, and the house was both. In the years that she'd worked for Gwen, Ava had seen multiple extensions and renovations to the house. She liked the way it looked now, the way it felt both spacious and lived in. It had little touches of personality—photographs on the walls, Luke's comic books scattered on coffee tables, Gwen's soft gray cardigan draped over the back of a chair. It felt like a home.

The door was opened by a small, round Hispanic woman in her late fifties. Ava didn't recognize her. Gwen was notorious for hiring and firing housekeepers.

"I'm here for—"

"Yes, yes," the woman nodded, ushering Ava in. "Señora Knight is in the back."

"Thank you." Ava smiled at the woman, who seemed surprised and offered one in return.

Ava made her way through the entrance hall, past the living room, into the kitchen, and out through the patio doors.

She loved the garden. It was slightly overgrown, green, and lush—filled with fairy lights and a little chipped fountain. There was a hammock where Luke would read for hours, and a little table where she would sometimes run lines with Gwen.

It was where Swiftwing had first visited Gwen, all those months ago, and where she returned over and over again as the masked superhero, inexplicably reluctant to abandon the strange sort of relationship they had formed while Ava was wearing the suit.

Ava wasn't sure why she'd started visiting Gwen as Swiftwing. At first, it might have been to thank her for the kind words Gwen had said about her during an interview. Later, it was to ask for advice on how to deal with negative backlash from the police department. And then, it became a sort of ritual. Gwen would spend evenings in her garden, and Swiftwing would fly down and visit.

Gwen would offer Swiftwing a drink, and she'd politely decline. They would sit in the wicker chairs where Ava the assistant ran lines with her boss.

When the light was just right and the air smelled of lemon trees, Ava was sometimes reminded of Zrix'dhor, where the humid, tropical weather made everything smell sweet and fruity.

In the late evening, the trees made it dark, but the lights around the pool were on, as well as the little lights strung up between branches. As Ava approached, Gwen looked up and blinked, as if she'd forgotten her summons.

Ava's eyes flickered to the martini glass on the little table in front of Gwen. It was half empty. And by the number of olives missing from the jar on the bar counter, Ava guessed that Gwen was at least on her third drink.

She was strangely nervous as she took those last few steps forward.

One glass and Gwen was wittier, sharper, and a little meaner. Two and she was argumentative and impatient; she'd pick a fight and win after two. Three and she was honest. Three made Ava nervous.

"Miss Knight."

Gwen sat up straight and stared at Ava for the longest time. Her eyeliner was smudged, her face all flushed, and she looked…sad. Garbo, who had been sleeping in the chair beside Gwen, yawned and stretched before hopping off and walking to the house, likely annoyed that they were bothering her sleep.

Ava smiled brightly, as if some of her shine could rub off on Gwen. "Can I get you anything, Miss Knight?"

"Cancel it." Gwen reached for her glass, took a too-big gulp of her martini, and pulled a face of distaste. "All of it."

"I–" Ava took a tentative step forward. "Cancel…?"

"The plans. The party, the cake, whatever."

"Everything?"

"Yes." Gwen sighed, seemingly too exasperated to come up with a sarcastic retort. "Everything."

Ava stood there for a second too long, feeling helpless. She was caught between running off to complete her task (which she imagined would be particularly satisfying) and stepping forward. But then what? How on earth was she supposed to comfort Gwen? A few placating words? A hand on her shoulder?

Swiftwing would have been confident. She would have echoed some wise Zrix'dhorian proverb and offered comfort. But as Ava, the idea made her stomach twist up with a strange kind of anticipation. It was the same feeling she got when she held eye contact with Gwen for just a moment too long, or when their fingers brushed as Ava handed over her coffee. It was a feeling she held close and tried her hardest not to analyze. She liked her job. She didn't want to complicate it with...things that were complicated.

She was saved from having to make the choice when Gwen stood, glass in hand, and sauntered over to the little bar area.

"You know he said that I was fooling myself?"

Ava swallowed, grounding herself. "He?"

"Ronald." Gwen poured clear liquid into her glass from the shaker, frowning in concentration as it filled up. She liked her martini cold and dirty. A splash of olive juice and she was all set. "Apparently he had a crisis of conscience." Gwen scoffed and whirled around; some of the drink escaped the glass.

"Maybe you should sit down," Ava suggested, only to be met with Gwen's most condescending glare.

Gwen sat anyway. "He said," she pointed her finger at Ava, "and— and this is the real kicker. He said that he didn't want to compromise his integrity. His *integrity*." She looked at Ava, as if waiting for a response. "This from a man who, up until two years ago, was doing shaving cream commercials. Who cares if it was staged? A relationship with me would have made his career."

Ava frowned and sat on the wicker chair opposite Gwen, not trusting herself to sit next to her. She might have done something stupid, like reached out and put her hand on Gwen's shoulder, or her arm, or her knee, right where her skirt was riding up. Ava narrowed her focus back to the issue at hand. One confusing revelation at a time.

"It was staged?"

Gwen hummed in confirmation and sipped her drink as if this wasn't the biggest entertainment scoop of the year.

"But, you were..." Ava started awkwardly. "You could have anyone you want. Why him?"

"Custody."

"Custody?" Ava repeated slowly, as if the word was foreign.

"My odious ex-husband is suing me for full custody."

"Of...of Luke?"

"No, of our pet Chihuahua." Gwen rolled her eyes and chugged the rest of her drink. "Apparently, getting married to someone half his age also robbed Alfonso of half his brain cells. He thinks that because wife two-point-oh has the luxury of spending her hours arranging fruit baskets and getting manicures that they'd make a better primary household. Apparently, all the traveling I do for work is disrupting my son's routine, which by the way, is ridiculous. He has…consistency. He knows I'm always here for him."

"Miss Knight." Ava wished now that she *was* sitting next to Gwen. She wished that she could reach out and steady her. "I'm so sorry."

"Don't be," Gwen said quickly. "They won't…I won't let it happen."

"Of course," Ava was equally quick to mollify her. "Of course not."

"The thing with Ronald was…" Gwen sighed and pinched the bridge of her nose. Ava made a mental note to greet her with ibuprofen in the morning. "Well, my lawyer thought that it would be a good idea to try and equalize the playing field. Alfonso's got his walking midlife crisis. I would have—"

"Ron," Ava finished for her.

"Two-parent households are still preferred by the courts." Gwen shrugged. "It wasn't going to be a permanent arrangement. An engagement announcement, a few weeks of cohabitation, cutting back on set hours, and by the time the deposition rolled around, Alfonso wouldn't have a leg to stand on."

Gwen ran her thumb along the side of the empty glass. "It's come to this. For six years, I've dressed my son for school, made sure he had his lunch, read him bedtime stories. Six years, while Alfonso was off winning Palme d'Ors and sailing yachts in the Greek Isles, making cameos as Luke's father. Now he marries a *Sports Illustrated* centerfold and I'm the one who has to prove competence. Can you imagine?"

As silence extended between them, Ava found she had nothing comforting to say. She felt a bit like a child, peeking through a door into a world where grown-ups had lawyers and custody battles, and the monsters didn't have horns or sharp teeth, and you couldn't just punch them to make them go away.

She stood and took Gwen's glass from her, then walked to the bar and traded it for a can of LaCroix.

Gwen accepted it wordlessly and took a sip. She didn't bat an eye when Ava sat in the chair beside her.

"You want to hear the worst part?" Gwen lowered her voice and leaned forward like she was about to divulge something awful. "My son—my smart, discerning, shy boy—actually *likes* living with Alfonso and *her*. He likes that she bakes him gluten-free brownies and that they go horseback riding while Alfonso is on set. He likes her and it…kills me."

It wasn't the first time Ava had seen Gwen drunk. But at this point, she was usually dispensing advice, or bemoaning the general idiocy of men. To see Gwen so vulnerable was jarring. She was almost too real. Raw nerves underneath layers of Chanel and expensive perfume.

Ava's first urge was to fix it, to stop the hurt. But the supersuit under her shirt wasn't going to solve this problem, and her urge to use jujitsu on Gwen's ex-husband wouldn't help anyone.

"Is there anyone else who could step in? I'm sure there are a hundred people—"

"Who I could trust to be discreet about this?" Gwen cut her off. "Don't be so naïve, Eisenberg. Ronald worked because we had something to offer each other. People know we occasionally move in the same social circles. The whole on-set romance would have sold like artisanal soap at a farmers' market. He needed a career boost; I needed a convenient relationship. It was perfect."

Gwen lowered her glass onto the table and it clattered against the metal coaster tray. "Maybe he's right," she muttered, her eyes focused on the rim of the glass. "I spend more time behind a camera than anywhere else. More time around these hair stylists and make-up artists than around actual people."

Ava wasn't about to mention the fact that they were very much actual people.

Gwen looked up then, as if sensing exactly what Ava was not saying. She narrowed her eyes in annoyance.

"God knows I see your pretty little face more often than—" The shift in Gwen's expression was slow and deliberate.

Ava was still too distracted by the fact that Gwen had just called her pretty to really notice it until Gwen straightened and looked at her with terrifying focus that seemed to push through the haze of gin and vermouth.

"Eisenberg."

Fidgeting under the intensity of Gwen's stare, she asked, "Miss Knight?"

"It's ludicrous," Gwen murmured, more to herself than to Ava. "It wouldn't be any better than what he's doing. You're so...young. It would likely do more harm than good." Gwen scowled at Ava as though she was somehow at fault here.

The first inkling of Gwen's idea became clear, and Ava's eyes widened. It was the alcohol talking. Gwen wasn't thinking straight. She couldn't possibly be implying what Ava thought she was implying.

"But," Gwen emitted a contemplative little noise, "it would cause a riot. It would make unfair discrimination a conceivable argument. We both know my last biography made the *New York Times* bestseller list because of the chapter about my flirtation with Portia back in the nineties. And besides..." Gwen sighed. "Luke likes you."

"It's late." Ava attempted a smile and stood on shaky legs, hoping to escape before Gwen pursued this any further. "I should go."

"Sit."

Ava sat.

Gwen studied her with careful consideration and bit at the edge of her thumbnail—a habit she adopted when particularly tense. "I should probably preface this by saying that your job with me is in no way at stake. Whatever you decide will have no bearing on your employment."

Ava shifted nervously. "Miss Knight, you're upset and—and not thinking clearly. You can't, you don't want...me."

"Oh, Ava." Gwen's smile was slow and calculated. "I think you're exactly who I want."

CHAPTER 3

"THIS IS INSANE." NIC WORE an expression of horror. "You know that, right?"

"It's not *the worst* idea ever," Ava protested for what felt like the hundredth time. There was a half-devoured slice of pizza in the box on the table, and Ava looked at it sadly, her appetite gone, thinking she should have eaten it before she brought up Gwen's little proposal.

"Isn't she, like, fifty?" Nic's voice went shrill.

"Forty-four," Ava corrected. "Not that it should matter."

"And Rachel. What the hell is she going to think?"

Ava cringed. She hadn't even thought about her adoptive mother's reaction.

"She's always been supportive about this sort of stuff." Ava hated this. She hated being on opposite sides of anything with Nic.

"I don't mean the—the gay thing." Nic paused, squinting at Ava. "Although we need to talk about that too. I'm more concerned with fact that you're considering betrothal to Tinsel Town royalty."

"We wouldn't actually get married." Ava hugged a throw pillow to her chest as Nic barreled forward with her rant.

"It's going to be everywhere. I thought you wanted to protect your privacy. You do this, and Ava Eisenberg is going to be on more covers than Swiftwing."

"Gwen can manage the media. If anyone can limit the exposure, it's her."

"This is..." Nic gave an exaggerated shrug as she trailed off helplessly.

"I know it sounds crazy. It did to me too."

"I'm hoping you have a really convincing 'but' in that sentence."

"*But* I can help. I can help a friend."

"She is not your friend, Ava." Nic's voice softened as the initial freak-out subsided somewhat. "She's your boss. You've told me time and time again how little she respects and underappreciates you. God, she won't even call you by your name."

"That's not actually—"

"Did she give you a choice? Did she threaten your job?"

"What?" Ava straightened. "No, of course not. I mean," she took breath, "yes, she gave me a choice, and no, she didn't threaten anything." She thought back to how pleased Gwen had looked when she'd laid out her strangely convincing argument.

Nic did not look convinced. "She shouldn't have roped you into this at all. Are you sure the kid isn't better off with his dad? Gwen's judgment is clearly lacking, if this is anything to go by."

"Okay." Ava sighed. "Obviously, I haven't painted her in the best light. But I swear, she's an amazing mom. And…and what's happening to her is completely unfair. Luke needs her. He needs his mom, and if I can help keep them together, if I can…"

"Oh, Ava." Nic's voice did that thing where it sounded both condescending and comforting, and Ava didn't know if she wanted to hug her or yell at her. Instead, she put her hand up to ward off whatever pity was being directed at her.

"I know what you're thinking. You're thinking that I'm projecting, that this is some way for me to feel better about losing my mom and brother."

"Am I wrong?"

"This is about Gwen," she stated definitively. "And Luke. And what they deserve. I want to do this."

That was truth of it. Simple and honest. She did want to do this, even if the thought was a little terrifying. Or a lot terrifying. Ava wasn't exactly sure what Gwen would expect of her, or how far this was supposed to go. But she trusted Gwen, more than she'd realized.

Nic threw her hands up in defeat. "I guess you've made your decision."

Ava shrugged and felt small again. "Well, I don't want you to be mad at me."

"I'm not mad," Nic was quick to say. "I'm just struggling to understand. Why did it have to be you? Why not one of the pieces of eye candy she's always parading around at swanky functions? I'm sure there are a dozen people who'd kill to marry Gwendolyn Knight."

"Because they don't know her like I do. And she trusts me with this."

Nic raised her eyebrows. "And Swiftwing?"

"What about her?"

"I'm guessing Gwen's next UN appearance isn't going to be about advocating for the rights of her alien girlfriend?"

Ava got a strange little thrill at the word "girlfriend" and shrugged it off. "At least we know she's alien-friendly."

Alien-friendly was a vast understatement. Gwen had spent the last ten years championing the rights of the Andromeda Orphans. She was, in many respects, the celebrity face of the Andromeda Orphans Equality Movement. She and her ex, Alfonso Moretti, had received acclaim for their documentary on the children of refugee aliens. It had made an outstanding impact on the way people thought of AOs. It was one of the reasons Ava had been drawn to her, and one of the reasons she so admired Gwen. For all Gwen's sarcasm and caustic wit, she cared deeply.

But Ava said, "She can't know who I am, about where I come from. This is completely platonic. We won't even spend that much time together. It's like a business arrangement."

"A skeevy business arrangement," Nic added. "If the truth comes out—"

"I won't let that happen."

"There's more at stake here. I know you want to help…a friend." She pulled a face, as if the last word had been a struggle. "But you're putting too much at risk. You've got to think of the bigger picture. There are other jobs, other bosses."

Ava made a little sound of frustration. "Nic, you know I don't want to be a PA forever. But this job is good. I get to be part of something I love. And I get time to work on my writing."

"Barely," Nic groused. "Look, I know it's a sweet job, okay? But I also know that you take your role as Swiftwing seriously. Remember what you said when you first convinced me and Rachel of this superhero thing? You said that you had a purpose, and that you needed to fulfill it."

"I also said that if I could help, I should help, and I can help Gwen." Ava fell back against the couch, feeling defeated.

"So, help her another way. Find another willing sucker. There's gotta be someone else out there willing to fake-date Gwen Knight."

"Finally." Gwen didn't open her eyes as Ava lowered the coffee cup onto the counter. It was 7:02 a.m., and Gwen was already in the make-up trailer, hair curlers and all. She looked decidedly less hungover than Ava would have suspected given the previous night's gin party. "I thought you'd flown halfway across the world to pick the beans yourself."

Ava's eyes went wide, and she was about to launch into a ramble when Gwen opened her eyes and looked at her with a hint of a smile through her snail-slime infused face mask. An honest-to-goodness smile.

"No, no flying, just traffic."

"Hmm." Gwen took a tentative sip. "Well, at least it's hot." She leaned back in her chair and removed her mask, presumably so that her raised brow could have maximum effect. "So?"

Ava looked down, suddenly very interested in the toe of her new shoes. Despite what Gwen had said the night before—and she had said a lot—Ava couldn't help but wonder if refusing your boss's fake marriage proposal was indeed grounds for termination.

"Eisenberg, I have an outstanding number of admirable qualities, but I think we both know that patience is not one of them. Last night I…" Gwen took a slow breath as she found her words. "I asked you a question. You told me you would have an answer by morning. It is now," she made a show of glancing at her watch, "seven minutes after seven, and you have yet to accept."

"A-accept?"

"Don't be obtuse; it isn't a good look for you."

"Miss Knight." Ava steeled herself and subconsciously crossed her arms over her chest before she realized that channeling her Swiftwing power stance might not be the best option. "I did think about it. A lot, actually—"

"Excellent." Gwen reached forward for her face mask, as if the conversation ended there. "You can call Georgia and schedule a meeting for—"

"I can't do it."

Gwen blinked. "Excuse me?"

"I'm uh, declining. Politely." Ava cleared her throat, feeling like the words were still stuck in there. "I'm sorry. I really am. But it just wouldn't be right, and not for reasons you'd think, or—or because I don't want to help, but I just… Well, I don't think I'd be good at it."

"Oh." Gwen's voice dropped an octave. She was surprised. And something else. Disappointed, Ava thought. Of course she was disappointed. She had drunkenly placed her faith in Ava.

"It's just that the more I thought about it, the more I realized that there were far more suitable candidates."

"Suitable candidates?"

"You know, um…people who would be more convincing."

"I see."

"I know you thought that my knowledge of, well…that I would be useful, but there must be someone who knows you better than me. I'm mean, I'm just your assistant, right? There's got to be—"

"Enough."

"—someone else who… What?"

"That's enough." Gwen had pulled out her phone and was scrolling through her Twitter feed as if this was the most casual conversation in the world. "Thank you, Eisenberg. You can go now."

"But I—"

"Go. Now."

Ava walked out of the make-up trailer with slumped shoulders and an air of defeat. This wasn't how it was supposed to go. This was the opposite of how it was supposed to go. Gwen was supposed to agree with her. She was supposed to blame the martinis and say something disparaging about Ava's outfit and how ridiculous it was of her to ever consider that Ava would make a suitable substitute for pretty-boy Ron Gooding. Then, because Ava was the only one privy to this little scam anyway, they'd look over other options. Images of the two of them sitting in Gwen's trailer poring over faces of possible candidates played through Ava's head like a slow-motion montage.

She hadn't expected Gwen to look disappointed. It was stupid how much it upset her, like she'd just let a bad guy get away. Worse, she felt like she *was* the bad guy, which was crazy, because everything Nic had said the night before was true. A fake engagement would be a bad, bad idea. No one would buy that Gwen and Ava were… Ava couldn't even say it in her head. Engaged? In love? And probably doing all of the stuff that engaged people did. The thought of pretending to touch Gwen in ways that Ava had only ever thought about in her deepest 3 a.m. fantasies, was…terrifying. Exhilarating.

It would never work. Nic was right.

There *was* more at stake. She'd have to double the subterfuge if she was seeing Gwen after hours as Ava. The flimsy excuses she made when she was missing from set wouldn't hold up if she was late for a dinner or whatever social event Gwen would want them to attend. She couldn't exactly hang her cape in Gwen's guest closet. Everyone would be looking at her. It was the antithesis of everything she'd taught herself to be. She couldn't be a wallflower *and* be Gwen Knight's date, and so she couldn't be Gwen Knight's date. Ever.

Wouldn't. Couldn't. Shouldn't.

She said it under her breath like a mantra—as Gwen ignored her for most of the morning, as she shot into the sky around noon to help with a forest fire just north of the city, as she trudged back into Gwen's trailer, determined and terrified, and still smelling mildly of smoke.

Gwen barely looked up from her novel (the newest offering by Andromeda Orphan Yanus Hakk) as Ava entered. "Eisenberg, you have been dismissed. Now, unless the Academy Award nominations have been announced or Dev Patel has finally replied to my text, I do not want to be—"

"We should date."

Gwen's head darted up from the book. "Excuse me?"

"Date." Ava nodded resolutely. "We should date."

"A few hours ago, you were convincing me of how utterly unconvincing you would be in this role and now—"

"I don't think an engagement would sell, at least not right away." She paced in front of the coffee table, rationalizing it to herself as much as to Gwen. "But if we dated for a while, not for real, of course, because that would just be…silly." She hazarded a glance at Gwen. "But if we pretended to date for a while, it might come off as more realistic. It might give people a chance to ease into the idea that we're in a relationship and that we're stable."

"And how is this different from my idea that we announce an engagement?"

"Because it's stability you're aiming for. So, we do it slowly, give them constancy. That's what your ex-husband is using as leverage, right? No one would let them take Luke from you if they saw how happy he was at home, what a good life you've created for him. If we date, then you get to showcase that life. It's like—like a PR strategy."

Gwen smiled, as if Ava had said something extraordinary, and Ava's heart did a little flip. "A PR strategy." She actually looked impressed. "That's good. That's really good. And you'd be willing to go along with that?"

"I—yes."

Nic's disapproving face flickered through her mind like a bright red light.

"If we do this, it'll be public." Gwen always seemed to know exactly what Ava was thinking. It was unnerving. "You do understand that? Your family and friends are going to know. And you will have to sell it. You can't tell anyone that this is just a ruse."

"Well…" Ava shuffled restlessly.

"Who else knows?"

"Just my roommate-slash-best-friend," Ava said quickly. "I needed another opinion. You know, to talk it through."

"You mean you needed someone to talk you out of it?"

Ava winced. "She's not exactly thrilled with the idea."

Gwen watched her carefully. "And you're doing this anyway?"

"I am." Ava smiled, hoping she looked convincing. "I want to help."

Gwen nodded, seemingly appeased, and Ava wished she knew what Gwen was thinking.

"All right. Good," Gwen said. "We'll go to dinner and discuss the terms."

The terms (as Gwen put them) were that they would tell Luke about their relationship as soon as possible to prevent him from finding out via gossip. They were to be seen in public, but to make no official statements about their relationship. Public displays of affection were to be discussed beforehand to avoid crossing any boundaries. Ava was to remain Gwen's assistant and perform her duties as normal. Neither party would have any outside romantic entanglements during their dating period.

Gwen didn't specify how long this dating period would be, but Ava knew that Alfonso was pushing to have the deposition at the beginning of November, which gave them just over a month. After that, Ava supposed they'd play it by ear. She didn't want to ask Gwen how long their arrangement was supposed to last. She didn't want Gwen to think that she was impatient for it to end or not entirely on board.

In truth, Ava didn't know how much more on board she could be. They were sitting side by side in a dimly lit booth in one of LA's most expensive restaurants, which catered to discretion and, based on the little floating candles and flowery centerpiece, romance. When Gwen had suggested an after-work dinner, Ava had envisioned going to the café on the lot, not being ushered into Gwen's car with a curt, "Come along, Eisenberg."

Gwen, a vegetarian, ordered the charred radish and quinoa salad, and Ava reminded the waiter to hold the pine nuts. Gwen didn't like pine nuts. Ava, who looked at the three-figure prices on the menu and almost broke out in hives, went for a hamburger with fries. It took her a second after the waiter left to realize that Gwen was still watching her with a contemplative expression.

"What? Do I have something on my face?" Ava reached for her napkin and Gwen shook her head.

"I made the right decision, didn't I? Trusting you with this."

It was more of a statement than a question, but Ava answered anyway. "I think so. I'll do my best, Miss Knight."

Gwen's lips moved up into a soft smile, the kind that Ava had rarely seen directed at anyone who wasn't Luke. "I believe you will. And Ava?" Ava's breath caught. It was a strange, almost giddy feeling to hear Gwen say her name.

"Yeah?"

"It's Gwen now."

Ava nodded, her heart in her throat. "Okay."

Dinner arrived on expensive plates, with little squiggles of sauce on the sides, and Ava thought it might be the fanciest hamburger she'd ever seen. She made a conscious effort to not inhale it in seconds.

The silence was awkward when Gwen was not directing the conversation, and Ava wondered what they were supposed to talk about. She wanted to ask more about what they were going to tell Luke, and about what exactly they were eventually going to say to the media. She liked having this secret, this project that was for just the two of them. Gwen, for her part, seemed content to let the whole thing rest as she picked at her salad and replied to a text.

"Was it important?" Ava asked, watching Gwen drop her phone back into her purse, looking more pleased than she had all evening.

"That was Daniel. Apparently, Cate has committed to some silly play in Melbourne this winter, which means Sofia's unnamed project is without a lead." Gwen smiled slowly, and Ava was reminded of a cartoon villain twirling their mustache. "Karma for accepting an award for a film by that slimy weasel of a man. I told Cate not to work with Allen, and she just didn't want to—"

"Do you like sunsets?" Ava wanted to kick herself the second the words left her mouth. Of all the inane questions to ask…

But Gwen answered. "Not particularly. They remind me that I don't have enough hours in the day. Sunset always seems to take me by surprise." Gwen pushed her plate away and took a sip of wine. "Speaking of surprise, a quick glance at my schedule tells me that you've booked me for—"

"Miss Knight?" Ava smiled nervously and shook her head. "I mean, Gwen. Could we…um, try to not talk about work?"

Gwen blinked and looked at her. "What do you suggest we talk about?"

"I don't know." Ava glanced up at their waiter, who seemed to materialize out of thin air to remove their plates and refill their glasses, only to evaporate again. "Maybe we should try to get to know each other?"

"Okay." Gwen's gaze was intense and absolute. Ava could feel herself blushing. "Tell me something riveting about you that I don't already know."

"Well, you can't just demand a fact."

Gwen frowned. "Why not?"

"Because that's not how it works."

That earned an eye roll. "Well, then perhaps you'd like to enlighten me as to how this works. I've never pretended to date my assistant before, and clearly you have all the—" Gwen laughed a nervous, tinkly laugh and scooted closer until she was practically sidled up against Ava.

"What are you—"

"Jess Cagle just walked in." Gwen leaned in, and her breath was warm against Ava's ear. This might be the closest they'd ever been to each other, and Ava fought back a shiver.

"Jess Cagle?" Ava whispered back because it seemed like that was a thing they were doing. "As in *Entertainment Weekly*?"

Gwen nodded. "If we do this right, we may just be able to make a little noise."

"I thought you wanted to keep it quiet." Gwen was still so close. Close enough that if Ava were to turn her head just a fraction, she'd be able to press her cheek against Gwen's mouth.

Gwen tutted against her ear. "I want them to think we want to keep it quiet."

Ava thought of Nic. So much for limiting exposure.

Gwen pulled back to look at her, and she was still too close. Ava could almost count her eyelashes. "Last chance to back out, Ava."

She wasn't sure if it was because of the way Gwen's perfume seemed to invade every one of her senses, or if it was the way Gwen had just said her name, all soft, rounded vowels. It might have been the fact that she was starting to realize that maybe this wasn't *just* about helping Gwen. Whatever the impetus, Ava snuck a cursory glance at the man at the table across from them and then placed her hand over Gwen's, making sure it was visible from his table.

Gwen glanced at their joined hands. "Okay then."

"What now?" Ava asked, barely breathing.

"Just wait for it," Gwen replied, stroking her thumb against the side of Ava's wrist.

And then it happened. He looked over at them. It made her feel nervous and surprisingly giddy.

She stopped breathing entirely when Gwen moved closer and pressed her lips to the spot just below Ava's ear.

It was fleeting, and barely there. A butterfly kiss. Ava's skin buzzed from the sensation. When Gwen pulled back, her expression was unreadable. Then she smiled, and Ava wasn't sure if it was for show or not.

"It was either that or be branded gal-pals for the next three months," Gwen finally said, finishing off her drink.

Ava nodded, not quite trusting herself to speak.

Gwen looked almost amused, and patted Ava's hand lightly. "Come on. Let's go before you start to swoon."

They got the check (Gwen paid, of course), and Ava watched her smile and flirt with the maître d' who came over to make sure they had enjoyed their meal. Ava was used to people fawning over her boss, but as they stood to leave and the squat little man kept talking, his shifty eyes darting between Gwen's face and her neckline, Ava felt compelled to press her palm against the flat of Gwen's back and lean in to say, "We really should be going."

Gwen stiffened for a moment and then relaxed. She turned and smirked at Ava, who felt a rush of warmth replace the nerves.

"Yes, you're right." That smirk still flickered at the corners of her mouth.

The car ride was quiet. Gwen gave her driver, Jonah, Ava's address, and then leaned back against the plush leather interior. They did not speak about the events of the evening.

The journey home took them from Sunset Boulevard onto Laurel Canyon, and Ava sighed, staring out at the colorful lights and the cars passing by. She felt restless. She needed to fly, to clear her thoughts. The car stopped outside Ava's building, and she waited for Gwen to make some quip about the ever-present smell of urine on the sidewalk, but all she said was, "That wasn't entirely disastrous."

Ava opened the door before Jonah could step out and do it for her. "You think so?"

Gwen made a noncommittal sound. "You'll come over to the house tomorrow night and we'll go from there."

"Okay."

Not for the first time that evening, Gwen's expression was unreadable.

"Okay," Ava repeated, under her breath, as she climbed out. And then the door was shut, and the car pulled away, and she was left on the sidewalk wondering what the hell she had just gotten herself into.

CHAPTER 4

Ava flew around the city, trying to wrap her head around her evening with Gwen. It was weirder than she'd imagined, and at the same time, not weird at all. There was an easy sort of familiarity at the base of all the newness. She knew Gwen. Knew her expressions, her voice, the scent of her perfume.

Of course, she'd never quite experienced Gwen's hand over hers, or the specific reverberation of Gwen's voice when her mouth was just a hairbreadth from Ava's ear. She'd never seen Gwen smile at her with unguarded amusement. Ava was caught up in this tangle of new and complicated feelings, and at the heart of it all was a sort of anticipatory sadness at the fact that this thing, whatever it was, was pretend and temporary. It felt, suddenly, like she was doomed to a relationship of pretense, whether she was seeing Gwen as Ava or as Swiftwing,

She was so caught up in her thoughts that she barely felt the vibration against her wrist that meant she was being summoned to help with a rogue alien. The band only ever displayed the location where Ava was supposed to race. Alien retrieval and combat were really the only times the LAPD willingly asked for her help. Most other times, it was a game of who got there first.

Ava had struggled initially with blowback against what the police chief called vigilantism. Of course, she wasn't the first of the Andromeda Orphans to put on a cape and declare themselves a superhero. She'd been in her teens when Captain Crusader started making headlines in Chicago, and a dozen or so had followed from there.

Ava had never met any of the others, but she'd been emailing with Sushri Sunhera—a young superhero from Pakistan. They'd met on a forum, and she and Ava had connected immediately. The most successful heroes were the ones who worked with their local law enforcement. And so, Ava was working hard to establish a relationship with the police department. For the most part, they worked well together.

When her wristband vibrated with an address—the Irwindale quarry—Ava sprang into action, no questions asked. She was ready for a good fight to take her mind off things. She was not, however, ready to get drenched from head to toe in noxious slime.

After an hour-long game of secure-the-alien, Ava helped sedate the fat, squelching, worm-like creature and maneuver it into the glass cells in the LAPD precinct basement, where alien prisoners were housed until they received representation.

Ava was still in the cell when Officer Barre removed the shackles and the panicked creature started spraying them with the thick, black stinger that emerged from the center of its body. No one was seriously hurt, but the sulfurous smell of alien goo permeated the corridor leading up to the containment area.

The shower ran cold in the tiny basement bathroom, which she'd been directed to after emerging from the cell dripping slime and smelling of sulfur.

"This is so gross," Ava muttered to herself as she threaded her fingers through her hair, trying to get the worst of the slime out.

Each state had a containment facility. In most cases of AO crimes, suspects were contained for as long as it took the Bureau of Alien Criminal Acts to assign them a lawyer, and move them to another containment facility if they were particularly violent or denied bail.

The crimes were as varied as the aliens that committed them. They were as violent, as depraved, as destructive as any human crimes. And even seventeen years after the crash, Andromeda Orphans were still feared, still marginalized. The non-humanoid ones were hunted and practically forced into hiding. For AOs like Ava, it was easier. They could blend in, hide their "abnormalities," or "extraordinaries," as Rachel called them.

Ava felt a twinge of guilt every time she put an AO away. Most of them were not as lucky as her—a kid who'd escaped the military assault and interrogation by realizing she could fly. A kid who'd landed in the backyard of a middle-class family from Compton, who'd taken one look at the skinny white kid in their yard and called the one person they knew would help—a human rights lawyer named Rachel Eisenberg.

The Riley family—mom, dad, and eleven-year old Nicole—had figured out almost immediately that Ava was one of the survivors from the *Andromeda*. After watching the media circus, neither the Rileys nor Rachel had had any desire to put Ava through that. And so, Ava'Kia Vala of the planet Zrix'dhor became Ava Eisenberg of Lakewood, California, daughter of Rachel Eisenberg, best friend of Nicole Riley.

It was years later when Ava discovered that Rachel had essentially forged a number of documents to make it look like she'd legally adopted Ava.

Ava was still thinking about the worm-like creature as she stepped out of the shower, all pink-cheeked and wet-haired, smelling less like alien excretion and more like industrial-strength, lavender-scented soap.

She was sure that she had seen something like it on one of the holoslides in biological genetics studies, but for the life of her, she couldn't place the species.

Ava ran a towel over her hair and considered her options. Her suit was worse for the wear. She'd managed to wipe most of the goop off of it, but it retained the sharp smell of rotten eggs. This was one of the few times she wished she didn't have a secret identity and could just change into jeans and a T-shirt. With a sigh, she pulled her suit back on.

Ava was greeted by an "out of order" sign on the elevator and had to take the stairs, which meant wandering down the corridor, past the holding cells where half a dozen imprisoned AOs were sleeping, pacing, snarling, and spitting.

"I know what you are," said a tall, green-haired Keela, responsible for the forest fires that had been ravaging northern California for months. Ava had fought him weeks before, and she could still remember the smell of her singed eyebrows.

"Hello to you too, Flame-O."

"I said I know who you are," he repeated, ignoring the nickname.

"Yes, you're very astute," Ava replied. "We met a few weeks ago. My fist became well-acquainted with your jaw."

"You're the Star-Chaser's little runt."

Ava stiffened. "You knew my mother." She kept her voice as unaffected as possible, but it trembled.

"She told them to go through that dwarf star." He pressed his palms against the glass of the cell, and Ava knew she should walk away, that nothing he said would make her feel better, but he was talking about her mother. Her *mother*. "Didn't know that, did you?" He sounded particularly gleeful. "She was the reason we went into that storm. The reason we crashed."

Ava had heard this version of the story before. Over the years, the more socialized of the AOs, the ones whose bodies allowed for human speech, the ones who looked fairly "normal," had done interviews with everyone from Christiane Amanpour to Oprah. They'd mentioned that the core team of the *Andromeda* was comprised of crew from Haas-7 and Star-Chasers of Zrix'dhor, and the ship was days away from mutiny. They'd talked about how Lei'Ya Vala, leader of the Star-Chasers, Ava's beloved mother, had convinced them to do a hyper jump into the Milky Way, and, unwittingly, into the meteor storm.

She tried not to think about it. For the most part, she succeeded. For the most part, she could pretend that her mother wasn't responsible for all of those deaths. She couldn't have known—she would never have put those innocent lives in danger if she had. Most of the time, Ava could shut out that little voice that whispered that her proud, adventurous mother might have preferred death to the shame of mutiny and insubordination.

Ava walked past the Keela, hating that she'd given him the satisfaction of her attention in the first place.

She hurried up the stairs and almost into Captain Fernandez, who looked tired and annoyed. Ava knew it was supposed to be her night off. She'd heard one of the other officers whispering about it. Ava was not the captain's favorite alien. But then, Captain Fernandez had no favorite alien. Bianca Fernandez was known for her black-and-white approach to the Andromeda Orphan Equality Movement. In her opinion, many of the AOs were physically superior to humans, and therefore dangerous. Anything that posed a threat to humanity was bad. Bad things needed to be stopped.

Swiftwing's assistance was only allowed because she'd been instrumental in taking down one of the biggest threats to the city the previous year—a psychopathic Shoksnar who wielded electricity and had plunged LA into two days of darkness. After that, Ava was tolerated.

"Bet this wasn't in your plans for this evening, huh?" Ava smiled, trying to lighten the mood.

Captain Fernandez grunted. "No. I'd planned on a quiet night in with my husband."

Ava tried a different tactic. "How is Agent Barre?"

"Quarantined for now," Captain Fernandez replied, crossing her muscular arms over her chest. "Although whatever that thing secreted doesn't seem to be toxic—to humans, at least."

"I'm fine too," Ava said, feeling a bit useless. She ran her hand across the back of her neck, discovered a smear of goo she'd missed, and made a noise of disgust.

The captain didn't look concerned. "That overgrown maggot's been burrowing under highways, causing giant potholes. We had a six-car pile-up because of this thing."

Ava wrinkled her nose. Humans tended to animalize any AO that wasn't humanoid-shaped. "Has he been scheduled for transfer?"

Captain Fernandez shrugged. "The suits from DC have ruled this a non-priority transfer. They'll be down on Thursday to get that foul-mouthed fire-breather first. Looks like the worm's staying for a while."

"Good," Ava said, immensely relieved that the Keela was being transferred. Facing an unstable creature that sprayed noxious slime was way easier than facing the questions she was too scared to ask.

The next morning at work, running on no sleep and pretty sure that she still smelled like sulfurous alien gunk, Ava realized that she seemed to be the target of a dozen curious glances.

She sighed. Either she really did smell, or news about her and Gwen had spread very fast.

It didn't take Ava long to come to the conclusion that it was the latter. Stares, whispers, and more "Hey, Avas" than she'd ever received in a day.

Halfway to the trailer lot, her phone rang. "Flight of Bumblebee," which meant one thing—publicist-in-chief Daniel Cho was about to start yelling. Ava reluctantly answered the call.

"Hey," she answered, trying to sound casual and instead sounding strangled.

"Ava, what the fuck? Every goddamn entertainment publication from Perez to the *LA Times* is asking what the hell is going on between you and Gwen. Please, please tell me you two are not sleeping together."

"I—" *Shit*. "I mean, we're not *not* sleeping together."

"And no one thought to tell me this piece of information? What happened to Ron?"

"He…he was a smokescreen?" She phrased it as a question, not sure whether he would buy it.

A string of profanities and what seemed to be a few breathing exercises before Daniel very calmly said, "Put her on."

Ava mentally checked the day's schedule. "She's shooting until noon. I can go and see if she has a moment."

"Yeah, you do that," Daniel replied. "And Ava?"

"Yeah?"

"You have no idea what you're in for."

Ava sighed as he hung up. She knew Daniel meant it as a warning, but somehow, it sounded like a threat.

Changing direction, Ava hopped into one of the nearby golf carts and drove through the lot to Stage 5.

The light outside the soundstage blinked red, indicating that they were shooting, and Ava slipped in, going to her usual spot at the back, where she had a pretty clear view.

It was the final courtroom scene, where Gwen's character realized that the blackouts she'd been having since childhood were actually repressed memories of her early life on another planet, implying that, like her client, her character was an alien.

It was an emotionally harrowing scene, and Ava had run the lines with Gwen at least half a dozen times. She knew both sides by heart, and yet, seeing Gwen deliver them with such intensity, such heartfelt emotion, left Ava spellbound every time.

Gooding played Gwen's former lover, and the prosecuting lawyer. He sat behind his table, watching Gwen perform her monologue, his face meant to react to her revelation. He wasn't bad, Ava conceded grudgingly, but he was no Gwendolyn Knight.

The scene ended with Gwen on her knees—a sobbing, shuddering mess of emotion. It was acting. All fake. Just pretend. And still, Ava curled her fingers into fists and willed herself not to run and comfort. It was the strangest urge.

The director yelled cut, and Gwen's magic fizzled and retracted back inside of her. She stood up, blinked wet eyelashes, and exhaled a breath, immediately becoming someone else. Sometimes Ava wondered how much of her was left in the character after the movie ended, and if she ever got it back. Barely sparing Gooding a glance, she walked off to her seat and unscrewed a bottle of water.

"Miss Knight," Ava called, running up to her. Gwen's head was tipped back as she drank, and her eyes went to Ava.

"Yes?" An eyebrow raise. No smile or any acknowledgement of the night before. Around them, Ava could have sworn the set went quiet as everybody not-so-surreptitiously watched their interaction.

"You, uh…" Ava cleared her throat. "Daniel wants you to call him."

"I'm busy," Gwen said shortly. "You do it."

"He's already spoken to me. I think he's freaking out about…" Ava waggled her finger between the two of them. "You know."

"I'm sure." Gwen's reply was sardonic.

"Why haven't you told him?" Ava asked, under her breath, aware that she may have been crossing the line, but annoyed by a morning of negative comments, lack of sleep, and now Gwen's attitude.

"Danny's a terrible liar."

"He's a publicist. *Your* publicist."

Gwen's mouth flickered into what might have been a smile for just a moment. "He'll do better if he believes this is real."

Gooding watched them from the opposite side of the set; Gwen didn't even look in his direction. Ava wondered if she was projecting her own anxiety onto Gwen. But she knew Gwen well enough to sense when something was off.

"You're hovering," Gwen murmured.

"I was wondering if we're still doing dinner. Tonight, I mean."

"Do you have some other pressing engagement?"

"Me? No, I just wasn't sure if I should bring anything, or change."

"Well, the fact that you have a cartoon otter on your shirt doesn't do you any favors." Gwen frowned in Ava's general direction. "Honestly,

Eisenberg, if you're going to be associated with me outside of work, could you at least attempt to dress like a grown-up?"

Ava straightened and tugged at her T-shirt, upon which a cartoon otter was indeed claiming to be "otterly adorable."

"I like this T-shirt," she grumbled.

"Thankfully, we're going straight home, so you won't have to interact with the outside world."

Ava waited a beat, considering her words. "Is everything okay? You seem a little—"

Gwen watched her expectantly, poised to sneer.

"A little off."

To Ava's surprise, Gwen didn't roll her eyes or deride Ava for her observation. "We'll talk later," she said softly.

Ava was in the middle of confirming Gwen's appointments for that week when her wristband vibrated. All it said was *Crystal Lake*.

"Finally!" Captain Fernandez called out as Ava hit the ground with a whoosh and a thump, sending a cloud of sand onto the shoes of the surrounding officers.

She walked toward the team, all kitted out in their retrieval gear in front of the large cliff face that framed the beach. "Is it bad?"

"We're not sure yet." Captain Fernandez held up her complicated black beeping device that Ava could never quite figure out. "We've traced this thing from the quarry to this cave. It's moving in circles, like it's disoriented or lost."

"Same species as the one we detained last night?"

"You mean Norman?" Another officer had come up behind them, holding a similar device to Captain Fernandez.

Ava frowned at him. "Norman?"

"It's what we've been calling the little squish monster." The officer grinned.

"DC seems to be having trouble identifying it," Fernandez explained. "For now, its species-type is unclear."

"And this one?" Ava gestured to the cave.

"Based off its hormone signature, we're guessing it's a Mantapodis," the officer replied. "What is it about summer and bugs?"

"Man*ti*podis," Ava corrected. "I remember reading about them. They aren't a violent race. I could go in there. Try and talk to it."

"We're not sending you in there alone," Captain Fernandez said. "In the dark. To face off with some bug."

"Captain." Another officer appeared next to them. "We think it might be tunneling again."

"I'll just check it out," Ava said, glancing over her shoulder as she made for the cave. "No fighting, I promise."

In hindsight, she realized it was a stupid promise.

The Mantipodis in the cave was big. A lot bigger than Ava had anticipated. Its spindly gray-green body was covered in small, bristly hairs that quivered as Ava approached. She held out her hands, squinting in the dark. Going into a mystery cave without a light may not have been her brightest idea.

The Mantipodis straightened up as she neared and cocked its head until it was almost completely horizontal. Ava would have tried to talk to it in Zrix'dhorian, but she'd barely opened her mouth before speaking became secondary to punching as it charged toward her. Ava had no time to pull her elbow back before it had her pinned against the hard cave wall with a talon-like stinger driving through her shoulder.

Ava wriggled her shoulders and willed her body to start twitching fast enough to begin vibrating, causing the Mantipodis to pull back in alarm. The distraction allowed her to break away and fly up. She used her energy burst to break through the ceiling of the cave, creating a window of light above them. Unfortunately, this also allowed the Mantipodis opportunity to burrow further into the ground.

Ava emerged from the cave barely five minutes after entering, covered in goop and with a giant hole through her shoulder.

"How's it feeling now?" Nic leaned back against the arm of the couch beside Ava, who was sitting ramrod straight with bandages wrapped around her chest.

"Like I got stung by a giant alien bug."

Nic had picked her up from Clinton Medical Center, where she'd been transported to the private wing. It was where they sent all injured AOs—a specialized section where the doctors and veterinarians had all signed non-disclosure agreements. Ava wasn't in there often. Despite the whole doctor–patient confidentiality thing, she still felt uncomfortable removing her mask in front of other people.

The year before, RainnTech had perfected a non-invasive, laser skin-grafting tool. It looked like a fancy barcode scanner. Nic had been able to "liberate" one of the earlier models. It healed most of Ava's invasive wounds—bullets, cuts and bruises, and so on. But every once in a while, she'd get speared by a giant pincer, and off to the hospital she would have to go.

Nic had once explained how Ava's cells regenerated at an abnormally fast rate, accelerating her healing ability. To Ava, the words mostly meant that she was hard to kill. Which, she supposed, had its benefits.

"I don't get it." Nic leaned in and studied the bandaged area. "How did it even pierce your skin through the suit? I developed that suit. It's made out of graphene thread."

"I don't know," Ava admitted. "But that insect thing was big, Nic. And last night when the slug went nuts in the precinct cell, I got covered in gunk and my skin felt weird after, like I was buzzing."

Nic looked concerned. "What about your powers?"

"All fine." Ava rolled her shoulder experimentally. She could almost feel her muscles stitching themselves back together.

"You should take it easy. I vote *Star Trek* and too much take-out."

"Uh, yeah. I sort of have a date tonight."

Nic schooled her face into a neutral expression. "So, after everything we said, you still went ahead with this thing?"

"I was going to tell you. It's not the same as what we talked about."

"Oh, so you're not compromising your integrity by pretending to be sleeping with your boss?"

"I…" Ava sighed. "I know you've always protected me. But I'm twenty-seven, not seventeen. You don't have to save me from being stuffed into lockers anymore."

"Fine." Nic shrugged. "You make your own decisions, but I don't have to agree with all of them."

"I wish you would though," Ava muttered.

"*You* still haven't come around on anchovy and pineapple pizza. We all have our things."

"Yeah, but your thing is gross."

Nic's expression suggested that Ava's thing was too, and Ava laughed despite herself.

Putting her hand on Ava's now mostly healed shoulder, Nic said, "I just don't want you to get hurt."

Ava wanted to shrug it off, to make light of it, but this was Nic, and lying to her was impossible.

"I could do pizza and *Star Trek* tonight. Gwen can wait."

CHAPTER 5

AVA DRUMMED HER FINGERTIPS AGAINST the armrest as she bounced her knee up and down. She absently scratched at the little red splotch on her wrist that she'd attributed to stress. She was fairly certain she couldn't actually break out in hives, so it was definitely psychosomatic.

It'll be fine, Ava thought. *He's just a kid. How bad could it really be?*

"Stop fidgeting." She glanced at Gwen, on the opposite end of the long backseat, leaning against the door. She was peering out the window, and Ava's eyes traced the long, delicate curve of her neck.

"I'm sorry. I know I was the one who put this off last night, but now I sort of wish we'd gotten it over with. I'm…a little nervous."

"Well, don't be." Gwen turned to look her. "He likes you."

"He likes Ava, your assistant. I don't know how much he'll like me as your girlfriend." It was still weird, saying that word out loud.

Gwen didn't seem fazed. She was less antagonistic but more distant since Ava had called to reschedule the night before. "Has the transition caused you to change character?"

"No, of course not."

"Then, he likes you. My son is as fickle as any pre-pubescent boy, but there aren't many people he…" Gwen struggled for the word, "takes to. Trust me. We'll be fine."

There was something about that offhand *we* that made Ava's heart clench. She wanted to reach out and touch Gwen's shoulder, or her knee. But they were so far away from each other, even in the confines of the backseat.

Making a conscious effort to remain still despite her nerves, she found herself thinking back to the Mantipodis in the cave, and the way it had gone from curious to aggressive in a beat. There was something they weren't quite getting. She was caught by surprise when Gwen's voice broke through the din of traffic around them.

"I received a phone call from Alfonso yesterday morning."

It took Ava a second to place the name. "Oh."

"Yes." Gwen was back to facing the window.

"How is he?" Ava assumed that he hadn't called to offer his congratulations or send them a fruit basket.

"Unhappy."

"So that's why you've been—"

Gwen finally looked at her. "What?"

"Nothing." Ava pursed her lips and shook her head. "Um. What did he say?"

"A number of unpleasant things. To sum it up, he's appalled that I'm putting you and Luke through this façade."

"He knows?"

"No." Gwen pursed her lips in a tight smile. "But he knows me, and he knows I would never—"

"Date someone like me," Ava finished softly.

Gwen looked at her with sharp surprise. "That I would never allow him to take Luke away from me."

"Gwen." Ava's voice was soft and uncertain. There was so much she wanted to say.

"He's right." Gwen uncrossed her legs and allowed her head to fall back against the bolster. "The things they're already saying. That I'm 'going gay' as a publicity stunt, that you were seduced by the big, bad boss. God, was I really this naïve?"

Ava frowned a little and made a decision based purely on instinct. She scooted closer, which made Gwen sit up straight and face her completely, seemingly startled at the invasion of her personal space.

"I *wanted* to help," Ava stated. "I still do. I knew going into this that people might say awful things, because that's what people do before they understand something."

Gwen scoffed. "That makes no sense, Eisenberg. Of course people don't understand it. All they see is a predatory older woman going after her much younger assistant."

"Well, what if I was the one who went after you?" Ava sounded affronted. "I'm not a kid. I knew exactly what I was getting into. Maybe I'm the one getting the better deal here. I mean, how much better was I gonna do than Gwendolyn Knight? One of the most powerful women—"

"People."

"*People* in Hollywood. Tell *that* to the press."

Gwen conceded with a hum.

"If you've taught me anything in these last few years, it's that you've got to fight for what you believe in, despite what people say. This is your cause. O-our cause. I'm not going to give up." Ava fixed Gwen with a determined stare. "And neither should you."

"Well." Gwen cleared her throat. "You do have a point. And I suppose," she shrugged, "failure is not an option here."

"*TMZ* is already calling us Eisenknight."

Gwen scoffed. "An absurd portmanteau. If anything, my name should come first."

Ava grinned and fell back against the seat. She was suddenly feeling a lot better.

Ava entered Gwen's house with a sort of quiet reverence, afraid to talk too loudly. It was different now. Before, Ava had been sure of her place and her role. Now, she was tentative and a little lost, taking cues from Gwen.

The silent reverence broke within seconds as a small, skinny, ten-year-old boy with a thick shock of black hair and bright brown eyes came barreling down the hallway toward his mother.

Everyone knew Luke was adopted. It was hard to keep that a secret when your kid was black and you were obviously not. Still, it always surprised Ava how like Gwen he was—the way he bit his lower lip when he was frustrated, the way he was constantly moving his hands, gesticulating as he spoke, and the way he crossed his arms over his chest when he was impatient.

Gwen shrugged off her coat and handed it to Ava on habit, then brushed past her.

"Mom, Mom, Mom! Can Jacob come over this weekend? The new Swiftwing comic comes out on Friday and I wanna read it with him. He can't get it 'cause his mom thinks it's 'too mature.' She sucks."

Gwen's sharp intake of breath was followed by a reprimand. "Luke!"

"That's what Jacob said."

"I'm not sure you should put much stock into what Jacob Levinson says, sweetheart. Besides, you know you'll be with your dad this weekend while I'm shooting in Vancouver. Maybe next week."

Ava hurried to catch up.

"But—" Luke's attention was caught by Ava's footsteps, and he turned to her with surprise. He seemed to withdraw a little, which made Ava think that he might not have been as vocal had he known she was there from the start. "Oh. Hi, Ava!"

"Hey, Luke." She gave an awkward wave. "How's it going?"

"Fine, thanks. How are you?"

Ava smiled widely. He was a curious combination of well-mannered breeding and wild kid energy. "I'm great."

Gwen glanced between them before disappearing down the hallway, heels tip-tapping on the polished hardwood floors.

"Are you staying for dinner?" Luke asked.

"Yup."

He puffed out his cheeks and stared at the floor, and Ava remembered how it always took him a while to warm up.

"Any idea what's on the menu?"

Luke shrugged. "I think there's sorbet for dessert."

"Lemon? It's my favorite."

Luke looked up at her with a serious expression. "I think peach is the superior flavor, but Mom likes lemon too."

"Peach?" Ava grimaced comically. "You've obviously never had a three-citrus scoop from *Jessie's*."

"Where's that?"

"Oh. Near my home in Lakewood."

"Your house is near a lake?"

"No, it's just called that. *Jessie's* is just down the road from where I grew up. They have the best sorbet in the known universe."

Luke pulled a face. "Have you *tasted* every sorbet in the known universe?"

"Of course," Ava teased, extracting a grin from him.

"Ava, would you like something to drink?" he asked suddenly, remembering his manners.

"Sure."

She followed him to the kitchen, which was decorated in pale colors—whites and lime greens. Ava's eyes went to the metallic *Swiftwing* fridge magnet holding up a notice about an upcoming parent–teacher night.

It was always a little disconcerting for Ava to see her symbol on T-shirts and baseball caps. It was weird to be a brand, when all she'd set out to do was make a difference. It was even weirder to be a brand on Gwen Knight's refrigerator. She knew that Luke was obsessed with the comics, and she supposed, by extension, Swiftwing. To be fair, there were a bunch of other superheroes he liked too.

More bizarre was Gwen's relationship with Swiftwing, though relationship may have been too strong of a word. The fact was, in many ways, Gwen was the reason that Ava had become Swiftwing, the reason she'd finally committed to this insane thing she'd been thinking about since she'd realized the extent of her abilities.

It was just over two years ago. Gwen was speaking at an AO equality rally when the first few gunshots scattered the crowd. Ava remembered it in slow motion. Seeing the shooter in his "America for Americans" T-shirt, seeing the bullet travel from the barrel of the gun, through the air, toward Gwen's heart. Ava saw the trajectory from a mile away. The rest was just instinct. Running toward Gwen, picking her up off the ground, depositing her out of harm's way, and flying away to double back before she was missed. It had happened so fast that Ava was merely a blur.

There was no going back after that, especially when Gwen—on every talk show, at every rally—had hailed Ava as her swift savior. The name Swiftwing had followed soon after.

Ava used to wonder what Gwen would say if she knew that she was talking to her loyal assistant and minion. Sometimes she was tempted to pull off her mask and reveal herself—but only sometimes.

Luke opened the refrigerator and stuck his head in. "There's chocolate milk and juice and diet soda and seltzer and—"

"I'll see to Ava and myself." Gwen came into the kitchen wearing flat, comfortable shoes. She'd changed into a thin, fuzzy sweater that had Ava imagining how soft it would feel between her fingers.

"Sit, sit." She waved her hand at Ava, who perched on one of the island stools. Gwen moved past Luke and pulled two beautiful glasses down from a cupboard.

"Wine?"

Ava cleared her throat, distinctly *affected* by this casual, relaxed version of Gwen. "Sure."

"Mom, do we still have lemon sorbet? It's Ava's favorite."

Gwen gave Ava a curious look, as if amused that this was where their conversation had landed. "I think we're out of sorbet. But we do have the peanut brittle gelato."

"Awesome." Luke turned to Ava. "It's not the *best* gelato in the known universe, but it's good."

She grinned, charmed. "I guess I'll just have to test it and see."

"Mom, can we go to Lakewood?"

Ava's gaze moved between Luke and Gwen, who was expertly opening a bottle of a white, fruity-smelling wine. She lowered the bottle opener. "Why on earth would you want to go to Lakewood?"

"Ava said there's a sorbet place that serves the best sorbet. It's where she grew up."

"Well, it's just my mom there now," Ava interjected.

Gwen's eyebrows drew together for a second. "I'm sure you can find just as wonderful sorbet around here, sweetheart."

Ava accepted a glass of wine from Gwen with a soft "thanks" and turned her attention back to Luke.

"Ava, did you know that spadefoot frogs smell like peanut butter?"

"I did not." She grinned at him. "Hey, do you think they hang out with jellyfish?"

Luke laughed loudly, causing Gwen to turn her head in surprise. "I can show you this book I have about amphibians and reptiles. It's pretty neat."

"You know my best friend had a salamander when she was younger. His name was Sylvester, and he was really polite."

Luke was delighted. "No way."

"Way."

"Mom, can I have a—"

"Absolutely not."

Luke practically hopped on the spot. "A newt?"

"What did you do?" Gwen shot Ava a death glare.

"I'm going to get my book. It's so cool." He bounced past them.

"Sorry." Ava turned to Gwen with a smile, not really sorry at all.

Dinner was take-out from a five-star Vietnamese place halfway across town. Ava hadn't even known *Saigon Kitchen* did delivery, but she supposed Gwen Knight was always the exception.

They sat at the table, candles lit and the television off. It was nice, not too formal. Ava wondered if this was how Gwen and Luke usually ate dinner, and she thought of herself and Nic holding cheesy pizza slices, their feet on the couch, watching old episodes of *Arrested Development*.

They talked a bit about Luke's day and the science test he'd taken. Gwen suggested that they go to an upcoming talk by Bill Nye at the UCLA science campus.

Ava was halfway through her ice cream when Gwen said, "Luke, there's something Ava and I want to discuss with you."

Her heart began a heavy thud.

"Am I in trouble?" Luke asked

"No, sweetheart." Gwen ventured a glance at Ava. "This is about us."

"Oh." He dropped his spoon into his bowl and watched Gwen expectantly.

"As you know, Ava and I have been working together for a while, and we've gotten to know each other really well. We've become close. And recently, our relationship has developed into something more."

"More what?"

Gwen glanced at Ava briefly. "More romantic."

Luke swirled his spoon into his ice cream until it was a gloopy mess. "Like, dating?"

"Exactly like that."

He didn't look up at them. "Ava is your girlfriend?"

Gwen inhaled. "Yes."

"Oh."

"Do you have any questions? Anything you want to ask us?"

Luke eventually looked up from his dessert. "Do you still work for my mom?"

"I do. Nothing's changed." She was eager to make this as normal-sounding as possible.

"So, my mom is your girlfriend *and* your boss?"

"Well." Ava fiddled nervously with her napkin. "We're very careful to keep work and home separate."

"Lisa Yu has two moms." He turned to Gwen. "They're lesbians. Is that what you guys are?"

Ava choked back a cough and glanced at Gwen, who looked pale.

"We haven't really..." Gwen pursed her lips, studiously *not* looking at Ava now. "It's not something we... I mean, I have had, in the past, with... women, and I suppose if you wanted a word, uh, I think bise—"

"I think labels are great for some people," Ava interjected. "But I also think that, you know, there's a—a spectrum, and it doesn't really matter how you, um—" She shot a panicked glance at Gwen, who watched her with a raised eyebrow and offered no guidance. "...how you identify. Or at least, it's not that important to me—us."

"My girlfriend, the millennial." Gwen muttered under her breath.

Luke absorbed this and then frowned. "Does Dad know?"

"He's aware, yes."

Luke knocked his spoon against his bowl as he played with his ice cream. "So, are you trying to beat him?"

Gwen's eyebrows raised slowly. "Beat him?"

"You know, he married Stephanie and she's like, younger and stuff. Now you're gonna marry Ava." Gwen didn't correct him. "And she's even prettier than Stephanie, so you'll win."

"Honey, this is not a competition." Gwen lied through her teeth. "This has nothing to do with your father."

"Dad said I'm gonna be spending more time at his house. Is he mad at you?"

Gwen's face moved in micro expressions: the subtle flare of her nostrils, the twitch of her jaw. Ava was attuned to the little things.

"Your father is mistaken." Gwen replied calmly. "And no, he's not angry."

Luke narrowed his eyes at his mother in an expression that was so *Gwen* that Ava wanted to smile, despite the tension. "You're sure?"

"Yes." Gwen said in a tone that left no room for discussion.

"Is Ava going to be over more?"

"Only if that's okay with you," Ava jumped in.

Luke went back to staring at the table. "I guess."

"Is there anything more you want to know?" Gwen pressed on.

"No." He pushed his ice cream bowl away. "Can I go now?"

Gwen looked like she wanted to say more, but she sighed. "Yes, all right."

Luke walked away from the table, and then stopped and turned. "Hey Ava, will you come say bye before you leave?"

She gave him a small smile. "Sure."

"He's always been so perceptive." Gwen tucked her legs underneath her. They were in the living room, across from each other on two soft gray couches. Garbo had waltzed in the moment Ava sat down and hopped onto her lap, demanding to be petted. This was a standard occurrence.

"Do you think he'll be okay?"

"Well, he's not thrilled. That much is clear." She leaned forward to put her glass on a pretty beaded coaster. "But he likes you, Ava. That hasn't changed. As long as we're sensitive, I think he'll come around. We're the adults here, after all." Gwen sounded like she was reciting lines from a script.

Ava watched her carefully. "You're thinking this was a mistake." She ran her fingers through Garbo's thick fur.

"What I'm thinking is really not your concern right now."

"Right, sorry."

Gwen closed her eyes and pinched the bridge of her nose. "No, I am. You're not my assistant in here. You're my guest. And you're, well, you're putting a lot at stake for me."

"It's okay," Ava said softly.

"I am grateful." Gwen seemed so intense suddenly. "For everything."

Ducking her head, Ava laughed off her discomfort. "It's nothing, Miss Knight. I mean, Gwen." She gave a sheepish smile. "Old habits."

Gwen exhaled with a little sound of relief. "Well, the worst is over. The tabloids have sunk their teeth into this. Both my son and ex-husband are aware and disapproving, and I assume your friends have already warned you off."

Ava took a big gulp from her glass. The wine was good, better than she'd ever had. Which, considering the price tag, wasn't surprising. "They're actually coming around. They just want me to be happy."

"And that's what you've told them?" Gwen looked amused. "That I make you happy?"

"You told me to sell it." Ava heard the defensiveness in her own voice.

"Mmm. And how exactly do I make you happy?" Gwen's smirk had Ava's insides twisting up.

"I don't understand."

"Going back to our conversation in the car. Why does this relationship work? Hypothetically speaking, of course." There was a glint of challenge in her eyes. "Let's say you had to answer some inane question for an interview, which, depending on how long we're forced to keep this up, is a very likely possibility."

"But you'd deal with that, right? I don't want to be on any covers, or-or on any talk shows."

"Relax. I wouldn't trust you near a microphone. You'd nervously chatter everyone to death."

Ava was not about to dispute this fact.

"Even so, if you were caught by some or other media hound, tell me how you'd handle it."

"I'd tell them the truth."

"Oh, well." Gwen fluttered a hand dramatically. "I can't imagine why I was worried."

"Every good lie contains an element of truth," Ava explained.

Gwen looked intrigued and lowered her glass. "Agreed."

"So, I'd tell them how inspiring you are, how you've taught me so much." Truth. "That after working so close for so long, it was impossible not to fall in, um, love with you." Truth?

"All right. You don't want to oversell it." But Gwen seemed pleased. "How do you feel about the fact that I'm your boss? Or that I'm nearly twenty years your senior?"

"Our work lives and our personal lives are two very separate things." Ava answered as though she was being quizzed. "In fact, we work better because we're so in sync with each other. I can anticipate your needs before you ask."

"You didn't answer the age question."

"Because it doesn't matter."

"Don't be so earnest. You'll be chewed up and spat out by them." Gwen finished off her drink. "Of course it matters. You were in diapers when I was graduating college. You don't think people are going to focus on that?"

"What matters is who we are now. Love isn't..." Ava frowned, trying to articulate herself perfectly. "It isn't about facts and figures. It's about the way I feel when I look at you. It's about not caring about stuff like age and race and species... Well, okay, maybe not that last one, but my point is that no one can dictate the rules. It is what it is. And what it is," she shrugged helplessly, "is everything I've ever wanted."

Her heart pounded in her ears throughout the entire speech, but it was a strange relief to say it out loud, even in the context of playing pretend.

"Well." Gwen watched her with a rare kind of appreciation. "Maybe you should give that interview after all."

"I-I don't think I'd be very good," she said with a self-deprecating laugh.

"I disagree. You've practically convinced me that we're perfect for each other, and I know this is just a ruse."

Ava said nothing. She felt unbalanced, as though they were crossing into something dangerous and unknowable, and she was the only one who could see it. Gwen was oblivious, because for Gwen, this was a means to an end.

"We'll be leaving the day after tomorrow," Gwen interrupted her musings. "We should make an effort to spend some personal time together while in Vancouver. I know of a number of decent restaurants. And we'll share a room, of course. I'll leave it up to you to arrange."

"O-of course."

"It's all about keeping up appearances, Ava. People believe what they see, and the more they see us together, well...that's half the battle won."

"Appearances." She nodded. "Got it."

Ava was considering feigning a yawn, because it was almost eight and she wanted to try for an evening sweep of the city before bed, when her phone vibrated against her thigh. With a start, she grappled for it.

It was an email from Captain Fernandez. Ava read quickly, her heart sinking.

"I, uh. I need to make a quick call." Her eyes flickered nervously toward Gwen, who watched her for a moment, then stood to take their glasses to the kitchen. Garbo followed, clearly hoping for food.

Ava scrolled to Nic's number and waited for her to pick up.

"Are you okay?" Nic answered.

"I got an update from the unit." Ava walked to the furthest end of the room and hunched as she spoke. "The officer who was in the cell with me is under sedation. His kidneys were failing. They think it's related to whatever he was exposed to by the alien we caught in the quarry."

"Oh God. You were exposed too."

"Nic." Ava gripped the phone a little tighter. "I'm okay," she whispered. "Alien DNA, remember?"

"I know, I just…" Nic sighed. "After what happened yesterday—"

"I need you to do something," Ava interrupted. "The database in DC can't find anything on the alien. Could you hack into the AO census and see if you can find anything they didn't? Anything about insectoids or venomous species. Maybe it'll trigger something I learned as a kid."

"It's the worm thing, right?"

"Right."

"On it," Nic promised. "But don't obsess over this, okay? I know you. There's nothing you can do for that officer right now."

"Yeah, okay. Thanks."

Ava stared at the phone for a second after Nic hung up, sighing heavily. Nic was right. There wasn't anything she could do at this stage, and that knowledge killed her. She looked up to find herself alone. Gwen had disappeared, and Ava was suddenly exhausted. That was strange, because it was still so early, and alcohol didn't particularly affect her.

She meandered down the corridor and found Gwen in her study, wearing her glasses and frowning at a script.

"Everything all right?" Gwen asked without looking up, as if she didn't really care one way or the other. But her tone was softer than it would have been at work.

"Just roommate stuff," Ava replied, stepping further into the room. "Is that the Hedy Lamarr biopic?"

Gwen made a noise of confirmation.

"Is it any good?" Ava took another step forward, desperate to read the script. It had been penned by one of her favorite writers. She knew it was going to be good.

"I can't tell yet," Gwen answered. "Daniel thinks it would be good for me to do something silly and light after we wrap, but…" She looked at the script thoughtfully and then handed it to Ava. "Here, have a look. Tell me what you think."

"You want my honest opinion?" Ava took the script from her.

"Well, you're the writer, aren't you?"

"You remember that?" Ava didn't think Gwen knew anything about her besides how good she was at getting ice cream at 2 a.m.

"You wouldn't shut up about it your first few months on the job. I assume you're still aiming for a screenwriter position."

"Yeah." Ava suddenly felt defensive. "I am. I just, I got busy."

"Hmm." Gwen appraised her and then gestured toward the chair across the room. "Make yourself comfortable. I have to go over tomorrow's lines."

Some time later, Luke moseyed into the study to announce that he was out of his favorite bubble-gum-scented shampoo. Gwen directed him to her bathroom, telling him to use hers until she could get more.

Gwen's gaze was fond as Luke walked away, grumbling about how he was going to smell like *mom*. There was nothing particularly profound or intimate about the moment. In fact, it was boringly domestic, but Ava understood how special it was to be allowed here, to be invited into Gwen's private world.

Luke's interruption broke whatever spell had been cast over them, and Gwen leaned back against the couch to have a languid stretch.

"So?" She gave Ava an expectant look. "What do you think?"

"I think," Ava put the script down, "that you'd be remarkable in this. It's brilliant."

Gwen narrowed her eyes. "I'm going to have to fight both Rachel Weiss and Kate Winslet tooth and nail for this."

"You'd win."

Gwen laughed, loudly and with abandon, and Ava found herself grinning in response. For a moment, as Gwen's laughter died down and Ava's smile faded, they stared at each other, and something felt heavy, different.

Gwen cleared her throat and held her hand out for the script. "Well, I'll certainly take your opinion into account."

When Luke yelled that he was going to bed, Ava assumed that this was the point where Gwen left to tuck him in. It made her think of her own mother coming to say goodnight—and to check that she wasn't up late reading with her Lexicube (which happened more often than not).

"I should—" Ava jutted her thumb in the general direction of elsewhere.

Gwen stood. "Yes, it is getting late. You probably have—" She made a face. "What *do* you do, when you're not fulfilling my every command?"

Save the city from crime and alien threats brought down when my ship crash-landed seventeen years ago. "Oh, you know...stuff."

"Well, far be it from me to keep you from *stuff*."

Ava took a moment to say goodbye to Luke, and almost laughed out loud when she stepped into his bedroom and saw the blown-up, framed print of Swiftwing next to what looked to be an autographed poster of *The Empire Strikes Back*. Ava wasn't sure if she was freaked out or flattered.

Luke smiled at her. His hair was wet, and he did smell like Gwen's shampoo.

"I like your stars," Ava said, pointing up at the ceiling.

"I tried to get all the constellations." He moved past her to switch the light off, and the room came alive with the neon glow of a hundred stars. "Mom did the Milky Way." He pointed to the stream of stars that crossed the ceiling. "See?"

Ava imagined Gwen on a little stepladder, painstakingly placing every sticker in its proper position. She thought about what Gwen was fighting for, and how her own role in it, as strange and confusing as it was, really might make a difference.

"It's really cool," Ava whispered in the dark. "You've got your own little galaxy here."

When Luke turned the lights back on, he was frowning. "Hey Ava?"

"Yeah?"

"If you're dating my mom, can we still be friends? Will you still like, help me with homework and stuff?"

Ava took in a breath, surprised at the twinge in her chest. "Of course," she replied honestly. "Of course I will. We're friends no matter what."

"Okay." He looked down and kicked the toe of his sock against the rug. "Thanks for coming to say goodnight."

"I'll see you soon, okay?" Ava smiled warmly.

Luke grinned and waved at her as she left.

Gwen walked her to the door—another first. They were quiet as the evening settled down around them.

Ava stepped onto the front step and turned to Gwen, who was leaning against the doorframe. Her hair was slightly tousled from where it had met the back of the couch. The bridge of her nose had two fading indents from her glasses, and she looked suddenly smaller—human and delicate.

Ava knew she had to say goodnight, but that would mean the end of the interaction, and she wanted to live in this moment for a while longer.

And all at once, she was overcome with the suicidal urge to lean in and kiss Gwen goodnight. She thought back to that moment in the restaurant, the softest press of lips against skin, the resulting tingle.

The inclination took Ava by surprise; perhaps it shouldn't have, but she'd never explicitly thought about *kissing* Gwen before. And suddenly, she was standing in Gwen's doorway, after spending the evening together, and it felt natural, almost inevitable. And really, it would have been so easy to just lean in, close the space between them, and see what happened.

"The car is waiting downstairs," Gwen said briefly, knocking Ava out of her reverie.

"I, um." Ava shrugged, relieved to be pulled out of the insanity. "I had a good time tonight, you know, considering."

"Considering," Gwen echoed, smiling wryly, and Ava thought that she could get used to Gwen looking at her like that.

Ava asked Jonah to drop her at a coffee shop a few blocks away from the house, and flew the rest of the way, aware of her heavy limbs and eyelids. The evening replayed in her mind—conversations and expressions—the sound of Luke's laughter, Gwen's indulgent smiles. Appearances were half the battle won, Gwen had said, and Ava wondered about the other half and just how far they'd have to go to go make sure they won.

Nic was right, she thought, with a hint of panic. Someone was going to get hurt, and she suspected that it wasn't going to be Gwen.

CHAPTER 6

THE PLANE RIDE FROM LA to Vancouver took two hours and forty minutes. They flew in Gwen's private jet, the one she'd "acquired" from her last marriage. It was supposedly the same kind of plane that Beyoncé had given Jay-Z, but Gwen claimed hers was bigger. Ava had flown in it countless times, but never had the privilege of sitting across from Gwen. She was usually a couple of seats behind, pretending to listen to Daniel describe the new house he and his husband were redecorating.

Sitting with Gwen was remarkably boring; she read through most of the trip. Ava alternated between staring out the window and fidgeting on her laptop, looking for Michelin-star restaurants in Vancouver. Of course, they were all booked out for months in advance, so she'd have to wait until she was on the ground to name-drop and get a reservation. Not for the first time, she thought about how absolutely insane it was to be arranging a date for herself and Gwen.

They were booked into a boutique hotel a little outside of the city. It was close to the shooting locations, but far enough away that Gwen would have a modicum of privacy if she wanted to go out. Sometimes she was lucky, and a scarf and oversized sunglasses hid her well enough. Other times, it was like fighting off a pack of rabid dogs; the paparazzi were ruthless—provoked, more often than not, by Gwen's icy refusal to play along.

Gwen stepped off the plane and shivered, pulling her parka closer around herself. "God, did we arrive during the revival of the Ice Age? Why the hell is it so cold?"

"We're experiencing some crazy gales this season," the captain said, stepping out onto the tarmac. "It's supposed to die down next week."

"Lucky us," Gwen deadpanned and pulled up her hood.

For Ava, the wind nipped and bit at her skin, and she shivered, surprised that she was so sensitive to it. She rarely felt cold the way humans did, and quickly decided that she did not enjoy the novelty.

The hotel was as beautiful as it had looked on the website, but a lot more remote than Ava had anticipated. Along with Gwen and Ava, Nancy the director and two producers were also staying there. Gooding was not. Despite the fervent speculation about Gwen and Ava, rumors about Gwen and her co-star persisted. Most were thanks to "sources" who claimed the two could barely stand each other on set, despite their "sizzling chemistry on screen." Ava was particularly annoyed by one article, which suggested that since they shone so brightly in front of the cameras, surely they must be sleeping together.

For the most part, however, tabloids were abuzz with gossip about Gwen and Ava, or as *US Weekly* put it, the Queen of Hollywood and her lady-in-waiting.

Gwen was ensconced in the presidential suite, of course. Ava had made sure of that. She had also made sure that the room was equipped with two beds.

The bell boy, who looked about twelve, deposited their luggage, and Gwen tipped him generously.

"Well," Gwen breathed out once they were alone, and turned her gaze around the room. It was big enough that they'd be able to spend an entire day together and not have to see each other. The second bed was up a wooden staircase on a little loft platform. Ava would be far away enough to sneak out if Swiftwing was needed. It was perfect. Perfect, except for the fact that she and Gwen were going to be forced to play the doting couple.

The first day of shooting was cold. It was cold and beautiful, and the ideal location to shoot the planet's surface. They were on set for almost eleven hours as the crew rushed around aligning and realigning equipment. Ava spent most of it clutching a cup of coffee and arranging Gwen's schedule for the following week.

Gwen's rented trailer was nowhere near as fancy as the one in LA, but she was in her chair or in front of the camera most of the time anyway. Location shoots were always exhausting.

They got back to the hotel around 8 p.m.—still early enough go out to dinner, although Ava suspected that Gwen was as tired as she was. When they entered the room, Gwen strode wordlessly for the bathroom. Ava thought she heard singing as she sank into the couch.

The next thing she knew, Gwen was standing over her, wearing pajama shorts and a thin, oversized T-shirt with a cat demanding kisses for being cute. It was such a bizarre image that Ava blinked a few times to make sure she wasn't still dreaming.

"Uh, hi," she rasped, and Gwen raised an eyebrow, somehow managing to look as intimidating as ever despite the cartoon kitten on her shirt.

"You were talking in your sleep."

"Oh." Ava sat up and ran the back of her hand over her cheek, which to her mortification was damp. "I, um..." she cleared her throat. "What did I say?"

"Nothing intelligible," Gwen assured her, and walked over to the room service cart by the door.

Ava's eyes followed her ass, still somewhat perplexed by her sleep attire.

"Are you hungry?" Gwen lifted two trays and the smell of food filled the room.

"Starving," Ava admitted. "I think I've been running on coffee all day."

"That makes two of us." Gwen brought the trays over to the little dining area. It was weird, Ava thought, seeing Gwen in this context. So...normal.

Dinner was hamburgers and fries and panna cotta, which Ava thought was really just fancy chocolate pudding, but whatever. They spoke about filming and the following day's schedule, until Gwen asked, "Why writing?"

"Excuse me?" Ava swallowed the last of her pudding.

"You want to be a screenwriter. Why writing, and not, I don't know, producing or directing?"

Ava shrugged. "I guess I like the idea of creating worlds and people within those worlds. In movies," she thought for a moment, "you get to step into someone else's life. It's a safe escape. I want to create those stories. I…" Ava shook her head. "It's silly."

"Tell me," Gwen demanded softly.

"I want to write movies where the good guys win, and people are loyal, and parents don't die, and heroes live happily ever after."

"That doesn't sound very realistic."

"Exactly," Ava replied.

Gwen smiled softly. "You're a romantic, Eisenberg."

"I know. It's outdated."

"It's refreshing," Gwen countered. "Heroic even."

Ava was about to argue that there was nothing particularly heroic about idealism, when Gwen stood and began piling the plates back on the cart.

Ava stretched and realized that she probably smelled like a day of work. "I should probably—" she began.

At the same time, Gwen turned and said, "How do you—"

"You go first," Ava said as they watched each other uncertainly.

"Well, sometimes after a long day, Luke and I wind down by playing UNO, and I thought…" she trailed off, uncharacteristically hesitant.

"Sure! Just let me grab a quick shower first." Ava tried to sound more excited than confused, and hoped it showed. She wondered what the rules were about beating your boss at cards.

"So, you're surviving, huh?" Nic took another bite of the maple donut Ava had brought her from a 24-hour bakery in Vancouver.

They were in the lab, where Nic was pulling an all-nighter working on a new project—a basically indestructible protective canvas for parked cars around LA. The rate of AO-related damages was so high that insurance companies were rioting. The year before, an AO from the outer planet Tokaatshu had reached her age of maturity and ballooned to a massive 160 feet. She'd destroyed a good chunk of K-Town before Ava was able to calm her down and sedate her. Nic's shield would have hypothetically saved a bunch of cars from being squished.

"It's been fine," Ava said honestly. "I mean, a little weird, but fine."

"Weird like she asked you to be her surrogate baby mama?"

"What!" Ava nearly choked on her sprinkle-covered donut. "No! That's…no."

Nic shrugged. "Don't sound so offended. The woman clearly has no shame."

"Come on, Nic." Ava sighed. "I thought you were cool with this. She's not a bad person."

"I know," Nic conceded as she squinted into a microscope and adjusted the coarse focus. "I know, okay? Her foundation has done some awesome stuff for AO equality, and she's down with the gays, and her kid is black. So, she's a good person underneath all of that make-up and meanness. But, you're a freakin' superhero. You literally save lives. You deserve," Nic moved another slide under the microscope, "…more."

Ava finished her donut in silence. She knew Nic was just looking out for her. Nic was always looking out for her. But she didn't see Gwen the way Ava did. She hadn't been there earlier that evening when Ava had won at UNO and Gwen had dramatically tossed up her cards in protest, causing Ava to laugh. She hadn't heard Gwen call Luke before his bedtime to read him the next chapter of *Howl's Moving Castle*.

"I should get going," Ava finally said, standing. "We've got a 6 a.m. call time."

Nic looked up from her microscope. "Hey, will you send me our Hulu details again? I'm having trouble logging in."

Ava grinned. "Genius hacker-slash-chemical-engineer-slash-mad-scientist, and she can't figure out how to log into Hulu."

Nic made a face and gave Ava the finger. "Get out of here, Swiftwing."

The following day was miserable. It rained all morning, followed by gale force winds. They got through a third of the scenes before the weather made filming impossible. Gwen and Ron Gooding, who were stubbornly ignoring each other between takes, had two big scenes that had to be moved to the following morning when the weather was due to clear. Gwen looked annoyed and cold, wrapped in her parka with the hood up and the fluffy trim framing her face. There were raindrops on her eyelashes, and Ava wanted to wipe them away. Instead, she handed Gwen a mug of hot tea.

"I'm meeting a friend for lunch," Gwen said, her tone offhand, once they were in the car back to the hotel. "You'll need to entertain yourself today."

Ava's first inclination was to ask if Gwen needed her to book a table somewhere before she realized that Gwen wasn't telling her this as her boss. She was merely discussing her plans.

"I'll be okay," Ava answered. "This place is so beautiful, and I haven't really taken any pictures. How will my Instagram followers know that I'm still alive?"

Gwen scoffed. "How indeed." A minute or so went by before she added, "We should take a selfie."

"Huh?" That sentence coming from Gwen's mouth was so bizarre that Ava wasn't sure she'd heard correctly.

"A selfie," Gwen repeated as if the idea pained her. "For your Instagram. That's what millennials in relationships do, is it not?"

"Uh, I guess." Ava turned to Gwen. "Do you wanna do it now?"

"No time like the present."

Ava whipped out her phone and held it up. The seatbelts were keeping her and Gwen pretty far apart, so they both leaned in, heads touching, and when Ava said, "Okay, smile!" Gwen actually did. God, she was good at that, Ava thought, as she snapped the photo and chose a filter. They actually looked like a couple—happy and goofy and normal.

"What about..." Ava turned the phone to Gwen so she could read the caption. *Experiencing the best of Vancouver* followed by the heart emoji.

Gwen made a face. "It's awful."

"It's Instagram," Ava countered and shared it. By the time the car reached the hotel, the photo had over four thousand likes, including one from Taylor Swift.

"Miss Knight, we've got a slight media issue," the driver said as he opened the door for them.

Ava saw flashes before anything else, and then there was a burly security guy at their side, helping Gwen out of the car, shielding her from the general chaos. Someone had leaked their location. Ava was distracted by the sound of clicking when she felt Gwen's hand in hers, pulling her closer. Ava gripped it tightly, and didn't let go until they were in the hotel elevator.

Ava spent the rest of the afternoon in Peru. She had discovered the little Aymaran village almost a year before, when they were almost wiped out by a flood that was all over the news. Since then, Ava had been back many times. They treated her as a friend to the village, and she often went there to escape for a while.

Her nickname was Pajarita—Little Bird.

Ava sat by the fountain in the dusty square, playing hand clap games with a few of the little girls. One of them ran up to Ava with a praying mantis on the back of her hand.

"*Un mantis religiosa!*" she said excitedly, transferring the little creature into Ava's palm.

Ava studied it and thought about the Mantipodis in the cave. It was still on the run, and still unstable. Ava couldn't understand it. She didn't have extensive knowledge, but she did know that the Mantipodii were not a violent race. Something was aggravating the one she had encountered.

She had received an update from Captain Fernandez earlier that day. They had deduced that whatever Norman the worm had sprayed was a kind of defense mechanism, a toxin intended to poison its attacker. Things did not look good for the officer in quarantine. Ava couldn't shake the feeling that there was a connection between Norman and the Mantipodis that had attacked her in the cave. It couldn't be a coincidence that they'd both appeared around the same time.

By the time she flew back, it was almost sundown in Canada. She managed to make it to the hotel room about ten minutes before Gwen, who waltzed in, tossed her purse on the couch, and announced that they would be going to a party on their last night in town.

"You don't have to come," Gwen quickly amended. "This is a rather intimate gathering of people I actually tolerate. Some of them I even like. And I wouldn't want to monopolize your precious free time. You'll have until tomorrow to decide."

Ava didn't know if Gwen actually wanted her to come, or if this was her way of asking Ava not to. After all, these were Gwen's friends. She might not want a pseudo-girlfriend tagalong in the company of her peers. But then Gwen said, "Of course, if you do want to come, it might be fun. Though I can't promise anything."

And Ava beamed, because Gwen wanted her along. "Yes. I'd love to."

CHAPTER 7

AVA WORE A DRESS THAT she'd packed on a whim, in case they went to a fancy restaurant. The longer they kept this up, the longer her clothes rack would need to be. She hadn't quite taken into account the cost of being Gwen Knight's significant other. Of course, Gwen paid when they went out, and Ava had no doubt that she'd fund a wardrobe too. But Ava didn't want Gwen buying her clothes that she'd never wear again once their little charade ended.

The party was as intimate as Gwen had predicted. Not more than fifty or so people, gathered under fairy lights and heat lamps on the deck of a beautiful lake house.

Gwen introduced Ava as her partner, and no one cried foul. They offered inquisitive glances, and whispered amongst themselves—some whispers simply curious, others snide.

That's the assistant, right?

The one who survived against all odds?

Well, it seems now we know why.

God, look at those arms.

I say good for Gwen.

Don't you think she looks a bit like…never mind.

Ava smiled at them all, staying close to Gwen, who kept a steady hand on her back and steered her into safe crowds, where people said things like, "Gwen Knight, where are you hiding that fountain of youth?" and "Darling, will you be at this year's UN summit for refugees and migrants? You know we could use your voice."

Every so often, Gwen leaned in close and whispered something salacious about someone in the crowd. "That's Louise Heyer," she murmured, her breath warm against Ava's neck. "She just landed the lead in HBO's new drama. She also happens to be dating the producer's son."

"Who's that?" Ava asked, nodding toward a strikingly attractive young man who seemed to dominate every conversation. She only asked because she had overheard him talking about his date with Swiftwing the previous week, and either she'd sleepwalked through said date, or he was talking out of his ass.

"Marcus Moore. Broadway actor. Perpetual playboy." Gwen's scowl deepened as she watched him preen. "I suspect he's your type." She glanced back to Ava.

"He is not." Ava scoffed dramatically. "Besides," she amended quickly, "I'm sort of learning that I don't really have a type."

Gwen narrowed her eyes, contemplating Ava for a moment before shrugging, as if she couldn't care less.

At one point, Gwen left her to speak to some beautiful person or other, and Ava found herself with a glass of champagne in her hand, caught up in conversation with the creator of one of her favorite shows as a kid.

It was a world removed from beer and charades at the apartment, and she couldn't imagine doing it every Wednesday night, but it was exciting, being surrounded by so many people who were actively shaping pop culture. She wandered from conversation to conversation, not really engaging, but soaking it in.

Gwen found her at the bar and kissed her.

It was fleeting, just a brush of lips that unraveled Ava completely. She stiffened and almost shattered the glass in her hand.

"Relax," Gwen murmured. Ava felt the press of Gwen's breasts against her side and wondered just how the hell she was supposed to do that.

"S—sorry," Ava whispered, her heart racing.

"Alfonso's golfing buddy is here. I'm almost certain that he's already been through the gossip mill, but I wouldn't mind giving him something to add to the grapevine."

"What—" Ava cleared her throat, suddenly convinced that the champagne was making her dizzy. "What do you have in mind?"

"Come on." Gwen took her hand and led her to the little open area, where five or six other couples were already swaying to the music.

"I don't…" Ava began to panic when Gwen's arms encircled her neck. "I'm not really good at this."

"Just follow my lead," Gwen murmured as she stepped into Ava's space, fitting their bodies together. "Traditionally, you would have to put your arms around me as well."

"Oh. Yeah." Ava tentatively splayed one palm and against Gwen's back and placed the other on her shoulder. She felt like an awkward prom date.

"Now you move," Gwen gritted through her teeth. Ava began to sway, gently, acutely aware of the curves of Gwen's body, which seemed intent on shaping perfectly against hers.

"Better," Gwen whispered, tilting her head up and nuzzling her nose against Ava's cheek.

In the end, it wasn't the nose nuzzle or the closeness, or even the fact that Gwen's fingers were tracing soft patterns against the nape of Ava's neck.

It was the very loud, very telling sound of Gwen's heartbeat speeding up, and the crazy thought that maybe Gwen was actually enjoying this.

That was what made Ava stop in the middle of the dance. That was what made her flinch when Gwen touched her arm. That was the reason they left the party early and drove back to the hotel in awkward, stilted silence.

Gwen walked in ahead of Ava, heels clicking on the shiny hardwood floor of their room. She expertly tossed her coat over the rack, along with her small glittery purse.

Ava wobbled in a step behind, trying to keep up while balancing on her ridiculously high heels. They were uncomfortable, even for someone with an incredible pain threshold, and just the act of shoving her toes into that narrow space seemed wrong. She was grateful to slip out of them.

Gwen had kicked off her own heels by the time Ava struggled out of her jacket—much less gracefully than Gwen—and found her way to the kitchenette area. Gwen had her back to the counter, drinking a glass of water, looking so much smaller without her shoes or her long coat. Smaller, but no less intimidating.

Ava took a tentative step toward her. "Gwen, I—"

"You can't wince every time I touch you." Gwen lowered the glass against the marble countertop with a hard clink. "You were the one who convinced me that you could sell this, Ava. If you can't even…" Gwen shut her eyes and pressed her palm against her forehead. "What am I doing?"

Ava was filled with rising panic. She'd messed up. She knew she'd messed up, and now Gwen was standing there, questioning this entire thing, and it was Ava's fault. Because the thought of Gwen's hands on her, of Gwen's mouth against her skin exhilarated her—which, okay, was sort of terrifying. But how did she tell Gwen this without coming off like some opportunistic pervert?

She thought back to the party, to Gwen's lips against hers, the way Gwen's fingers had felt pressing into her side.

Half in tears, and frustrated that she couldn't articulate just why dancing with Gwen had been one of the most terrifying things she'd ever done, she said, "I'm sorry. It's…it's still a little weird. Not because you're my boss or, or because you're—" She took a chance, pre-empting Gwen's insecurities. "… older." Gwen's brows rose slowly, but she didn't say anything, and so Ava continued her fumbling explanation. "Anyone would be lucky to be with you. And to be touched by you would be… This is coming out wrong. I know you said it was okay, and to follow your lead, but I don't want to cross any lines. I don't want to…" *Forget that this was just pretend.* "I don't want to make you uncomfortable."

Gwen's expression changed from annoyance at this inarticulate ramble to something like disbelief, and then something even softer than that, almost tender. "You're concerned about me in all of this?"

Ava shrugged in a sort of helpless motion.

Gwen shook her head and strode past Ava, to the living area just adjacent to the kitchen. "Come with me."

The plush couch seemed to swallow Gwen up until she was half couch cushion, half person. She patted the space beside her and Ava sat, obedient.

Gwen watched her carefully, and the moment, for all its uncertainty, was charged with a strange sort of electricity. Ava couldn't quite explain it, except that it made her feel all restless and tingly. She sat with her back straight and faced Gwen, who had reclined back against the arm of the couch.

"For now," Gwen crossed her legs, and her already short dress rode up her toned thighs. Ava's eyes flickered down before she dragged them back to Gwen's face. "Just for now, let's forget about those pesky lines and boundaries. Is that all right with you?"

"I guess."

"Okay." Gwen smiled.

Was that supposed to be reassuring? Because it had her heart beating at twice its normal rate, and now she was feeling all breathless—and had the temperature been turned up?

"Now, have you ever slept with a woman?"

Ava choked on air. "No." And because this felt like some sort of test she was already failing, she added, "But I don't see how that's relevant."

"You will." That smile. "You've slept with men I assume?"

"A couple of times." She tried to sound casual, because she really didn't want to get into her generally pitiful sexual history.

But Gwen seemed amused. "And how was that?"

"F-fine." At best.

"Hmm." Gwen moved closer, and her knee bumped gently against Ava's thigh. "So, you know what you enjoy. What feels good?"

"I...this..." She reminded herself to breathe. *Breathe.* "I'm not really comfortable talking about this."

Gwen's gaze was thoughtful, and she nodded slowly. "All right. I'm not going to push. Not here. If you're still up for this, then I suppose we could dial back public appearances from now on. That way you don't have to look so utterly panicked every time I come close. And people won't begin to assume that I have the plague." Gwen patted Ava's knee absently and stood.

She was barely a step away when Ava found herself jumping up and blurting, "I do."

Gwen spun around, her expression coy. "Do what?"

"Um. Know what feels good," Ava whispered.

"Well." Gwen sauntered back toward her, until there was barely any space between them.

Ava resisted the urge to fall back down against the couch, despite her trembling knees.

"That's a start." Gwen's eyes trailed down the length of Ava's body, and she imagined that Gwen could see the way her heart thudded against her chest, as if trying to make a run for it. "Now, imagine you knew what I liked."

The pause went on long enough for Ava to swallow down a panicked squeak.

"Imagine," Gwen continued, "you were as familiar with the curves and contours of my body as you are with yours. Imagine that I was as comfortable with you touching me as you are touching yourself."

Ava inhaled through her nose, not trusting herself to speak.

"So, when we dance," Gwen put her arms around Ava's neck, like they had been an hour ago, before Ava had clammed up and frozen. "You wouldn't put your hands there," Gwen stepped into her, pressing their bodies together.

Automatically, Ava moved to encircle Gwen's waist, her touch gentle and tentative.

"You'd put your hands..." Gwen looked at her.

"Here." Ava ran her palms against the soft fabric of Gwen's dress until her hands rested on Gwen's lower back, fingers dangerously close to the subtle curve of Gwen's ass.

Gwen hummed in approval and pushed up on her tip toes. "And when I lean in like this to whisper in your ear?"

"I'd kiss you," Ava replied in a breathless rush. "Right," she pressed her lips to the juncture where Gwen's shoulder met her neck and murmured, "here."

It was like she was in a trance that she couldn't pull herself out of.

Gwen exhaled a small sigh and nudged Ava until she fell back against the couch, then followed immediately, her knees on either side of Ava's hips, holding herself up so that she wasn't quite in Ava's lap. "What else?"

"I-I'd place my hand on your leg." Ava breathed. She was trembling as she closed her fingers around Gwen's exposed knee.

"And then?"

Ava slowly trailed her fingers up. "I'd go higher."

Gwen inhaled sharply, but her voice was steady when she asked, "And do I like that?"

"Yes." Ava was transfixed, watching the slow ascent of her fingers up Gwen's thigh. "Your skin is so soft. And I can't help going just a little bit further, even though I shouldn't." She got to the hemline of Gwen's dress and pushed until the material gave, allowing her access to more skin.

Gwen was swaying a bit, struggling to keep herself raised up. "Why shouldn't you?"

"Because we're in public, and you have rules about what we do in public." Ava stopped, more than mid-way up Gwen's thigh. "Then you put your hand on mine."

Gwen slipped her hand under Ava's and linked their fingers.

Ava looked down, and the image had her hot and flushed. "And you just hold it there."

"Now you're getting it."

"And I can't stop thinking about how much I want to brush my fingertips against your skin, or how…" Ava stopped, the words stuck in her throat, caught between the erratic beats of her pulse.

"How what?"

Ava shook her head, still looking down at their joined hands. "I can't."

"Say it."

"Gwen." She looked up. Gwen's cheeks were flushed, her pupils dilated, her lips parted. That image alone had Ava pressing her thighs together.

Gwen canted her hips, ever so slightly. "Tell me."

"How wet you'd be."

She'd never experienced anything as erotically charged as this moment. Ava half-expected Gwen to leap off of her and demand she leave.

But Gwen only pursed her lips together, as if physically restraining herself from replying. She removed herself from Ava's lap with expedient, graceful movements and murmured, "Good," before she walked away, leaving Ava wrecked and trembling.

When Gwen returned a few seconds later, she handed Ava a glass of cold water and sat down on the opposite couch. "I expect our next public appearance to go much better."

"I-I don't…" Ava took a gulp of her water. Her blood was throbbing in her ears. A loud *bah-bum, bah-bum, bah-bum*. Her thudding heart. Gwen's thudding heart. "What just happened?"

"Every good lie contains an element of truth, Ava. I think we just found yours."

Ava was up seventeen minutes before the alarm. She'd spent the night circling the city, trying to outrun, or outfly, the thrumming desire that seemed to be twisted through her veins.

Her initial panic that Gwen could see every one of her infatuation-tinged thoughts had died down after Gwen had said, "Sexual desire is a perfectly natural thing, Ava, and it's no secret that I'm, well…desirable." She'd accompanied that statement with a perfect "What can you do?" expression.

So, Ava was off the hook in some ways. She'd rather have Gwen think that this was just a physical thing than have her suspect what Ava was only beginning to come to terms with.

Luckily for Ava, there was no time for awkwardness as they got ready to leave for the airport that morning. The flight had been moved up an hour, and everyone was frantic.

"Have you seen my—"

"In the front pocket of your purse."

"I need you to call Barry and—"

"Already done," Ava replied. She'd had a very productive morning of intensely *not* thinking about the previous night.

Gwen spent a significant part of the plane ride on the phone. With Daniel, with Luke, with her stylist. Ava stared out the window, trying not to watch Gwen out of the corner of her eye. Trying not to feel her insides clench with nerves and excitement, even as she convinced herself that the previous night meant nothing.

Ava turned away from the window at the sound of Gwen sighing and shifting in her seat. She was watching Ava with an unreadable expression.

"That was Shayne. He'll have a few selections for us at the shop tomorrow."

"The shop?" Ava was confused.

"You need a dress for BAFTA LA, darling. We'll go tomorrow afternoon."

Ava's eyebrows raised. "You're coming?"

"Well, I can't trust you to know what works, and besides," Gwen's lips curved up into a slow, feline smile, "I'd like to see all of the options."

Ava bit down on her inner cheek to keep herself from grinning back. "Of course."

They were less than an hour outside of LAX when Gwen removed her glasses and leaned back with a sigh.

"How are the rewrites?" Ava asked, motioning to the script in Gwen's lap.

Gwen hummed her approval. "Better. A lot more…organic."

"They added those two new scenes with you and Gooding, huh?"

"One must suffer for one's art, I suppose. And…" She made a pained face. "He's not a terrible actor."

"Yeah, but that doesn't make up for the fact that he's an ass," Ava mumbled.

"Oh, is he now?" Gwen raised an eyebrow, but she looked amused.

"I just, I mean because, you know," Ava continued ineloquently.

Gwen allowed Ava to ramble for a moment longer before saving her. "Would you mind running the lines with me?"

"No, of course not." Ava stumbled over her words, still thinking about Ronald Gooding and his stupid, perfect face. She took the script from Gwen and adjusted in her seat.

"Act three, middle of the third scene," Gwen directed. "From 'I can't do this.'"

Ava cleared her throat and prepared to read.

"I can't do this anymore, Alice. I can't pretend." Ava's eyes flicked from the page to Gwen's face, but she was completely transformed and in character.

"Pretending is the only thing I'm good at. Do you think I enjoy this, James? Do you think I like being up there defending people I know deserve to be punished? This is the only thing—"

"My job," Ava interrupted, and Gwen looked confused. "The line is 'This is my job' and then it goes into 'the only thing.'"

"This is my job," Gwen corrected. "The only thing I've ever truly been good at. If I can't keep Samir out of prison, then it's all for nothing."

"That's not true. You were good with me. We were good together."

"That was a long time ago."

"You might be okay with pretending, but I'm done. I can't watch you up there every day and know what it feels like to—" Ava stopped suddenly, her heart in her throat. Part of her wanted to shake her fist at the universe and yell, "Seriously!"

Instead, she recovered her place and continued before Gwen could question her. "…know what it's like to kiss you. To have you in my arms."

"James, stop," Gwen implored.

"I can't," Ava continued, her heart pounding as the words hit too close to home. "You know how I feel about you. When you stop pretending, you know where to find me."

Ava looked up to see Gwen watching her with an expression that was intense and vulnerable.

"Did I skip a line?"

"No, you were good." Gwen's voice was soft. "I uh, I think we can stop there."

"If you're sure," Ava replied, relieved that she wouldn't have to continue.

Gwen sat back and took the script from Ava. "I'm sure."

CHAPTER 8

GWEN WATCHED AVA EXPECTANTLY. "WELL? Do you like it?"

The dress was blue. A deep, rich blue, just a shade brighter than Swiftwing's cape. Ava's first thought was that wearing a blue dress would be a very, very bad idea. But the strangest thing was that she didn't look like Swiftwing in the dress. She didn't quite look like everyday Ava Eisenberg either.

Her reflection seemed to capture that in-between moment when her shirt was undone and her suit was peeking out from underneath. In this beautiful, overpriced, way too low-cut dress, she wasn't quite sure where she fit. Gwen was watching her with an eager expression, like it was important that Ava liked the dress.

And she did. She thought that maybe this was how Gwen saw her. Ava Eisenberg dressed up in potential.

"You're right," she said, suddenly overwhelmed. "This is the one."

Gwen smiled—a wide, pleased smile that reminded Ava of how Gwen sometimes looked at Swiftwing—and she was flushed with warmth. The boutique assistant, inexplicably named Bunny, helped Ava off the little foot stool, and to her relief, she instantly felt less like a talking mannequin.

"Despite what I told Luke," Gwen began as she strutted toward Ava, "this *is* a competition." She dragged her index finger under the delicate strap of the dress. "And I like to win."

"I know you do," Ava murmured, trying to keep her voice steady with Gwen standing so close. Gwen's brows drew together suddenly, and she ran her finger over Ava's collarbone.

"What happened?"

Ava angled her chin down to see, then realized that looking over Gwen's shoulder at her reflection was the better option. There was a bluish spot over the area where the Mantipodis had stabbed her. It didn't hurt or feel any different, but it was definitely discolored. Ava couldn't ever remember having a bruise for so long before.

"I, uh…" She tilted her head, confused by it. "I must have knocked into something."

"I thought you were—" Gwen looked at Ava as if alarmed, then shook her head. "I thought you were more careful than that." She frowned at the offending bruise. "Try not to walk into any more walls or fall down any stairs before the awards."

"I'll do my b—"

She was cut off by the ring of Gwen's phone. Gwen answered with a clipped, "Yes?" and moved away, leaving Ava with Bunny, who directed her to a changing room as big as Ava's bedroom and ten times as fancy.

Ava reached back to pull down the zipper, only to have it get caught in the material of the dress halfway down her back. She couldn't risk using more strength and unwittingly tearing the entire thing off, but she couldn't get it back up either, so she was left holding the wisp of fabric against her chest, in fear of it falling forward.

Poking her head out of the changing room door, she tentatively called for Bunny, feeling a little stupid.

Ava focused and heard her in the welcoming area, speaking in rapid French to someone on the telephone. "The one time you're actually needed, Bunny," Ava grumbled under her breath as she retreated back into the changing room.

She was trying the zipper again, tugging it down with the least amount of force possible, when Gwen rapped her knuckles against the door in three quick knocks.

"Some of us have day jobs, Ava." It was "Ava" now, more often than not.

"I'm almost done," Ava called out, and then sighed. "Actually, I'm a bit stuck."

"Stuck?"

She opened the door just wide enough to see Gwen's exasperated face. "The dress got caught."

Gwen rolled her eyes and pushed the door open, forcing Ava to hop backwards out of the way.

"What's wrong?" Ava asked when Gwen closed the door behind them. Her lips were pursed and her brow was knitted in that specific look she sometimes got after the thirtieth take.

"Nothing is wrong," she replied, motioning for Ava to turn around. Ava stiffened at the feel of Gwen's fingers curled around her waist as she struggled with the zipper. Memories of Vancouver flooded her mind, and she closed her eyes for a moment, trying to regain her composure. She felt like a horny teenager—it was embarrassing.

"What did you do?"

"I don't know. It just got caught."

Another exasperated sigh and Gwen finally freed it, zipping all the way down to Ava's lower back.

"Thank you." Ava stepped away, waiting for Gwen to leave so she could let the dress fall to the floor.

But Gwen didn't leave.

Instead, she leaned back against the door, apparently content to wait there until Ava had finished getting dressed.

"It was Alfonso on the phone earlier," Gwen finally said. Her head was tilted back, and she wasn't looking at Ava. "Today's accusation is that *this*—" She fluttered her fingers through the air between them, "—is a cheap fling. He..." She laughed humorlessly. "He actually accused me of using you for the sex."

Ava made a choked sound and nearly dropped the dress, suddenly very aware that beneath that fine silk, all she had on was her underwear. "I..." Ava watched Gwen carefully. "What did you say?"

"I told him that our relationship is none of his business. Of all the things..." Her expression was mildly accusatory. "And considering that you're barely able to make eye contact without blushing."

"That isn't true."

"Oh, come on." Gwen appraised her through narrowed cat eyes.

There was something about the challenge in Gwen's tone that had Ava fighting to push back. "I've been...well, I've thought a lot about what you said. About...practicing." She felt herself blush. She wasn't about to confess that since Gwen's demonstration, she'd been a mess of hormones.

"Really?" Gwen seemed amused and utterly disbelieving, which made Ava even more determined to prove herself.

"Really." She crossed her arms over her chest, trapping the dress against her body. And then, with a burst of courage, she asked, "You want proof?"

Gwen's expression still bordered on amusement, but she seemed interested rather than condescending. "And how exactly does one *prove* such a thing?"

"Like…" Ava swallowed, taking a leap of faith. "Like this."

She didn't mean to actually do it. There was no real thought process that preceded intent, except perhaps the overwhelming urge to prove Gwen wrong. But suddenly, she was moving forward. Suddenly, her lips were on Gwen's, moving gently, softly, swallowing Gwen's little gasp of surprise. Ava's fists were still between them, creasing the soft blue silk of the dress. It was barely three seconds before Ava pulled back, one hand clapped over her mouth in shock, eyes wide with panic.

"Oh my God. I…Gwen, I'm so sorry." She was fired. Done for. She'd never work in Hollywood again. "I don't know why I—"

But Gwen pushed herself off the door and snuck her hand around to tangle in Ava's hair, effectively fitting their bodies together. And then they were kissing again.

Like, *really* kissing.

Gwen moved to grip Ava's shoulders like she didn't know what to do with her hands, but then they were running down and up Ava's bare arms, looping around her neck, encouraging her closer.

The kiss was hungry and desperate and a little clumsy. Ava winced when their noses bumped together, but then Gwen was tracing her tongue along the inside of Ava's lower lip and sucking it into her mouth, and Ava stopped thinking altogether.

It wasn't like she'd never kissed anyone before. It wasn't like she'd never kissed a girl either (Grace Wu during her first and *only* college kegger). The act itself was both familiar and unique. Gwen was soft and delicate and so very human. Her perfume was subtle—floral, vanilla, hints of bergamot. And beneath the scent, warm skin and a racing pulse.

The realization that it was Gwen, *Gwen* against her, had Ava almost faint with desire. And as Gwen dug her fingers into Ava's scalp to urge her half-naked body *even* closer, Ava moaned loudly and involuntarily. She didn't have time to be embarrassed as Gwen scraped her teeth against the side of Ava's jaw and said her name on a flutter of breath.

"*Ava.*"

Ava arched into her, hot and flushed, and needing to be touched everywhere. She'd never felt so reckless, never been so utterly dazed with lust. And she was still barely touching Gwen, still afraid to take too much. Her fingertips ghosted against Gwen's waist and she flexed them, eager to feel Gwen's body, which moved against her, feverish and urgent. And for all her own urgency, Ava was terrified to touch, terrified of how much she wanted it.

She wasn't sure how long they kept it up, but she became vaguely aware of the way her stomach muscles were beginning to quiver as Gwen ran soft fingers up her side, past her ribs to cup her breast through the thin fabric of her bra.

As if of their own accord, her hands slid down to grip Gwen's hips, to anchor herself. She wrenched herself back almost immediately, already envisioning finger-shaped bruises on Gwen's perfect skin. The flimsy fabric fell to the floor between them, leaving Ava in her underwear, trembling and watching Gwen with an expression that was probably as panicked as she felt. Her lips were throbbing and kiss-bruised.

Gwen's chest heaved and she closed her eyes for a second, as if trying to collect all the pieces of herself that had gone splintering off.

When she finally looked at Ava, her eyes were wide and dark and unfocused. "The car," she rasped, and cleared her throat. "I'll be waiting in the car."

Ava didn't get a chance to answer before Gwen opened the door and slipped out. She heard her tell Bunny that the dress was fine, and that she wanted it delivered by the following day. The entire conversation was punctuated by the erratic beat of Gwen's heart.

Ava heard it loudly and more clearly than anything else in the whole world.

She dressed quickly, despite the fact that her entire body would not stop trembling. She carefully draped the dress over a chair and buttoned her shirt up to her collar. She zipped up her jeans and laced up her flats. When she finally felt more like herself and less like a sentient column of raw emotion, she stepped out.

She had no idea how to navigate this. It wasn't like Vancouver, where there were cameras and excuses. There was no out here.

She had kissed Gwen. Gwen had kissed her back. And it was...it was everything.

The car was waiting outside the boutique, and Ava took a steadying breath before opening the door to the backseat and sliding in.

Gwen was on the phone, leaning against the opposite side of the car. She offered a wary glance as Ava shut the door, and held a finger up to indicate that Ava should give her a moment.

Jonah veered into the midday traffic, and they began the inevitable stop-start along the 405. Ava watched the greenish-brown hills go by while her stomach tied itself into knots.

She made a point of blocking Gwen out, and her voice became a soothing drone of white noise. She couldn't quite drown out the drumming of Gwen's heart, though, no matter how hard she tried. It was less erratic than before, but still loud, still insistent that Ava listen to that telltale thud.

Gwen eventually ended her call and leaned forward to tell Jonah to take them to Third Planet Productions, the company she co-owned with Alfonso. "I need to pick up a few things," she said, tone offhand.

Out of the corner of her eye, Ava saw Gwen glance at her, then away, before finally seeming to come to a decision.

Gwen's voice was calm and measured as she began. "There are rules, Ava. They exist for a reason. Rules allow for boundaries and limits."

Ava wondered where Gwen's boundaries and limits had been the night she'd pushed Ava down on that sofa, or where they were just now when she'd had Ava's lip between her teeth.

But Gwen continued. "And I suppose that after these past few weeks, I can't really blame you for losing sight of them."

"Blame *me*?"

"You were obviously a little...a little worked up."

Ava's face pinched in confusion, and the diluted frustration that had been simmering under her skin flared up. "You kissed me back."

"A mistake," Gwen said simply. As if two words, three syllables could erase what had just happened.

"Mistake?"

"This is an unconventional situation, and I understand how it might be confusing."

Here it comes, Ava thought. Gwen was going to tell her that they should end the charade before anyone got hurt. When it started, Ava might have agreed, but now, now she was a mess of chaotic feelings, and nothing made sense. The only conclusion she could come to was one that she could not admit, especially with Gwen looking at her with that unreadable expression that could only precede the breakup of their fake relationship.

"I think from now on it might be better if we stick to the rules."

"You kissed me back," Ava repeated weakly, because suddenly it seemed like that was the only thing that mattered, the only thing she had to hold on to.

"I may have misjudged the situation. I thought you could handle it. I was wrong."

"Thought I could..." Ava trailed off in disbelief.

Gwen's voice was infuriatingly calm, and Ava wanted to yell, "I can hear your heartbeat! I know you're as affected by this as I am!" But of course, she couldn't yell it, and even if kissing Ava like her life depended on it did get Gwen all hot and bothered... So what? Gwen was right—this was still all physical. Lines and boundaries had been crossed, but it didn't change anything. It didn't make it any more real. At least not for Gwen.

"It's better this way. No one gets—"

Hurt. Gutted. Annihilated. "Confused?"

"Precisely." Gwen's smile was quick and forced. "The deposition is coming up, and I don't want anything to... Well, it's important to remember why we're doing this."

Ava hazarded a glance at Gwen, fighting off the ridiculous urge to burst into tears. "So, you're not upset?"

"Not at all," Gwen looked down at her lap and smoothed out her skirt. "Because I know you understand that at the end of the day, it's all pretend." She looked up suddenly and searchingly. "You do, don't you?"

"Of course." Lying was as easy as breathing. As easy as flying.

Ava heard the click the moment they stepped out of the car. It took two more shutter sounds before Gwen whipped her head around. Her face was half hidden behind her sunglasses, but Ava didn't have that option and she had to blink a few times before she identified at least two men, on either side of the building, both equipped with telephoto lenses. Gwen ducked her head on instinct but Ava froze, surprised by the flashes.

"Come on," Gwen murmured fiercely, her grip firm on Ava's arm, steering her toward the entrance. "I want them gone," Gwen muttered through clenched teeth to the security guard at the desk, who sprang up and spoke into his walkie-talkie.

Gwen strutted to the elevator, still holding onto Ava, and jabbed her finger against the button to close the doors with more force than necessary.

"How did they know we'd be here?"

"They didn't. But they know my production office is here, and they're trying their luck. They're parasites."

"I guess I forgot—"

"Who you were dating?"

"I don't think that's possible. I just forgot how ruthless they could be."

"I'll make sure they're gone when we leave. I refuse to deal with bottom-feeders inside my own building." And then, as an afterthought, "I'm sorry." Gwen plucked off her glasses and dropped them into her purse. "You shouldn't have to deal with this either."

Ava made a noise of indifference. She wanted to tell Gwen that she'd become used to the flashes and the yelling of her name (not her real name, of course), but that she'd never be entirely comfortable being the center of attention. She wanted to tell Gwen a lot of things that she knew she shouldn't. It was becoming more and more of a problem. Instead, she said, "It comes with the job, right?"

Gwen turned to her then, with something like curiosity. "Right."

The elevator stopped on the thirteenth floor and Gwen took her hand. Ava wasn't sure if she was doing it for Ava's sake or her own, but it was a comforting gesture.

The elevator doors slid open and they walked out, with Ava very aware of heads snapping up and quickly back down. If anyone was not caught up on the gossip before (unlikely), they were now. Gwen Knight did not hold hands with just anybody.

Ava followed dutifully as Gwen walked toward Daniel Cho's office.

"Ah, the prodigal couple returns." Daniel stood as they entered, and made his way around his desk and over to Gwen, who graced him with an air kiss on each cheek.

"Nice to see you too, darling." Gwen sat down and crossed her legs, completely unaffected.

"Ava," Daniel offered her a strained smile.

"Hey." She inclined her head and sat on one of the couches near the door. Her usual spot during these meetings.

She watched as Gwen spoke to Daniel about a new Todd Haynes project. She took down notes as instructed, and it was all so very normal. As if it was just an ordinary day.

As if they had not been pressed up against each other an hour before.

As if Ava had not just come to the crashing realization that she was falling, completely and desperately, in love with Gwen Knight.

CHAPTER 9

"No Gwen tonight?" Nic's voice was casual, almost tentative.

Ava shrugged. "Not tonight. She's working late. And we had a..." she cleared her throat, "a long day." She couldn't tell Nic about the kiss. Not now, not yet, not until she could wrap her head around it.

They were sitting on the roof of RainnTech, where anyone looking up would have seen a young woman in a white lab coat and bright purple Converse sneakers casually talking to a masked superhero. They were on the edge, their legs dangling 900 feet off the ground.

Nic slurped the last of her bubble tea through a straw and leaned back. "So, Horatio's got a few new tricks up his sleeve."

Ava glanced at her and smiled. "He's a robot; he doesn't have sleeves."

"Maybe I decided to give him some."

Ava turned, eyes wide with excitement. "Please tell me you finally did it."

Nic snorted and rolled her eyes. "I did not dress him in a Hawaiian shirt and shorts."

"Missed opportunity," Ava lamented, chewing on her boba.

"I did, however, give him some new armor. You're going to have work hard to dent his new plates."

"I look forward to it."

"So, uh," Nic scraped her nail against the concrete. "When do you think you'd want to train? You've been sort of...absent."

"I know. And, I know you think it's cause of Gwen, but it's not just that. This thing with the Mantipodis on the loose, and Norman—"

"Norman?"

"The worm. That's what they're calling it. *Him*, I guess."

"Huh." Nic seemed to think about it. "I like it. And, speaking of good 'ole Norman, I couldn't find anything that matched his profile. Are you sure this thing was on the *Andromeda*? He could be a hybrid."

"I have no idea." Ava brought her knees up to rest her chin on them. The cape flapped listlessly behind her. "You know what's weird?"

"What?" Nic leaned all the way back and rested on her elbows, completely relaxed.

"I think I've been dreaming about him."

"About Norman the worm?"

"Yeah." Ava sighed. "And the Mantipodis too. I keep having these dreams that fade almost immediately, and all I feel is sad after."

"What do you think it means?"

"I don't know. Maybe Norman's psychic. Maybe he's trying to tell me something. Maybe all of this is in my head and I'm going nuts."

"You're not going nuts." Nic sat up and looked at Ava with a serious expression. "Who doesn't have weird tragic dreams about five-foot alien slugs?"

Ava laughed. "I guess."

"What?" Nic asked with a hint of suspicion. Ava was still grinning at her.

"Nothing. I just missed you."

Nic threw an arm around her. "You're a sap, you know that?"

"Yeah, yeah." Ava rolled her shoulders, half-heartedly shrugging Nic off.

Nic looked at her for a moment, as if deciding whether to speak before saying, "So, Rachel called earlier."

"Why?" Ava's stomach swirled nervously. She'd been very deliberately avoiding her adoptive mother.

"She's, uh, a little concerned." Nic paused. "Remember Hilda, that weird librarian with all the pugs? Well she read something in one of those gossip rags, called my mom, who called Rachel, who called me to ask if you've been pressured into something because you're so...easily fascinated by people. Her words, not mine," Nic was fast to clarify.

Ava groaned, suddenly embarrassed and awkward, despite the fact that Rachel was nowhere near. "Hilda has always been…nosy."

Nic pursed her lips in amusement. "Well, don't hold back."

"Rachel shouldn't have called you."

"You know that's not how it works."

Ava sighed. "What did you tell her?"

"I said that your choices are your own, and if she's concerned she should speak to you about it."

"Do you think she'll call me?"

"I hope so. You guys need to talk about this. What you're going to say to her is another matter."

They sat in silence for a while, and Ava mulled over what she was going to tell Rachel. She didn't want to lie to her, but the truth was getting even more complicated.

"I just don't know where to start with her. How do I even—" She stopped when her police scanner buzzed. It was a 133—a possibly dangerous person in Lincoln Heights.

"Up and off?"

Ava shot her a quick smile. "See ya." And then she was shooting through the sky, a shadow against the splatter of stars.

The "dangerous person" turned out to be a fourteen-year-old kid in a tracksuit, walking home with his earphones on. Ava intercepted before anything got out of hand and flew the boy home.

"I'm sorry," she said, as if those two words could solve anything. As if they could make him less afraid of walking through his own neighborhood.

He shrugged, as if he knew those words were as useless as she did. But then he asked for a selfie, and Ava posed with him for several.

The city was quieting down—as quiet as LA could be at 10 p.m. on a Friday. She flew past windows where kids were getting ready for bed, and couples were catching up on their favorite shows. The scent of food and car fumes permeated the air. Somewhere, someone had burnt rice.

Ava flew in lazy circles, her thoughts restlessly churning, and she found herself at the harbor, where the odor of salt and fish overpowered any human smell. She roosted on the roof of a warehouse overlooking the port and pulled out her phone.

The urge to call Gwen was overwhelming and unexpected. Ava wasn't used to *missing* her after work. But it was different now that Ava knew what Gwen felt like pressed up against her as they swayed; now that she'd seen Gwen curled up on a sofa, or licking peanut brittle gelato off a spoon; now that she'd had Gwen's hands on her, felt her body arch and twist with desire.

However their charade ended, they couldn't go back to what they were before. The knowledge was unsettling at best. Ava didn't want to leave her job, but she also didn't want to be fetching lettuce wraps and lattes while pretending that she wasn't hopelessly in love with her boss.

She wiped her thumb over her screen and scrolled down. *Gwen Knight.* It was a stupid idea. What would she even say? The twist of nerves in her stomach at the thought of texting Gwen made her feel like a high school kid with a crush.

She was still staring at her phone when it rang. Gwen's name appeared on the screen, accompanied by "Imperial March," and Ava was momentarily disoriented.

She answered with a tentative "Hello?"

"Where are you?" Ava automatically straightened up, panicked that she'd forgotten some or other engagement.

"Um. I'm—" The horn of a passing boat drowned out most of her sentence, and of course, Gwen noticed.

"Is that a tug boat?"

"What? No. Um, yes. In a movie. I'm, uh, watching a movie."

Gwen made a little sound of acknowledgement, but didn't say anything to suggest why she'd called.

"Can I... Is there something you wanted?"

"Where are the minutes from this afternoon's meeting?"

"In Dropbox," Ava said in confusion, because she was sure she'd seen Gwen open the email earlier. "I copied the file in there like I always do."

"Well, obviously you didn't, because I don't have it." Ava strained her ears, listening to the click of the mouse and then Gwen's annoyed tut. "Here it is. Why you would name the document with the date first is a mystery."

Ava was pretty certain that Gwen had specifically requested that format months ago. Some more clicking, followed by a sigh, and Ava began to ask, "Is that all?" as Gwen said, "Is it good?"

Ava was confused. "What?"

"The movie." She was impatient now, and Ava couldn't quite figure out what she'd done to provoke it. "Is it good?" Gwen repeated.

"Um…not really." A seagull landed next to her and began shuffling about, and Ava prayed that it wouldn't squawk. "I was thinking of going to bed actually."

"Oh."

Ava almost convinced herself that Gwen sounded disappointed. "Unless there was something else I could do?" She had the brief, crazy thought that Gwen might ask her to come over.

But Gwen said, "No, no. I'm perfectly capable." She sighed, and Ava could picture her clearly—sitting in her study, glasses fixed, a small frown line between her brows, a script in one hand, a cup of tea in the other.

"Gwen?"

"Luke is home this weekend and I thought I'd take him to the observatory," Gwen began, and Ava held her breath, suddenly and stupidly hopeful about where this might be going. "And beyond that, I don't have much planned. So, I suppose…"

A pause, and Ava actually craned her neck, waiting. *Hoping.*

"Well, there's no reason why I should monopolize your time over the weekend. We've done enough publicity for now."

"Oh." Disappointment was heavy in the pit of her stomach. "You don't want me to come around?"

"What would be the point? You don't want to spend your off day with your boss."

Your boss.

Gwen was punishing her. For what, Ava couldn't imagine.

"I guess." There was a beat of silence, and Ava wished that she was there, that she could see Gwen, *touch* her the way she had touched her that afternoon.

"Oh, don't sound so sullen." Gwen's voice was softer now—almost tender, imploring.

"No, I mean, if that's what you want." She knew she was being childish, but she was heartsick and frustrated, and Gwen was pushing her away. Ava was annoyed with herself more than anything. She wanted everything that Gwen had never offered, and reality hurt over and over again.

"I—" Gwen paused, and then, "I'll see you on Monday."

"Goodnight, Gwen."

Gwen hung up and the seagull squawked.

It wasn't like she was *trying* to fly past Gwen's house. It just happened to be one of the easiest routes home. So, the fact that Gwen happened to be out in the garden, and the fact that Ava happened to be flying close enough to see the slump of her shoulders and hear her tired sigh was coincidence. Total coincidence.

Ava hovered above a lemon tree, careful not to fly in too quickly and startle her.

Gwen looked up. The change in her expression was subtle, hardly perceptible, but Ava knew to search for it—the little spark, the quickly suppressed wonder that flickered across Gwen's face before she schooled her features back into impassiveness. It filled Ava with a thrill she was generally reluctant to acknowledge.

"Swiftwing." Gwen raised her empty martini glass and inclined her head.

"Hello, Gwen." Ava smiled at Gwen in a way that she couldn't when she was getting lattes and scheduling interviews. "You're up late."

"So are you."

Ava floated a little closer. "Mind some company?"

"Not at all." She motioned to the empty chairs, and Ava was hit with an unexpected twinge of resentment at how easily Gwen shared her space and time with Swiftwing in comparison to Ava "Yes, Miss Knight" Eisenberg. It was ludicrous to form the divide in her mind. She was as much Swiftwing as she was Ava. But Gwen didn't know that. And while Ava received impatient, confusing phone calls full of weird mixed messages, Swiftwing was invited into Gwen's private garden with the hint of a smile.

Ava chose to sit in the chair right beside Gwen instead of the one across from her. Behind the mask, it was so much easier to be who she wanted to be and say what she wanted to say. Around them, lights twinkled in the trees and Nina Simone crooned softly out of the strategically hidden speakers. In the distance, someone blared their horn and yelled an obscenity out their window. Ava's ears pricked for trouble, but the offender drove on without incident and Ava lamented that her powers didn't include preventing people from being assholes.

Ava liked being quiet with Gwen. She turned her head and studied Gwen's profile—the curve of her forehead, half hidden by a wisp of perfectly styled hair, the gossamer lines that feathered out around her eyes and dared to hint at her age, the dip of her nose, the perfect swell of her lips. She was beautiful.

It was an obvious statement. Gwen Knight was beautiful.

But, in that moment, in the late evening air, surrounded by the lights and sounds of the city, Ava was struck by this simple, undeniable fact.

Gwen tilted her head, and Ava was caught staring. She flushed and looked down.

It felt suddenly as though Gwen could take one look at her and know everything that even Ava wasn't sure of, as if Gwen would know that she'd been playing their kiss on a loop in her head for hours, trying to recall all of the little things lost in the flurry of the moment—the way Gwen had sighed against her cheek, the scrape of her blunt nails against Ava's ribcage, that breathless exhale of her name. *Ava.* She had whispered it like it was the only word she knew in some forgotten language.

Gwen's gaze didn't linger, and she glanced away as if she, too, was uncertain. Ava didn't think she'd ever seen Gwen uncertain.

Ava found herself suddenly possessed with the ridiculous urge to tell Gwen everything. To start from the beginning with Zrix'dhor and her mother's decision to join the research team, ending with fire raining past stars and a broken ship in a desert. She wanted to tell Gwen about the flowers her grandmother grew in their sunhouse—big white and red blooms that smelled like nothing she'd ever encountered on Earth.

Suddenly, Gwen was the only person in the world that she wanted to tell.

But she couldn't tell her. She couldn't risk Gwen knowing. If she was honest with herself, she might have admitted that it was because she was selfish and scared, and not ready for everything to change between them. Again.

"I saw the little interview you gave for the foundation's newsletter," Gwen said, dragging Ava from her thoughts.

"It wasn't really an interview," Ava replied. "I happened to see one of your staff members, and she happened to ask me a few questions."

Gwen's lips turned up in a thin smile. "You happened to be flying very low and very slowly, over last month's charity benefit, posing just long enough to allow a picture that would make any curious reader subscribe to the newsletter?"

"I…" Ava shrugged. "Yes?"

"Anyway," Gwen continued in a voice that suggested she didn't believe her for a minute, "I wanted to thank you."

"Thank me?"

"Hmm." She turned back to the vista. "For what you've been to the foundation. For allying yourself with us."

"It's an important cause. And," Ava waited a beat, "I've always felt sort of indebted to you."

"How so?"

"Well," Ava turned in her seat, facing Gwen fully. She could smell Gwen's shampoo and the citrus of her moisturizer. "You were my first real save."

"You know, I always wondered about that. Huh. Your first."

Ava smiled a cocky smile. "And you know what they say…"

Gwen breathed out a laugh. "Indeed, I do."

Garbo chose that moment to hop up onto Ava's lap and rub her face against Ava's arm, demanding head scratches. Ava laughed awkwardly and used her gloved hands to scratch behind Garbo's ears.

"You know, there are very few people she allows to pet her," Gwen mused, watching them.

"I'm…good with cats," Ava replied, as Garbo purred like a truck engine. "It's my most powerful superpower."

Gwen laughed.

They were quiet for a while after that. The silence was warm and companionable. Ava felt closer to Gwen in that moment than she had all day, closer than she'd felt with Gwen's hands all over her. She wondered if she could ask Gwen about the rumors of dating her assistant, but she wasn't sure how she'd start that conversation, and she *was* pretty sure there was an ethical boundary somewhere there.

Eventually Gwen broke the silence. "Trust is a funny thing, isn't it?"

Ava watched her curiously. "I suppose."

"When you first came out," Gwen continued, staring straight ahead at the garden that lay before them, "you had to earn the trust of thousands, millions of people who were prejudiced against the Andromeda Orphans. And you won them over."

Ava followed her gaze. "It helped that I had good people supporting me. The best people, really." What she meant to say was, "It helped that I had you supporting me." But Gwen had always been good at reading between the lines.

"Good people," Gwen repeated with a wry expression that Ava couldn't quite interpret. "You may not know this about me, Swiftwing," she began, "but I don't trust easily."

Ava watched her closely, wondering where this was going.

"I've recently entrusted someone with a secret."

Ava waited, but Gwen didn't say anything more.

"Are you're worried sh—they won't keep it?"

"Oh, I know she will. That's the trouble, you see. I worry that it's…" she paused, looking contemplative. "I suppose I worry that it's too much. That I'm asking her to compromise too much."

"How?" Ava's heart began a heavy thud in the pit of her stomach.

"Ava is…rare." Gwen took a while to settle on the word.

"Rare?"

"Good," she clarified. "Kind. She's not self-serving or indulgent." Gwen arched an eyebrow. "She's not like me."

"Gwen, you are one of the kindest people I have ever met."

She rolled her eyes, but didn't argue.

Ava went on, "And I'm sure she'd tell you if she felt…compromised. I'm sure she's happy to help. I imagine that anyone who's earned your trust would be happy to help."

Gwen turned to face her. "And what would it take to earn your trust, Swiftwing?"

"My trust?" Ava whispered, so close to Gwen she could count her eyelashes if she wanted.

"Hmm."

"You have my trust," Ava answered, and wondered why it felt false.

Gwen surprised her then, by reaching up and gently tracing her thumb over Ava's lower lip.

Ava wondered if Gwen could hear her heartbeat, which echoed loudly in her ears. She couldn't recall Gwen ever touching Swiftwing like this before.

"You're the real thing, aren't you?" Gwen looked at her with a hollow sort of amusement. "Earnest to the last."

She wasn't certain whether she should feel offended or not. Gwen didn't sound mean, only contemplative, and maybe a little sad. Ava wished she knew what Gwen was thinking. She wished Gwen would tell Swiftwing what she wouldn't tell Ava.

She heard the sirens a second before Gwen looked out into the distance.

"I think they're playing your song."

Ava's muscles begin to twitch in anticipation as she prepared for flight. "Sorry, I've gotta—"

Gwen waved her off. "Go, go."

And she did.

It wasn't until much later, when Ava fell into bed, yawning and exhausted after helping rescuers with a two-truck accident, that she recalled something that Gwen had said to her. She had called her earnest twice in the space of few weeks. Once as Ava, the night they'd had dinner at Gwen's house, and then tonight as Swiftwing.

It was a ridiculous thought. There was no way that Gwen suspected anything. If she did, Ava would know.

Ava was pretty sure she would know.

Mostly sure.

CHAPTER 10

She woke up in agony.

Ava gasped and gulped at the air as her lungs closed up. It felt like fire racing under her skin. She wasn't particularly lucid as she sat up, fighting back a cry. She was about to call out for Nic, when it ended as suddenly as it began.

Ava just lay there for a moment, trying to get orientated as the excruciating pain subsided. She was terrified for the first few seconds that it would return. After a minute or so, she threw her legs over the side of her bed and stood, shaken and scared.

She shouldn't feel pain like that. That wasn't something that happened.

Tentatively, she tried to float an inch or two off the ground. Her heart sank. She had felt it the second she woke, that something was different, wrong.

She was completely powerless.

Ava sat on the edge of a very cold metal table, swinging her sneakers impatiently.

She could feel the loss in her limbs, in her muscles, in her bones. She felt…less. The absence of her abilities was acute.

Dr. Shepard, the resident physician of the AO hospital wing, had a stain on her white coat. A yellowish-brownish splotch just below her collar. It might have been mustard; it might have been alien intestines. One never knew in this part of the hospital.

Ava had arrived in her civilian clothes and was admitted under a pseudonym. Dr. Shepard was one of the few staff who knew her real identity. To everyone else, she was just a pretty blonde twenty-something with a high-security access pass.

"It seems that whatever is affecting Officer Barre is also affecting you," Dr. Shepard said. She'd been head of the officer's care unit since he'd been brought in. "The toxins in the creature's secretion have been slowly poisoning you, but your immune system is a lot stronger than Barre's."

"Is it," Ava swallowed down a bubble of fear, "temporary?"

"We're hoping so." She offered Ava a small, comforting smile. "We've managed to extract antibodies from the specimen in custody."

Ava eyed the syringe of bright orange liquid on the table.

"Officer Barre has been responding positively to it, and in theory, if your cells are behaving like a human's in response to the toxin, they should be as receptive to the cure. You're lucky. This creature seems to be immature. It isn't at full strength." Dr. Shepard tapped the needle a few times.

Ava decided then and there that she hated needles. "What's going to happen to me?" she asked.

"We're working in hypotheticals here, Swiftwing. Officer Barre started showing symptoms a few hours after he was exposed. For you it took much longer to reach this stage, and all it's done so far is strip you of your powers."

"That's not exactly a minor side effect."

Dr. Shepard wiped an alcohol patch over Ava's upper arm. "What I mean to say is, you aren't in any biological harm yet."

Ava gritted her teeth as the needle was inserted. Looking down, she was fascinated and horrified as the luminous liquid slowly disappeared out of the syringe and into her body.

"How long before it kicks in?"

"A few hours at best. I've doubled the dose, hoping it's enough."

"And if it isn't?" Ava asked in a small voice.

"Then we make more." Dr. Shepard set down the syringe. Her face was kind when she looked at Ava. "The toxin is so slow moving that it can't do any real harm for a while yet, and now the antidote is actively fighting back. You may experience some nausea, fatigue, maybe a nosebleed." She patted Ava's arm gently. "We'll get you back to normal, before real harm becomes a risk. I promise."

Ava managed a smile. "Thank you."

Back in the main waiting room, Nic was sitting tensely. She had been there for almost two hours, since Ava had woken her up with a yell and Nic had raced to her bedroom, bleary-eyed and concerned.

Nic waited until they were in the car before she said, "I hate the thought of you walking around with poison inside of you."

"It's fine, Nic. I guess I feel a bit tired, but nothing dire. Although I guess this explains why I was able to get a stinger through the shoulder. And why I didn't—"

"What?"

Ava thought about her fingers, curled over Gwen's hip, the way she'd held back, scared that she'd bruise that perfect skin. She thought about how she could have held on a little tighter, pushed a little harder. It wouldn't have been safe, not really, not when her control was already frayed and compromised. But she couldn't help but stray to *what if.*

"I think my powers have been deteriorating without me even realizing it." She sighed heavily. "I miss being me."

"I know." Nic put a hand on her shoulder. "We'll get you home, okay? I'll even make you pancakes, and we can watch morning cartoons and—"

Ava's phone vibrated against the cup holder with dull *gzzzz*. The screen lit up with Gwen's name, and Ava winced internally at the bad timing. She reached for it with a quick glance at Nic.

"Hello?"

"Can you be here in twenty minutes?" Gwen was in a hurry; Ava didn't need heightened hearing to know that she was rummaging around.

"What's wrong?" she asked warily.

"Nothing is—" Something fell, broke, and Ava heard Gwen's muffled, "Goddamn it!"

"Gwen?"

"I'm fine." Gwen replied shortly. "But this movie is falling apart."

"What happened?"

"Ronald fucking Gooding decided that now would be a great time to break his collarbone."

"Oh. Oh no."

"I have to go in. The studio is having a fit, and they want to see the producers immediately, which means that I have to trek down to Paramount on a Saturday morning and—" Gwen sighed, and Ava imagined her standing in the middle of her home office, hand on her hip, eyes scanning surfaces for her glasses. "I don't have anyone to watch Luke. I let the last housekeeper go because... Well, I thought I didn't need the help. As it turns out, I do. So, can you be here in twenty minutes? Alfonso is due to drop him off at any moment, and then he'll be here until Jacob's mother comes to collect him for the sleepover I promised him. I know it's Saturday, and we decided that you needn't come around, and I wouldn't ask if it wasn't—"

"I'll be there," Ava said in a rush, pointedly *not* looking at Nic. "Just," she swallowed down a bout of nausea. "It might take a bit longer than twenty minutes."

"Do you need me to send the car?"

"No, I'm—" Ava finally glanced at Nic, who frowned and shook her head. "I'm out. But I'll be there as soon as I can."

Gwen exhaled, and Ava couldn't tell if it was in relief or exasperation. "All right. I'll wait here until you arrive."

"See you s—" Ava was left listening to the dial tone as a distracted Gwen hung up.

"You can't go," Nic said the second Ava ended the call.

"I told you what Dr. Shepard said." She braced for an argument. "I'm pretty useless right now as Swiftwing. I might as well make myself useful somewhere—"

"You're sick. You're powerless. You're in no state to play assistant or babysitter."

"I'm not...she needs me. I can't just—"

"Why not? Gwen is not your girlfriend, Ava. And it's Saturday, so I'm pretty sure she's not your boss. Why does it always have to be you?"

"Because I want it to be! I want her to think of me when she's in trouble or needs something. I want to be her person, Nic. I—" Ava's eyes went wide, as she surprised herself with the outburst. "I like her," she admitted softly.

Nic's face drew into a frown. "*Like* like?"

"Yes?" Ava's voice was soft.

"Ava..."

"I know!" Ava threw her arm over her eyes and groaned. "You're weirded out, aren't you?"

"I'm not." Nic shook her head. "Okay, maybe a little." She looked at Ava helplessly. "She's just so…"

Don't say old, Ava thought. *Don't say old.*

"Mean."

"She's not," Ava protested weakly. "Okay, a lot of the time she's not. I think you'd really like her, if you ever, you know, got to know her."

"I…doubt that. Does she feel the same way?"

"About me? No. Definitely not." Ava shrugged her shoulders high. "And she doesn't know how I feel either, so there's no chance of you ever having to endure a meeting."

"Thank God for that. The sooner this is over, the better, and you can move on."

Ava gritted her teeth, suddenly flushed with annoyance at Nic, at Gwen, at the whole situation.

"Just…take me home, okay? I need to change."

"You're not in any condition to—"

"I'm not dying, Nic," Ava sighed. "I'm just…human."

"Finally," Gwen announced when Ava arrived at her door half an hour later. "No, not you, Jessica" she barked into her phone. "I'll speak to you in an hour. You've got until then to come up with reminders as to why I agreed to produce this godforsaken picture."

She disconnected with an audible growl and focused all of that residual intensity on Ava.

"Hi." Ava held up her hand in a little wave as Gwen ushered her into the house.

"I don't know how long I'll be gone for, but Alfonso should be here soon. I'm not sure when exactly Rebecca Levinson is arriving to collect him, but—"

"That's okay," Ava said, breathing in the specific, comforting scent of Gwen's home. "We'll just, hang out." She hoped that Luke wasn't in the mood for anything particularly energetic. She still felt like she might throw up at any minute.

"Just ask him about his books and you'll be fine. He's moved on to insects and other disgusting crawling things."

Ava thought back to the Mantipodis and shivered involuntarily. She looked up to see Gwen watching her.

"Are you all right? You look pale."

"Fine, just," she attempted a smile, "cold."

"It's 88 degrees outside."

"I—" She didn't have time to concoct a lame excuse before Gwen's phone began to ring and she glanced at it, looked annoyed, and pressed "reject."

"There's a takeout menu in the kitchen drawer. Although I'd rather you heated up last night's dinner. Oh, and Garbo might try and manipulate you into feeding her. Don't do it. She's getting fat."

She stopped, rolled her shoulders, adjusted her skirt, and faced Ava. "If you'd like to stay until later," she pursed her lips thoughtfully, "well, I don't think this catastrophe should keep me away all day."

Ava wasn't sure if Gwen was asking her to wait or not, but she nodded. "Okay."

Gwen looked hopeful. "Well, then."

And then Ava's heart stopped beating for a second as Gwen moved forward and pressed the lightest, briefest of kisses against her cheek. "Wish me luck."

Gwen was out the door before Ava could say more than "Good—"

Ava waited until she heard Gwen's car leave the driveway before slumping down on the couch and pulling out her phone. She planned to look over the following week's schedule, but ended up mindlessly playing Candy Crush for fifteen minutes. Garbo hopped up on the couch beside her and gently headbutted Ava's thigh, demanding attention. Ava buried her fingers in the cat's soft, gray fur, provoking a loud purr.

Ava was nodding off to sleep when the keypad on the front door beeped, jolting her into lucidity. She bolted up and walked into the entrance hall just in time to see Luke pushing the door open. She secretly hoped that Alfonso had waved him off from the car, but then she heard the knock of suitcase wheels up the front steps, and felt a twinge of panic. She wasn't exactly prepped for meeting the ex.

She'd taken a course on Moretti's films in college. He was a genius, arguably the greatest indie filmmaker of the nineties. His style had changed after he'd married Gwen and they'd started the company, and the movies got even better, until they got worse.

People cited Gwen as his muse. They said that after the split, Moretti's movies lost their heart. Ava was inclined to agree. And, while she appreciated the man as a filmmaker, he was still Gwen's ex, and Ava was not looking forward to the meeting.

Alfonso Moretti was a tall, annoyingly attractive man.

Ava hated him immediately. Okay, maybe she didn't hate him, but she hated the thought of him being Gwen's ex, the thought that they were married and had a kid and that they were once happy. She hated his stupid, smug, handsome face, and the stupid, charming way he said, "Hi. I'm Alfonso."

"Ava." She held her hand out and stepped to the door, wishing she had just a hint of her powers so she could give him a really firm handshake. "Ava Eisenberg."

"Hey Ava!" Luke smiled. "Are you hanging out with mom?"

"Your mom had to go to the office, so I'm here to hang out with you." She returned his smile, acutely aware of Alfonso's eyes on her.

"Okay." Luke took the small rolling suitcase from his father and turned to head for his room. "I'm going to go organize my rock samples to take to Jacob." He looked back. "Thanks for my new comics, Dad."

Alfonso bent down to give him a quick hug. "No problem, kid. I'll see you in a week, okay?"

"Cool!" Luke exclaimed, and took off, suitcase clattering behind. "See ya!"

"That moment when your son chooses rock samples over you." Alfonso's mouth pulled into an irritatingly charming smile as he fixed his gaze on Ava. "So, the rumors are true."

"I don't really pay attention to rumors," Ava said sweetly. "If I did, well, I wouldn't have a very good opinion of you."

He laughed—a full-bodied, boisterous laugh that was warm and inclusive, and annoyed her even further because she didn't want to be charmed by this man. "Oh, she knows how to pick 'em."

"Would you like to come in?"

He leaned against the doorframe, arms crossed over his chest. "That's all right. I'm a little worried I might disintegrate if I stepped over the threshold."

Ava didn't return his smile.

"Gwen's run off?" He continued to make conversation despite Ava's best "let's not engage" face. "Let me guess…a work emergency?"

"Yes, actually."

"And you're here to babysit my son while his mother is off playing pretend."

Ava swallowed. Her head was throbbing, and she hoped that she wouldn't pass out at any point in this conversation-slash-showdown. "I'm here because I want to be."

His stupid smile became a stupid smirk. "You're not going to win. You know that, right?"

Oh, she wanted to. Suddenly, she wanted to more than anything. It was different when he was just this abstract threat looming over Gwen's happiness and Luke's home. But now he was here, with his face and his teeth and his perfect hair, and she wanted to punch him.

"Your son is not something to be won or lost in some game." She used her Swiftwing voice and crossed her arms over her chest. It might not have had the same effect as it did when paired with the cape and the symbol, but she took some satisfaction in the way his smile faded. "Luke is happy. You should ask him yourself."

"Is that the line she's spinning?" He was a little less friendly now. "Did she tell you that when he broke his arm it took almost three hours for her to be notified because she was on set and explicitly told them not to bother her for any reason?"

Ava's heart fell. She imagined how panicked Gwen must have been. "Luke is always the exception," she said. "Gwen makes that very clear."

"Oh, I'm sure she does. Just as I'm sure she makes clear the fact that in the past year, his grades have dropped and he's had to start seeing a therapist."

Ava hadn't known that.

"But of course, giving him a happy, two-parent home is the real threat to his routine."

"You have no idea how much hurt you'll cause if you pursue this," Ava replied without missing a beat.

Alfonso looked as though he was about to argue, but just then, Luke ran down the stairs and into the kitchen. Alfonso seemed to deflate. "It was illuminating meeting you, Ava."

Ava straightened and forced a smile. "Likewise."

She did not wait for him to get into his car before shutting the door. She was unsettled by the encounter and wished Gwen had been with her, to guide her. Gwen was good when it came to emboldening Ava, whether she realized it or not.

They ordered pizza. Luke wanted the "thick, cheesy kind" like he'd had at his cousin Giovanni's birthday party, and not the thin cracker kind with goat's cheese and balsamic fig reduction that his mom preferred. Ava called Papa Pizza. It was halfway across town, but the wait was worth it. It was greasy and gooey and had zero nutritional value—Luke was thrilled.

Ava insisted on napkins, because while she was okay with stealthily discarding the boxes, a greasy fingerprint might be harder to explain.

"You know, this show is a lot deeper than I thought," Ava commented, as the next episode of *Adventure Time* began.

"Yeah, and in this one, Marceline's dad shows up, and lures Finn and Jake into the Nightosphere. He's a total douche."

"Hey. Should you be using that word?"

"Jacob uses it," Luke said, but he looked sufficiently chastised.

Ava debated whether to take it further, and eventually said, "From what I've heard, Jacob might not be someone you want to be emulating."

Luke paused the episode and turned to look at her. "Are you gonna be weird about stuff like that now that you're dating my mom?"

It took Ava just a second to realize that this moment was an important one, that Luke was testing her, checking to see where her loyalties lay. She'd said she'd always be his friend, but she wasn't about to let him get away with stuff that she knew Gwen would frown on. It was a weird thing, straddling the line between friend and adult. So, she pushed back. A little.

"Well, I'd like to think that I'd be weird about stuff like that even before I was dating your mom." She tried for a smile, and earned one in return.

"That's fair," Luke acknowledged, sounding ten going on forty. "I guess."

"So." Ava waggled her brows at him. "You'll think about using less Jacob-inspired language? I mean, what would Finn use instead?"

"He'd call him a whacked-out poo-brain." Luke giggled.

She scrunched up her face. "I...don't know if that's better."

Near the end of the episode, Luke turned to Ava with a smile that faded almost immediately. His eyes went wide in alarm. "Hey, Ava, are you okay? I think your nose is bleeding."

She swiped her index finger over her top lip and pulled back to look at the smear of bright red blood. "Oh, uh..."

"Hold on. I'll get an ice pack." Luke sprang up. "It's the fastest way to stop the bleeding," he called from the kitchen.

There was a small drop of red on her collar, but Ava managed to pinch her nose in time to stop the worst of it.

"Thanks, buddy," she wheezed out in a nasally voice when Luke rushed back with an ice pack and a mini box of tissues.

"You shouldn't tilt your head back like that," Luke said, holding the ice pack against Ava's nose. It was unbelievably cold on her cheek. "Lean forward a little."

"You're good at this," Ava said, when Luke moved the ice pack to the other side and offered her a tissue.

"Thanks. I have experience."

Ava couldn't help but smile at his very grown-up tone. "You get these often?"

"Yeah. Since I was little." He carefully wiped the cold moisture off the bridge of her nose with a tissue. "And once when this kid from school punched me."

Ava tried to turn her head to look his way, but the angle was awkward. "I'm sorry. I had to deal with bullies too."

Luke looked skeptical. "But, you're pretty and like...normal. Why would anyone pick on you?"

Ava laughed. "Oh, believe me, I was never normal. I was this scrawny, shy kid who always said the wrong thing at the wrong time and...I guess I just never quite fit in. And you know what?"

"What?"

"Normal is way overrated."

Luke smiled. "That's what Mom says."

Ava imagined Gwen having this talk with Luke. Encouraging him, letting him know that he was the most important thing in the world to her. Ava knew the feeling. When Gwen believed in you, you felt like you could take on anything. "Hey, thanks for showing me *Adventure Time*," she said when he removed the ice pack. "It's really cool."

"You think?" Luke settled back down beside her on the couch, and she continued pinching her nose.

"I do. Although…" She ventured a glance at him, wondering whether to pursue it. "That last episode with Marceline was kind of intense."

"Just wait until we get to 'The Lich.' That's the most intense episode. You have no idea." He was grinning so hard that she almost didn't want to continue with her line of questioning.

"Looking forward to it. But I meant, uh…" She experimentally let go of her nose. "I meant that stuff with Marceline's dad."

"Oh." Luke deflated a bit. "Yeah, but it was 'cause he wanted her to rule the Nightosphere with him and she wanted to stay upworld."

"It must be a hard choice."

"Nah, he just doesn't get it." Luke looked down and picked at a loose thread on his T-shirt.

"Get what?"

"That Marceline doesn't wanna move."

There it is. "You know, if she feels that way, then maybe she should talk to her dad about it."

"I guess." He went quiet for a while, and Ava wondered if bringing it up was a mistake, but then he turned to her with a smile.

"Hey, do you wanna play Heroes of the Beyond? I have the card game. Except it's based on comics, not real superheroes, so it doesn't have Swiftwing, but sometimes I pretend the Miss Power card is actually a Swiftwing card. I can teach you the rules. They're real simple."

"Yeah, sounds fun." Ava smiled widely, wondering how much brainpower this was going to take.

Half an hour, two juice boxes, and four cookies later, Luke was still explaining how your abilities card could double up as a justice card if the supervillain was a level three or below. Ava was utterly lost. She was concentrating so hard that she almost didn't hear the doorbell. Luke sprang up and ran to the front hall, where he pressed the little security monitor.

"Oh, hey, Mrs Levinson," Ava heard him say. "I'll buzz you in."

Luke turned to Ava. "Jacob's mom is here." He was still holding his deck of cards. "I guess we can play when I get back. Will you be here?"

Ava wasn't sure when Luke was coming back, or how long Gwen would want her hanging around the house, but she nodded and smiled.

Once she was alone, Ava cleaned up a little, getting rid of the pizza boxes and everything else she and Luke had gorged on. Food, she found, tasted different without her powers. Not better or worse, just different. Certain flavors were heightened, others dulled. With nothing better to do, she flipped through TV channels, bored and feeling low.

She thought back to what Alfonso had said, about Luke's broken arm and his grades slipping. She wondered why Gwen had never told her. She wondered if she was entitled to know these things, or whether at the end of the day, Gwen just saw her as a competent assistant doing her a favor.

She'd called her rare. The memory of Gwen's face as she'd described Ava Eisenberg to Swiftwing stayed with her. That expression was soft and faraway and conflicted all at once.

That was the image Ava held onto as she fell asleep in Gwen's living room, on Gwen's favorite chair.

CHAPTER 11

AVA WOKE TO THE TORTURED strains of Mozart's "Lacrimosa." She was particularly familiar with the piece due to years of listening to Rachel's old records. Soon after moving in, Ava had discovered the eclectic collection of dusty vinyl in the attic, ranging from Bob Marley to Bizet's *Carmen*. She had devoured them all, her ears eager to absorb the strange sounds that her new planet had to offer. The melodies were so unlike anything with which she was familiar.

Some of the really old stuff reminded her of home (one particular record called *Best of the Middle Ages*), but even the music they deemed "classical" was prone to wild melodies and chaotic rhythms. Some of it stuck; a lot was forgotten. Mozart, for no reason that Ava could explain, remained a constant favorite, even through her Backstreet Boys phase (she had Nic to thank for that) and that month she'd convinced herself that she liked jazz because a pretty girl in senior year played the saxophone. Mozart calmed her when everything became too loud and her head became too full. She still listened to it when she took public transport.

Ava blinked open heavy eyelids and pulled at the soft pashmina covering her. She nuzzled it against her cheek as she burrowed further into the couch with a contented little hum. It smelled warm and familiar—vanilla, bergamot. Gwen.

It took Ava a few moments to realize that if Gwen's shawl was covering her, then Gwen must be home.

She sat up reluctantly, feeling lethargic. She might sleep for another week if she could. Her head hurt in that dull, achy way that she had come to associate with the loss of her abilities. Except they weren't gone—not completely. She could feel the slow regeneration, the way her cells were working together, becoming strong. She could feel it, envision it—but she still couldn't fly, still couldn't hear the rush of the traffic over the music in the house. She felt contained and paralyzed, tempted to curl back onto the couch and just stay there until the antidote brought her back completely.

In the end, she was lured into action by the fragrant smell of herbs wafting from the kitchen.

The curtains were still open, and through the wide French doors that led onto the balcony, the sky was a palette of pink and orange. It was that in-between hour, when the stars began to push through, ignoring the fading sun. Ava knew exactly how the sky would smell from 3,000 feet above the sea at this time.

She imagined the crisp, clean air that would tingle her nostrils if she breathed in too deeply. She missed flying, missed the rush and the speed and the freedom of having the sky to herself. She wondered if one of the poison's side effects was ennui.

Ava meandered toward the kitchen, still clutching the pashmina. Music was filtering through the small speakers located throughout the house. It had changed to something less melancholy, a little lighter. Ava didn't recognize it, but she imagined how Nic would geek out if she ever got a look at Gwen's home entertainment system. The thought made her smile. Nic in Gwen's home was only a little less unbelievable than she herself falling asleep in Gwen's living room.

She wandered into the kitchen area to find Gwen, facing the stove, stirring something with a slim wooden spoon. It was an incongruous image. Ava was so used to seeing Gwen holding microphones and cell phones—a wooden spoon was strange and homely. She wondered if she'd ever get used to this domestic version of Gwen.

Whatever she was stirring smelled good, and Ava's stomach grumbled in response. Gwen knocked the spoon against the side of the pot with a quick tap and placed it on the little ceramic spoon rest. She cooked the way she walked, the way she talked—quickly, efficiently, interspersed with moments of flourish.

Ava was about to announce her presence with a modest little cough, but Gwen seemed to sense her and whirled around. She looked surprised for a moment, as if she'd forgotten Ava was there at all, which, of course, was impossible since she must have covered Ava with the shawl. Gwen's expression softened almost immediately, as if she was looking at something precious, and for a moment, Ava was tempted to look behind her to see what might invoke such an expression.

Her gaze flickered across Ava's face, but she made no attempt to speak, and Ava came nearer, into the bright kitchen lights.

"You let me sleep." Her voice was raspy and her throat hurt.

"You were drooling on my couch when I got back." It was her indulgent tone. "I thought you might need the rest."

Ava surreptitiously wiped the back of her hand against her mouth. "What time is it?"

"After seven."

She settled on a stool. "I didn't mean to be out for so long."

"You're sick."

It was an accusation more than a question, and there was no point in denying it, so Ava nodded. "Just a little."

"I sincerely hope you're not contagious." Gwen pursed her lips, and all wonder or tenderness or whatever it was that Ava had imagined was gone. "I will never forgive you if you've infected me with some virus you've picked up God knows where."

Ava might have smiled at Gwen's dramatics, but the headache, and the equally dizzying implication that Gwen might have picked something up while Ava's tongue was down her throat, had her looking down quickly, afraid she'd give too much away.

"No. Definitely not contagious." Ava hoped. She didn't know how she'd explain weird alien mononucleosis.

Gwen narrowed her eyes for a moment, as if not sure whether to believe her or not. "I'm making soup," she stated. "Chicken and corn."

"Um." Ava paused, not quite sure if Gwen was telling her that she was making the soup for her, or simply announcing the existence of said soup.

But then Gwen said, "You'll feel better after you eat something not drenched in grease and covered in cheese."

Ava's eyes widened. "How did you know?"

"There's a Papa Pizza napkin in the trash."

"Ah. Yes. That." She tried to look innocent, and Gwen shook her head, as if disappointed that Ava would even try.

"How was Luke?" She turned and reached for a glass of something clear and bubbly. Seltzer, Ava guessed.

"He was great. We watched some TV."

"I assume that Alfonso was his usual charming self."

"That was…less great." Ava considered leaving it there, but then added, "He's sort of a jerk."

"You picked up on that." Gwen's tone bordered on apologetic. "I'm ashamed to say it took me almost four years to catch on." She turned back to the stove and lifted the saucepan lid, filling the kitchen with the delicious smell of bubbling soup. "In fact, I think that might have been what attracted me to him in the first place."

"The fact that he's a douche?" Ava asked hotly, remembering that smarmy face.

Gwen spun around, amusement clear on her face. "A douche?"

Ava shrugged. "Jacob Levinson uses that word."

Gwen actually laughed—a real laugh—prompting Ava to grin back, and for a moment, she forgot that she was powerless and miserable and heartsick.

"Then by all means." Gwen turned back around. "What's wrong with you, anyway?"

There was no pause before the question and it took Ava a moment to realize it was directed at her. "I, um…I'm having a reaction to an autoimmune…thing." She panicked and circled the counter. "Um, can I help?"

Gwen backed away from her. "Are you going to sneeze on anything?"

"No." Ava managed to sound offended.

Gwen gestured at the chopping board with her spoon. "Then you can chop the parsley."

Ava chopped and Gwen stirred and Debussy fluttered out of the speakers. The scene felt surreal and a little whimsical. Gwen reached behind Ava to get the salt, Ava circled Gwen to run her parsley-stained fingers under the tap. They moved like they had been doing this for years. And, Ava thought, in a way they had.

"That smells good," Ava said, angling her head toward the pot.

"An old family recipe," Gwen replied. "One of the few I know by heart."

"Do you like cooking?"

Gwen seemed to think about it. "When my schedule allows it." She turned off the gas and pulled a bowl from a top cabinet, standing on her toes to reach it.

Ava was tempted to go up behind her and help, but she didn't think Gwen would appreciate the subtle jab at her height—she always seemed so much shorter without her heels. Instead, Ava leaned back against the counter, feeling significantly less woozy. She wasn't sure if the antidote was beginning to work or if just being here, with Gwen, was enough to make her feel better.

"I would bake with Luke when he was younger, but I was never very good at it."

"I can't imagine you not being good at anything."

"Oh, you'd be surprised. It's that waiting period between putting something in the oven and having it ready that I find insufferable. I, once," she laughed softly, "convinced Luke that oatmeal cookies were supposed to be charred at the bottom. Melted raisins, I said."

Ava chuckled, delighted at the anecdote. "The Knight Cookie. Slightly Burnt to Perfection."

"That's not a bad idea," Gwen teased. "I might market that. Except…" She tilted her head and looked at Ava. "We'd have to omit the raisins for you."

"They're pretty gross," she conceded. "Wait, how did you know I don't like raisins?"

"Honestly Eisenberg, you do so much inane rambling, it's hard to block it all out. I think you mentioned it once when I asked you to get me a health bar."

Ava was pretty certain that the last time she'd gotten Gwen a health bar was over a year ago.

"And anyway," Gwen deflected, "with this production mess, I doubt I'll have much time for anything."

"What happened today?"

"Nothing too dire. Insurance claims, reshoots, a tiff with Ronald."

"What did he say?"

"Far too much." She reached for the chopped parsley and sprinkled it over the soup in a bowl before motioning for Ava to sit.

Gwen placed a plate of warm bread rolls on the counter and settled on a stool opposite Ava. She didn't eat, but slowly sipped her water. "Pepper?"

"Please."

Gwen leaned forward to grind some over the bowl.

Ava swallowed a hearty spoonful and closed her eyes as the warm soup filled her up. It was just the right amount of everything. She blinked and smiled, about to compliment the cook, only to find Gwen watching her with narrow-eyed curiosity, as a documentarian might observe the strange habits of a rare primate.

"You might want to blow on it first," Gwen suggested softly.

Ava looked down and realized, upon seeing the steam coming off the bowl, that it would scald anyone else's mouth.

She looked back up at Gwen for one confusing, panicked moment and then, "Oh! Uh! Ha! H—hot!" Ava made a show of fanning her hand in front of her face.

At least she knew the antidote was working. She wasn't fully back. She couldn't feel the arc of power and restless energy zipping through her veins. But she was getting there.

"Do you need water?" Gwen asked in a strange, toneless voice, and Ava shook her head quickly.

"No, I'm fine. I'm...fine. It's, uh," she smiled widely, hoping she didn't look as panicked as she felt, "it's good."

"Hmm." Gwen took a sip of water.

"The awards show is coming up," Ava blurted, desperate to change direction.

"Tuesday," Gwen agreed. "We'll need a babysitter. I've considered rehiring Manuela on a part-time basis."

We, she'd said. As if Ava could dare to hope. It was easy to forget, especially when she was sitting here, eating dinner with Gwen as if this was their life. But Ava was painfully aware that this was temporary. She was painfully aware that the closer they got, the harder it would be when it all ended.

Gwen continued, oblivious to Ava's inner turmoil. "Of course, Alfonso's convinced that a nanny is a show of weakness."

"Is that why you fired Manuela?"

"I..." Gwen's shoulders moved up and down as she sighed. "I don't know. Perhaps I wanted to prove that I could do it alone."

"Gwen, no one could do it alone. Or no one should have to. Alfonso has no idea what he's talking about. And all that stuff he said about—" She paused, unsure if she should continue.

"About what?"

"Just…stuff."

"I forgot how articulate you can be. What did he say?"

"He, um, he mentioned Luke breaking his arm and…being in therapy."

"That was ages ago." She stood and took her glass to the sink, and Ava wanted to tell her to come back, that she was sorry for ever bringing it up.

"You didn't say anything about it," Ava said quietly, and Gwen turned to face her.

"To you?" She scoffed, and Ava couldn't remember what her smile looked like at all. "No, well, I'm not in the habit of sharing my failings as a parent with my employees."

"I just meant…" Ava swallowed down the hurt. "I think we know I'm not just your employee anymore."

Gwen raised an eyebrow. "Is this the 'you've always got a friend in me' pep talk?"

"You do." It was extremely important to her suddenly that Gwen knew this

"He was playing dodgeball in gym class," Gwen began softly. "He's not…athletic. Which is perfectly all right. Sport is highly overrated and leads to God knows how many concussions. Apparently he dove and fell and…" Gwen pressed her lips together for a moment. "I was on set. They didn't put the call through."

"I know." Ava watched Gwen carefully. "And I know you would have been there the second you could."

"I was. I mean, of course I was." Gwen said nothing for a moment, and Ava didn't push. "The therapy has nothing to do with his home life. He's… struggling with socialization. Therapy is not a bad thing." Gwen said, as if it was Ava who needed convincing. "And Luke, he's…"

"Exceptional."

Gwen looked at her with a hint of surprise. "Yes, he is. What his father fails to understand is that he's adjusting, even thriving. His grades took a bit of a dip because his curiosity extends beyond what they teach him at school. Shuffling him around now…" She bit down on her bottom lip. "If I thought that Alfonso having full custody was the better option, if I thought that was what Luke needed…" Gwen swallowed, shook her head. "I will not give up. I choose to fight for my child, however unconventional," she looked pointedly at Ava, "my methods may be."

"I wish I could do more to help," Ava said, causing Gwen to laugh—mirthlessly this time.

"I think pretending to date your boss at the risk of social and professional ostracization is plenty. Unless you're offering to fly Alfonso into space and leave him there. That might help."

"Fly? What do you—?"

"Silly, isn't it?" Gwen continued over Ava's flustered reply. "I thought, after all of this," she motioned to the soup, getting cold between them. "I thought now that we'd...well—" Gwen pursed her lips for a moment. "I suppose I thought you might finally trust me."

"I do," Ava whispered, echoing Swiftwing's line from the night before. It felt just as false now as it did then.

"How long have your powers been blown out?" Gwen asked softly.

Ava parted her lips to speak and found she had nothing to say. She didn't know how to navigate this without giving herself away, but she couldn't lie, not again, not when she was sitting in Gwen's kitchen, eating soup Gwen had just made for her, telling Gwen that she trusted her.

"They've been going for a while, haven't they? You had a bruise on your shoulder." She crossed her arms over her chest and pierced Ava with a stare. "And you don't bruise."

"Gwen—"

"You were flying around last night, and I didn't see anything on the news about any big fight, so it's slow-moving, whatever this is. Is it temporary?"

I'm not Swiftwing, weighed against *I'm sorry, I'm sorry, I'm sorry*. Excuses and apologies. Ava was saved from the choice by an ear-piercing screech that echoed through the night.

Ava recognized that scream. She heard it in her dreams.

She jumped off her chair as Gwen rushed past her, toward the window.

Toward the source of the sound.

Of course.

"Gwen, wait!" Ava ran after her.

Gwen was nearly at the French doors to the balcony when they shattered. A thousand glimmering shards of glass came exploding toward them, and Ava's first instinct was to grab Gwen by the back of her shirt, pulling her close, and turning them around so that Ava's back shielded them from the worst of it.

The pain was muted and barely there, but she wasn't fully healed, and she felt the glass pierce through her skin.

She brought her hand up to cup the back of Gwen's head, feeling glass in her hair. "Are you okay? Are you—"

"Ava." Gwen was looking past her shoulder, to the broken window. Her eyes were wide and disbelieving.

Ava turned.

The Mantipodis was silhouetted by the twilight sky. Its spindly body was tense and poised for attack.

"Run," Ava whispered, maintaining eye contact with the alien as she slowly disengaged from Gwen. "Get to the hallway." Ava could feel the trickle of blood winding down her temple from where a shard of glass had struck her. Not invulnerable, then.

"What is that thing?" Gwen's voice trembled and she kept her grip firm around Ava's wrist. Holding her back, keeping her close. Safe.

"Dangerous," Ava murmured. The Mantipodis seemed to be undecided about whether to attack or not. It keened forward, sniffing the air as its triangular head twitched and tilted. It was looking for something.

"The hallway," Ava repeated through gritted teeth. "Now!"

"We'll both go," Gwen whispered, her breath warm and close against Ava's neck. "We'll go toge—"

The Mantipodis spread its arms and launched forward. Ava ran toward it.

She could feel the current in her veins, the crackle of power. Not fully there, but almost.

"Ava!"

Gwen's voice was lost in the whoosh of air rushing past as Ava propelled herself up and toward the Mantipodis. She was a few feet off the ground before she fell onto her knees with a heavy thud.

No flight. Not yet.

The Mantipodis hulked over her, its stinger poised to strike, and Ava scrambled up and jumped high, over the creature. Her feet crunched on the shattered glass as she made for the balcony, drawing it away from the living room, away from Gwen.

The Mantipodis turned, cornering Ava against the balcony railing. She reached out and gripped the metal banister so hard that it began to give between her fingers.

"Wait!" Ava yelled desperately, looking up at the alien. "Wait! Tell me what you want! Let me help!" It was only after a moment that she realized she was speaking in Zrix'dhorian. Her native language curled itself around her tongue and settled behind her teeth, both familiar and foreign.

Surprisingly, the alien stopped and bent its head. Ava stood her ground as it angled its head toward her neck, caging her in with its elongated, bony arms. She held her breath, keeping herself steady as it sniffed her. It inhaled deeply as it neared her arm, nuzzling itself against the small gauze patch that covered up the area where the antidote had been injected, reminding Ava of Garbo the night before.

It was the antidote, she realized as the Mantipodis began to whine, its face inches away from her neck. It was attracted to her blood. And suddenly, the first fragments of understanding fell into place.

"It's Norman, isn't it?" she asked, her native language coming easier now, and the creature reared back, its glassy, black eyes appraising her questioningly. "You smelled him on me in the cave. And now, in the antidote."

The Mantipodis opened its mouth—her mouth, Ava guessed—and emitted a shriek. She was angry. She hadn't found what she'd been looking for. Ava made to duck out from under the Mantipodis's elbow when it extended a second stinger from its back and darted it toward her. She braced herself for a blow when the creature jerked and stumbled to one side. Ava looked up to see Gwen, holding a dining chair above her head.

She looked back at Ava with wide eyes and a helpless shrug. They had no chance to speak before the Mantipodis came skittering back.

Ava took a breath, closed her eyes, and propelled herself skyward. She almost cried in relief as her feet left the ground and she was filled with a familiar sense of weightlessness.

"Hey!" she yelled, hovering above the balcony. "Over here!" The Mantipodis moved her head between Gwen, who was still holding the chair, and Ava, now floating above their heads.

"I can take you to your baby," Ava called down, understanding now. Her heart was heavy with the knowledge of what they'd done. "That's who you're looking for, right?"

The Mantipodis shrieked in reply.

"You've got to come with me," she continued. "I can take you—"

With frustrated and impatient motions, the Mantipodis launched herself into the air and over the balcony railing toward Ava. She couldn't fly, but she could glide for a second or two, the thin skin connecting her elbows and torso acting as wings.

She landed on the ground below, and cars screeched, people screamed. The Mantipodis immediately tunneled into the asphalt road. Ava knew she needed to get it away from populated areas before it hurt anyone. She also needed to get herself into her suit before she was recognized.

For a brief moment, Ava allowed herself to look back at Gwen, still watching from the balcony. She imagined what Gwen must see: Ava in jeans and a sweater. Ava still in socks, with a messy ponytail. Ava hovering in the night sky like some kind of superhero.

Gwen was still breathing hard. Ava could hear that now-familiar staccato of Gwen's heart. Her pupils blown wide, her hair sprinkled with glass. There was a small cut on the bridge of her nose that Ava wanted to press her lips to.

But there was no time for that, and it was too late for an excuse or an apology, and even if there was time, Ava wasn't sure she'd have the words.

And so, she looked away from Gwen and darted down, following the Mantipodis into the ground.

Ava was thrown into darkness. The space was tight and smelled of burnt tar and sewage. The tunnel went far and deep.

She walked cautiously for a few minutes. She could hear it, but couldn't see it. It seemed to be employing some sort of camouflage—the same trick it had pulled in the cave after it stabbed her.

A high-pitched jingle echoed through the tunnel, and it took Ava moment to realize that her phone was vibrating in her back pocket.

She reached for it as her eyes adjusted to the darkness. Above her, she could make out the sound of tires running over the street, the sound of footsteps on the sidewalk. The sound of sirens and people. It was all back. She was back.

There was no time to celebrate as she was knocked against the tunnel wall by a long, spiny arm and her phone flew into the air, landing with a loud crack.

"I don't want to hurt you," Ava said desperately as she dodged the Mantipodis's two stingers. "I want to help yo—" She was whacked to the ground, and realized very quickly that fighting an alien bug in a confined space minutes after regaining her powers may not have been the best idea. Ava dodged the alien's angry limbs and gained enough space to build up force.

The dirt and rubble around her feet began to tremble, and a second later, Ava broke through the ground above and shot into the sky, leaving the Mantipodis in the tunnel below.

CHAPTER 12

"SHE'S A MOTHER." AVA STOOD in the precinct's meeting room, her arms crossed over her chest, cape hanging from her shoulders, mask perfectly set over her eyes. She felt more herself than she had in days. "That's why she attacked me. Norman's a Mantipodis larva. That's why we couldn't find anything on him. He's still a baby."

"I'm not following." Captain Fernandez frowned. "Why attack you specifically?"

"The first time was in the cave. That was the afternoon after Norman threw up all over me."

"She smelled her kid on you," Captain Fernandez inferred, and Ava nodded.

"Exactly. That's why she was so confused at first. And then she attacked. Then again, tonight at Gwen…Gwendolyn Knight's place. She must have somehow caught the scent in the antidote. In my blood."

"Wait," another officer—one Ava called "Officer Mustache" in her head because she could never remember his name—spoke up. "Why were you at Gwendolyn Knight's place again?"

"We were…discussing her foundation," Ava said quickly and changed the subject. "I'd never heard of the Mantapodii attacking people or each other."

"Tell that to Officer Barre," Captain Fernandez replied.

"And to everyone this Mantamama has come into contact with." Officer Mustache piped up.

"If she can sense the worm, why hasn't she come looking for it here?" Another, younger officer asked.

"I think she's been trying. I think she's been calling for it. And it's been trying to call back. They're doing it psychically. I've been..." She paused, trying to articulate what she'd felt in her dreams. "I've been dreaming about them. Sensing their emotions."

"They're trying to find each other," Captain Fernandez murmured in sudden realization. "But our cells are heavily insulated and soundproof."

"She must know she can't get close," Officer Mustache deduced.

"We're keeping them apart," Ava finished solemnly. "We're keeping a mother from her child."

They were quiet for a moment, guilt settling around them.

"We still have to bring her in," Captain Fernandez finally stated. "We'll put them together and decide from there."

Ava began to protest, and Captain Fernandez held her hands up in defense. "We can't let the little one out. It's too dangerous."

"So, we'll imprison them both?" It came out more sharply than Ava intended.

"For now," Captain Fernandez answered, her voice firm and commanding. "Unless you have an alternative, Swiftwing."

Ava glanced around the room. The officers looked sympathetic, but resolved.

"Just don't hurt her."

"This is a capture and contain mission only." Captain Fernandez motioned to the room. "No weapons are to be drawn unless absolutely necessary. Is that clear?"

There was a general hum of consent, and Captain Fernandez raised an eyebrow at Ava, questioning.

Ava nodded, satisfied, and crossed her arms over her chest.

"So, what's the plan?"

"Go home," Captain Fernandez replied, and Ava looked at her with confusion.

"But—"

"You were right. We wouldn't have figured this out without you. But you've done enough, and you need to rest. You're exhausted."

"I can help."

"We'll call you if we need you. This is our job."

"My phone got totaled. I won't have a new one until Monday."

"Fine. Email then."

Ava sighed. She was tired. Her powers may have been back, but her body still hurt. "You promise you won't hurt her?"

"I promise we'll try not to," Captain Fernandez replied, before leaving Ava alone in the meeting room.

It was almost midnight when Ava trudged up the steps to her apartment.

She had changed out of the suit to buy four candy bars at the little corner store. It seemed her appetite was back, along with her abilities. Ava wracked her brain, trying to remember if she still had half a pastrami and rye sandwich in the refrigerator, or if Nic had eaten it. Her housemate had texted her earlier after seeing the attack on the news. When Ava confirmed that she was okay, Nic let her know that she was spending the night at the lab. Ava suspected she needed some space after their fight that morning.

She imagined she wouldn't be getting much sleep, between worrying about the Mantipodis mother and worrying about Gwen. The first thing she'd done after leaving the station was fly to Gwen's house, but a quick sweep had told her that she was nowhere near. Ava assumed, based on the glass still scattered across the balcony, that Gwen had relocated to the Beverly Hills Peninsula for the night.

She considered calling every second minute and kept deciding against it. She must have found at least twenty different excuses, and the lack of phone made it easier to convince herself that she should give Gwen space—the night, at least.

She opened her door, annoyed at Nic for forgetting to lock it again.

In the dark apartment, she leaned against the door, lamenting that Captain Fernandez was right. She *was* emotionally exhausted; it *had* been a strange couple of days.

It took a second longer than it should have for her to realize that she wasn't alone in the apartment. She narrowed her eyes to make out the dark silhouette on the couch.

"Gwen?"

Gwen sat with her legs crossed, back straight, and expression bored. "I thought you'd be in the suit. Or at the very least come flying in through the window. How disappointing."

She stood as Ava came forward with a confused, "What are you doing here? In my apartment. In the dark. How did you get in?"

"Your landlady's a fan of my work." The half moon was casting just enough light into Ava's living room for her to see the frown on Gwen's face. "You didn't answer my calls."

"I…" Ava took another step toward her, hesitant and nervous. "I lost my phone in the fight."

"You didn't come back up." Gwen made it sound like an accusation.

Ava was confused for a moment, until she realized what Gwen meant. She'd seen Ava dive in after the Mantipodis, but had no way of knowing that Ava had resurfaced two blocks away after following the tunnel.

"I waited…" Gwen continued, in a voice still laced with anger that reached out and twisted at Ava's heart. "And then you didn't answer. You just…stayed gone."

"I'm sorry," Ava said. And the apology she'd been dreading came as easily as breathing. "If you'd just let me explain—"

"What is there to explain? That it took a giant insect smashing through my window for you to finally let me in on your little secret? Ava." Gwen clucked her tongue, disappointed, and something inside of Ava withered.

"It's not that simple. I couldn't. I didn't—"

"Trust me."

Ava felt the hot prickle of tears behind her eyes. She didn't want this. She wanted anything *but* this. And it wasn't the anger that got to her, but the betrayal etched into Gwen's face.

"I was scared," she answered honestly.

"Well, join the club." Gwen rolled her eyes and huffed, her empathy turned down to its lowest volume to accommodate her own hurt. "Do you have any idea what I thought when you failed to resurface? Can you imagine what I…?" She turned and exhaled a mirthless laugh, as if to herself. "No, of course you can't. You're the hero. You don't think before you go charging in after a homicidal bug. You don't consider checking in with the one person who…" She trailed off, still scowling.

Gwen pursed her lips and wrapped her arms around herself. She suddenly looked so small. Small and out of place in the middle of Ava's dark apartment. She had changed into a casual dress and washed the glass out of her hair, but even in the dark, Ava could see the small cut on the bridge of her nose. She still wanted to kiss it better.

She knew that if she pushed too far, Gwen would walk out and that would be that. But this was really the first time that Ava had gotten to stand in front of Gwen without any pretense between them, and she felt that stupid surge of misplaced courage.

"I don't even know why I'm here."

"Yes, you do." Ava said it tentatively, but she said it all the same.

Gwen seemed surprised, and she wavered for a moment, as if caught somewhere between staying and leaving.

"I wanted to call," Ava admitted. "I went back to your house after the… after the fight. I was worried."

"I'm fine, as you can see."

Ava motioned to the cut on Gwen's nose, the thumb-sized bruise on her shoulder from where Ava had held her after the window shattered.

"You're hurt."

"I'll live." Gwen watched Ava for a moment and then asked, "Should I be concerned about it coming back?"

Ava shook her head. "She was there for me. Well, because of me."

Gwen's silence unnerved her; she would rather have had yelling. She knew how to deal with a yelling Gwen, with a Gwen whose eyes blazed and whose hands cut through the air with dramatic gestures. But the quiet, heavy disappointment and hurt that emanated from the woman in front of her was unfamiliar and jarring.

"Would you like to—"

"It's late," Gwen said, cutting off Ava's desperate attempt at conversation.

She brushed past, and Ava panicked when her hand closed over the door handle.

"Gwen, please." Please what? Ava wasn't really sure what she was asking for. Understanding? Forgiveness? Any sign that everything was not completely ruined forever? "Can we just talk about this?"

"What is there left to say?" But she hovered at the door, not making any further move, and Ava took a step forward, forgetting rules and lines and boundaries, coming up behind Gwen, so close that she could see the strain in her neck, the tightness of her shoulders, as if Gwen was trying to hold herself together with sheer will.

"Stay." Ava's fingertips ghosted against the small of Gwen's back, barely touching, unable to stop herself from making a tentative connection. "Stay here with me," she implored softly.

Gwen's shoulders rose and fell in a deep sigh before she turned, an inch away from Ava. "How do you do that?"

"Do what?"

Gwen replied by leaning up and kissing her. It was an angry kiss, a bloody-lipped "don't you ever leave me" kiss. Gwen kissed Ava like she'd been thinking about it for a long time. Like she had watched Ava disappear into the ground and never come up.

When Gwen finally pulled back, flushed, she left just enough space between them for Ava to go cross-eyed trying to assess her expression. "Are you—"

"Don't talk." Gwen's breath fanned against Ava's cheeks. "You'll ruin it."

"Okay," Ava replied. And that was all it took for her to tilt her head and kiss Gwen fully, without hesitation, without question, eagerly taking everything Gwen was willing to give.

She pushed forward and Gwen's back met the door. The little jolt had Gwen pulling away, and her head hit with a soft thud. Ava took advantage of the break to trail a path of kisses down the side of Gwen's neck. She wanted to keep it slow and gentle, wanted to show some modicum of finesse, but the low moan of appreciation Gwen made when Ava sucked on her pulse point had Ava trembling and desperate.

She was suddenly as lightheaded as she'd been that morning, but this was a different kind of poison, and she was completely at the mercy of her want. They moved to the couch, and suddenly Gwen was on top of her, Gwen's heart drumming almost in time with her own. It was a reckless and terrifying rhythm, and Ava pulled back, overwhelmed by the rush of blood and heat through her body.

"Wait, wait." She rested her forehead against Gwen's, panting. They stared at each other for an infinite moment, the earlier anger in Gwen's eyes replaced with something more complicated and impossible to read, but just as intense.

"I need a moment to—" Ava closed her eyes, trying to find something to keep her grounded. There were so many questions she wanted to ask, so many things to say that were tangled up in her throat and evaporated by the time she exhaled.

"Are you all right?" Gwen was watching her with wide, lust-hazy eyes. She was just as flushed and breathless as Ava.

"I-I think so. It's just...a lot." Ava tried for a smile.

Gwen swallowed and exhaled shakily. Ava wanted to kiss her until she was steady and strong again. But it was Gwen who leaned back in just a little to kiss Ava softly against the little scar on her brow from when she was nine and chasing her brother through the metal corridors of the *Andromeda*, and then on her cheek, and then right against the corner of her mouth, as if she couldn't quite decide, couldn't quite commit.

There was a tenderness here, a softness that Ava had only ever caught glimpses of underneath all of that perfectly coutured armor.

Ava suddenly found that she couldn't continue, knowing that in a few weeks she'd never have Gwen's hands on her again, knowing that she'd have to go back to merely arranging meetings and fetching lattes. Despite the rush of heat, despite the very physical evidence of Gwen's desire, Ava was terrified. To have Gwen peel away her shirt and see her naked—not Ava or Swiftwing, but that fragile understanding of the two... No one, especially not any of her previous sexual fumbles, had seen her so utterly exposed. To have Gwen look at her and *know*...the thought made her panic, made her close her hand over Gwen's with a whispered, "Maybe we should stop."

Concern slowly morphed into understanding, and then that frown line appeared, and Gwen tilted her head, assessing.

"Ah."

When she rolled her shoulders and lifted herself off of Ava's lap, the loss was tangible.

"You don't have to go."

"No, I do," Gwen said. She didn't look at Ava. She looked anywhere *but* at Ava as she pulled down the hem of her dress and adjusted her bra strap. "This was obviously not what I—" She huffed in frustration. "Sex doesn't have to mean anything, Ava, and you're under no obligation here."

"But it does," Ava objected, standing up on wobbly legs. "It's just—"

"No, no," Gwen held up her hand, pursing her lips in a particularly Miss Knight way. "I don't require an explanation. In fact, it's best this evening is cut short. My living room floor looks like the scene of a bad action movie, and I need to get it cleaned up before Luke comes home. Besides, I left Garbo locked in my bedroom. She's probably ripped my curtains to ribbons."

"It's 1 a.m.," Ava pointed out, provoking another scowl.

"I'll get an Uber."

"You hate being exposed to Uber drivers."

"Are you offering to fly me home?" Gwen's voice was glass-sharp, and Ava flinched.

I would if you'd stop pretending. I would if I could touch you and not dread the moment it ends because I can't trust that it won't be the last time. I would if this could be something real.

But she said nothing, and Gwen nodded slowly, knowingly. "Mmm. Didn't think so."

Ava didn't stop her from walking away. She didn't call her name or ask her to stay. She watched Gwen close the door, listened to the ding of the elevator as it reached the first floor, waited to hear the halt of car tires. And only when she was sure that Gwen was safe and on her way home did Ava sit back down and allow herself to cry.

CHAPTER 13

AVA DIDN'T SLEEP. SHE DIDN'T retrieve her half-eaten rye and pastrami sandwich from the refrigerator. She didn't change out of her clothes, or turn on the TV.

What she did was sit on the floor, with her back against the couch, and her feet stretched out in front of her, while she watched the sky grow lighter as dawn broke over the city.

She vacillated between being angry with herself and angry with the entire situation. It wasn't like she'd wanted to fall in love with her hot, rich, unattainable boss. And there really was no way around it now. She might as well have screamed it from the rooftops. She was in love with Gwen Knight.

Stupid, scary, painful love.

Ava wondered whether Gwen had gone home to her damaged apartment and fallen asleep instantly or lain awake, remembering Ava with as much longing and intensity as Ava felt for her. She wondered if Gwen's memory was soured by the taste of Ava's betrayal. Because that was exactly how Gwen would see it—not as Ava protecting her identity, but as Ava lying to her for years. She wasn't sure how long Gwen had known, but it wasn't a recent revelation, she knew that much.

She wished she could properly explain how many times she'd wanted to tell and why, every time, she couldn't. Wished she could explain to Gwen that the more she had to lose, the scarier revealing her identity became. It wasn't just a job; it was Gwen herself. Gwen, who in these crazy past few weeks had become everything Ava never thought she could have.

Sunlight warmed her skin, wrapped around her bones as she replayed the night in its entirety, obsessively recounting every word, every phrase, and thinking about what she should have said, and how she should have acted.

How can I give you everything, every secret part of myself, when I'm only a means to an end? Even as she thought it, Ava knew she'd never really ask Gwen that. She didn't want the answer. She didn't want Gwen to roll her eyes and tell her that she wasn't really that interested in having all of Ava anyway.

By 6 a.m., the sky was crisp and blue, and Ava thought, *screw this*. She chugged a glass of milk and changed into her suit.

The sky smelled sweet. Once she got past the smog above the city, she flew north toward the mountains. Drought had painted the hills yellow and gold. They fringed clear blue waters, and Ava shot up into a wisp of clouds to dive back down, toward the lake, stopping just inches from the smooth, mirrored surface. She came down with such force that the water moved without being touched. It felt incredible to fly again, to stretch her muscles and open her arms to welcome the sun.

She flew back the long way, toward home—her first real home on this planet. She knew Rachel would be up for her Sunday morning run, and Ava landed in the backyard of her childhood home with a gentle thud.

"Hey, lady! Some strange girl just flew into your backyard!" Ava called out, grinning.

"There she is!" Rachel smiled widely as she opened the back door.

They hugged, and Rachel ushered Ava inside. The house always smelled the same, no matter what time of day or season it was—like old books and laundry detergent. It was comforting.

Ava made herself comfortable on one of the kitchen chairs, and hummed happily when Rachel presented her with coffee.

"Have you eaten?" she asked with her head buried in one of the top cupboards.

"Not yet." Ava sipped her coffee.

"I'm out of milk, so..." Rachel stuck two pop tarts into the toaster oven.

"Just like old times," Ava said, making grabby hands at the tarts when they came out.

"You know, I would have been more prepared if you'd told me you were coming." Rachel gave her a look, and Ava shrugged, half a pop tart already devoured.

"It was spontaneous."

"So," Rachel started as she settled herself on a stool across from Ava, "how's work? How's Nic? How's superheroing?"

"Fine, good, the same."

"Uh-huh," Rachel nodded. "And how's your boss? What was her name again? Gwyneth? Gertrude?"

"Gwendolyn." Ava shoved another piece of pop tart into her mouth to buy some time. "I know you know that. You own like three of her movies on DVD."

"All right." Rachel held her hands up in surrender. "Fine. Gwendolyn. Tell me about her."

"What's to tell?" Ava asked, her heart sitting in her throat.

"Ava'Kia," Rachel said softly.

Ava exhaled in frustration, knowing Rachel had won. Rachel was the only person who called her by her birth name. In the beginning, it was all Ava responded to, and then, it became something Rachel only used when she wanted to remind Ava of who she was, and who she and Rachel were to each other. Bonded by love, Rachel used to say.

"I don't know what to say," Ava whispered.

"Try starting at the beginning." Rachel reached out and put her hand over Ava's. "We'll go from there."

And Ava did. She told Rachel *almost* everything, opting to give her the more PG version of certain events. Ava told her about how Gwen had changed toward her, and about how smart Luke was, about Vancouver, and Nic's disapproval.

Rachel listened, stood up to pour more coffee for them both, and just let Ava speak.

When Ava concluded with a censored version of the previous night's events, Rachel reached out and swiped her thumb gently against her cheek. "I know what you need."

"A time machine to take me back to before Gwen thought I didn't trust her?"

Rachel smiled. "I was thinking Chinese."

Ava actually laughed. "You know it's barely eleven?"

"Sweetheart, I've seen you devour two whole pizzas at 2 a.m."

"I have a fast metabolism!"

"Ugh," Rachel groaned as she stood. "To be twenty-seven again."

Ava considered Rachel for a moment before asking. "Does the, uh, the age thing with me and Gwen freak you out?"

Rachel thought about it for a moment. "Not particularly. What about you?"

"Not if the alien thing doesn't freak her out." Ava sighed. "But it's pointless. I told you. She doesn't feel that way about me."

"Is that why she rushed over to your apartment after the fight? Or why she kept your secret for so long?"

"Okay, so maybe she cares about me," Ava conceded. "In like a fond, pat on the head, grateful for being the city's protector kind of way." Ava knew Gwen respected her, *liked* her even. After the previous night, she was pretty sure Gwen was attracted to her. But stupid, scary, painful love? That wasn't something Gwendolyn Knight did, and it certainly wasn't something she'd allow herself to feel for her assistant, even if said assistant was able to break the sound barrier.

"And..." Rachel still looked thoughtful, "that's not enough?"

"I guess it was." Ava stared down at the crumbs on her plate and mumbled, "But that was before I realized I might be falling in love with her."

Rachel exhaled a breath. "Ava, I know these have been an intense couple of weeks, but..."

"No, it was before this whole arrangement. I just...I didn't see it. Or I saw it, but I knew that it couldn't ever happen, so I never went there."

"And now?"

"Now I know that I might have had a chance to at least see where it could go and I blew it. She thinks I don't trust her." Ava gave a dejected huff.

"Do you?"

"Of course."

"Then why didn't you tell her about Swiftwing?"

"You know the answer. The fewer people who know the better."

"The people in your life who matter know. The Rileys know, your doctor knows. One more person wouldn't make that much of a difference." Rachel watched Ava carefully. "What's the real reason?"

Ava bit on the inside of her cheek and looked down at her lap. "I was scared."

"That she wouldn't accept you?" Rachel asked softly.

"That she'd only see me as a symbol. I wanted to be important, significant without the suit. I-I guess, I wasn't sure that I could..."

"Trust her?"

"Yeah," Ava admitted.

"And all this time she's watched you come up with excuses, and she hasn't said anything, or done anything besides keep your secret?"

"Yeah."

"And the only reason you know she knows is because she told you?"

"Yes?"

"Well, obviously you're important to her, or she wouldn't have protected you."

"What if I screw up?" Ava asked in a small voice.

"Hey." Rachel waited for Ava to look at her before she went on. "Do you remember when you first told me you wanted to put on that suit? You said you wanted to honor your old people and protect the new."

"I remember."

"I didn't understand it at first."

"Because I couldn't throw a punch to save my life?"

Rachel chuckled. "That, and because you spent so many years as a teenager wanting to forget your past, wanting to fit in and be like everyone else. I couldn't understand why you wanted to do this thing that would so obviously set you apart. Oh, I was proud of you," Rachel emphasized, "but I was confused."

"I guess I just wanted to do something with my abilities."

'No, not just something. You wanted to help people, Ava'Kia. You wanted to ease some of the pain and suffering in this world. And then, when you started focusing on AO crimes, I thought that maybe you were trying to make amends for your mother's choices. But you've always been such a hero. Ever since you were little. And I soon came to realize that you weren't fighting your nature by stepping into the light—you were embracing it.

And now," Rachel reached over and wiped a tear from Ava's cheek, "look how you shine."

Ava rolled her eyes, embarrassed by her tears. "I don't feel very shiny. I just feel kind of sad."

"Talk to her," Rachel said. "My little star."

Ava nodded and wiped her cheeks. "So, were you lying about Chinese? Cause I could really use some egg rolls right now."

Rachel smiled and went to get the menu.

It was almost sunset by the time Ava left Rachel's. They'd spent most of the day just hanging out. She'd taken a shower, had a nap in her old room, and then she and Rachel had watched reruns of *The West Wing* and eaten too much Chinese food.

When she landed in her living room—now sunny and awash with light, as if the previous night was nothing but a dream—Ava opened her laptop and found an email:

Mission unsuccessful. Mature Mantipodis displaying possible invisibility.

Ava read the email twice. She wanted to ask Nic if the census said anything about the Mantipodis's abilities, but she didn't know if she and Nic were in a place where she could ask anything right now. Other than a seventh-grade fight over who loved *High School Musical* more, this was the longest they'd ever gone without talking. Ava wanted to reach out, but didn't know how to begin. She felt helpless with Nic, with Gwen, with the Mantipodis.

She had to convince Captain Fernandez to allow her to help. No matter how hard she tried, Ava couldn't stop thinking of the baby Mantipodis separated from its mother. The older female must have been pregnant on the *Andromeda*, and the baby born on Earth. She wondered if that automatically made it a citizen of the United States.

When Ava was growing up, there'd been a large movement to acknowledge the offspring of AOs and humans. The AOs who were genetically compatible with humans were creating entirely new species—and the government was scared. That was when so many of the anti-discrimination laws started up.

Ava remembered seeing a picture of Gwen at one of the rallies. She was barely famous at the time. The thought made Ava smile.

She was lost in her thoughts until the screech of tires against asphalt jolted her into action. In 0.6 seconds, Ava established where the sound had come from, how far away it was, and how fast she needed to fly in order to get there before a collision.

Ava made it to the 4th Street Bridge just in time to stop a delivery truck from swerving and losing its cargo all over the bridge. Ava heard the blaring of sirens, and waited until the EMTs arrived, just to make sure there wasn't more she could do. They thanked her, a little starstruck as always, and told her they could take it from there.

She flew to the police station next, and Captain Fernandez agreed to let her come on their next sweep. The mission was simple. They would use the last of the junior Mantipodis's antivenom to draw out the mother. Once they had her, they'd contain her with an electromagnetic field. That would also knock her out long enough for them to relocate her to the holding cells.

They ventured out just after sunset. Office Mustache led, and Ava circled the skies above, listening for movement that the monitors couldn't pick up.

After almost two hours, Captain Fernandez's voice over their walkies said, "I don't think she's coming." A few of the other officers gathered at the helicopter, unofficially calling the mission unsuccessful.

The city was quiet, preparing for the week ahead. Ava told herself that she was just going to fly over Gwen's house, just near enough to check that the glass door was fixed, to make sure everything was all right before Luke came home.

On impulse, Ava closed her eyes and searched for one rhythm, one melody in a symphony of noise. She thought it had been a fluke before; there was no way she could actually differentiate one beat among thousands. But there it was—that specific cadence of Gwen's heart.

Ava swooped in low, and saw Gwen on the small private balcony of her bedroom—half empty glass in hand, forearms draped over the railing, looking across the city that had made her. It was an iconic image, one that

Ava wished she could capture and frame, except a static photograph could never catch the way Gwen lifted her face to the warm night breeze, or the way her delicate wrist swirled her glass.

Gwen gave a contented hum as she swallowed down her martini, and Ava smiled. She couldn't help it. Despite every tangled, conflicted emotion churning inside of her, the sight of Gwen, alone and content, made her smile.

"Are you going to hover there all night?" Gwen blinked up at her slowly, as if she'd been waiting for Ava this entire time.

"I didn't want to disturb you." Ava floated closer, blocking out the sliver of moon and casting a shadow over her.

"Too late."

"I can leave…" Ava said uncertainly and jabbed a thumb over her shoulder. Gwen pursed her lips in that way that suggested Ava had said or done the wrong thing. The way she had when Ava had first started and added Splenda to Gwen's latte.

"But you'd just come back, wouldn't you? We're stuck in this thing."

Ava came forward, floating directly in front of Gwen now, close enough to smell the notes of juniper and olives in the glass and on Gwen's breath.

"Gwen—" Ava began, with no real purpose.

"Ava," Gwen mimicked, and then tilted her head, as if a thought had just occurred to her. "Or would you prefer I call you Swiftwing exclusively? Is Ava even your real name?"

"It is." She crossed her arms over her chest, defensively. "Ava'Kia Vala of Zrix'dhor, only daughter of Dro'Gah and Lei'Ya Vala, both deceased. Sister of Hada'Si Vala, also deceased. Adopted by the Rachel Eisenberg of Lakewood California, so… Ava Eisenberg, if you want."

"Well then," Gwen swallowed back the last of her drink and grimaced. "Points for honesty."

"I'm sorry I lied," Ava said in a rush. "And I'm sorry I didn't trust you."

Gwen's expression remained wary and distrustful. "But?"

"No buts. I'm just sorry. You were right." Ava shrugged in defeat and flew right up to Gwen, landing softly beside her. "You were right. I didn't trust you. I was scared that if you knew my secret, you'd stop seeing me as your assistant."

"And that's what you wanted?" Gwen's frown deepened. "To be seen as an assistant?"

"I wanted you to see me as me." A light breeze whipped between them, and Ava brushed her hair out of her face. "I still want that."

"And aren't you Swiftwing as well? Or is it just this?" Gwen reached out and tugged at the cape billowing softly against Ava's back and around her sides. "Something you put on and take off?"

"I've never felt more myself than after I got to put on this mask," Ava said, aware of the irony. "But everyone is in love with Swiftwing, or at least the idea of her. And I guess a selfish part of me wanted you to…" Ava stopped suddenly, with a look of panic. She had said too much to backtrack now, but the thought of Gwen knowing everything made her stomach knot up with fear. How would she articulate what this meant to her? What Gwen meant to her? "To, um…"

"To fall in love with Ava the underpaid, undervalued wallflower?"

"I didn't mean… That's not what I…" But it was. Of course it was. And Ava deflected as best she could. "I didn't want to risk my job."

"Why even have a job?" Gwen asked sharply. "Why not be Swiftwing 24/7? You could make millions off licensing your brand. Like you said, the world is in love with the superhero."

"Because I like being able to think about schedules and call sheets, and when you're booked for your next facial." Ava's own exasperation came through. "I like the normalcy of waking up every morning and coming in to my job like a regular person. I like seeing you every day," she gestured toward Gwen, "and feeling useful in a way that doesn't involve putting out forest fires or picking up school buses. And whether you believe me or not, I wanted to tell you. So many times."

"But you didn't."

"No, I didn't. And I'm sorry."

"For God's sake, stop apologizing. You sound like an adulterous politician."

"Then stop pouting and making me feel like I have to." Ava answered, with a spark of temper.

"I do not pout." But Gwen looked sufficiently admonished, and Ava thought that maybe they had reached some sort of truce.

She should have left it there. She should have taken this as a win and gone to bed. But she couldn't help herself. The catharsis of truth was addictive, and she found herself whispering, "Are we going to talk about last night?"

Gwen watched Ava for a long moment and then asked, "Would you like to start with the Franken-bug that smashed through my window, or the way you had your hands up my dress?"

Regret was immediate and startling. She should have left it. Screw catharsis. "I…um."

"Oh, relax. Your chastity is safe." Gwen's lips twitched, as if Ava's discomfort amused her. "I'm not about to give a tell-all interview about my night with Swiftwing."

"That wasn't… I know you're not going to tell. And I'm not concerned about my…my chastity."

"Hmm." Gwen's gaze drifted toward her empty glass, and Ava the assistant resisted the urge to ask if she wanted a refill. "You could have fooled me. You seemed quite eager to end things last night."

"I didn't…" Ava exhaled another frustrated breath. "That isn't why I froze."

"Then why?" Gwen challenged.

"If I tell you, it'll ruin this." Very quietly, Ava added, "Ruin us."

"Tell me anyway," Gwen urged gently.

Ava's heart pounded against her chest, in her throat, in her fingertips. A frantic beat of *don't don't don't*. "I didn't want to go further because I want more. More than just sex and, and pretending that I don't feel the way I feel for you." And there it was. No going back now.

"How do you feel about me?"

"It doesn't matter."

For a moment, Gwen looked like she might just let it lie, and Ava thought she was off the hook, but then Gwen said, "Of course it matters."

"I feel…" Ava took a breath. "Too much…for-for you. And it terrifies me because I can do all these things. I can…I can move faster than the speed of sound, but I can't stop feeling like this. I can't talk myself out of what I know is a stupid, unrealistic fantasy—"

"Ava—"

"No, it's okay," she said quickly, fearing for her already battered pride. "It's…I just needed you to know. It's not because I don't trust you, and it's not because I-I don't want to. I just...I need to not fall any harder than I already have," Ava finished in a small voice that seemed out of place as she stood there in her suit, backlit by the night sky, a picture of power and grace.

Gwen opened her mouth, closed it again. *Shit.* She had made it worse. Gwen was speechless, and Ava had made it worse.

But then, with quiet deliberation, Gwen asked, "Do you want to end this arrangement?"

"No," Ava answered honestly. "I want to go to this BAFTA thing with you, and I want to go to the deposition with you, and I want to help you fight for Luke. Because this is about more than what I feel."

"Okay."

"Is..." Ava bit down on her bottom lip. "Have I ruined it?"

"No." Gwen shook her head slowly, and Ava was still half convinced that she was suffering from shock. "No, Ava. You haven't ruined anything."

"You're not mad anymore?"

"I'm..." Gwen seemed to think about it. "Tired."

"Oh." Ava swallowed down her disappointment. She wasn't sure what she was expecting, and part of her knew that this definitely wasn't the worst-case scenario. Still, some crazy, hopeful part of her wished Gwen would reach out and pull her close, and tell her that she felt the same and that she was only waiting for Ava to say it first.

Except Gwen took a small step back and gave Ava a strained smile that suddenly seemed worse than any sort of overt rejection. "I'll see you in the morning."

Ava tried to smile back, but her lips felt wobbly, and her throat burned. "Sure."

She watched Gwen pick up her empty glass and make to go back inside. Ava had begun to float backwards when Gwen turned.

"Oh, and Swiftwing?"

"Yes?"

"Goji berry juice tomorrow, not coffee." She shrugged. "I'm thinking of going on a cleanse."

Ava smiled, genuinely now. "Of course, Miss Knight."

Gwen's expression softened. "Good night, Ava."

And then, there was nothing left to say besides, "Night, Gwen."

CHAPTER 14

THE MORNING STARTED OFF SURPRISINGLY well. Ava got to Gwen's place early enough to wave Luke off to school and chat with the new housekeeper about the weekend's weather. She made sure that there were fresh flowers in Gwen's study, and that the fridge was stocked with LaCroix. She was armed with Gwen's goji berry juice and a bag of oatmeal cookies that were still warm and soft from the cafe.

There was no time for any awkwardness, as Gwen appeared only long enough to breeze out the front door. "We'll talk when I get back," she promised, taking the juice from Ava. "I shouldn't be gone too long."

Ron Gooding's snowboarding catastrophe had required Ava to do a fair amount of reshuffling. The shooting timetable had changed to accommodate the accident, so Gwen was suddenly open to take meetings. Since production was on a break until further notice, Ava would be working out of Gwen's home office.

She was sitting in the garden, sipping on bubble tea and making sure that everything was set for the BAFTA LA Gala, when she heard her name being called. She looked up to see Daniel coming toward her.

"I swear, I'm moving back east. I hate LA drivers."

Ava set her tablet aside. "Hello to you too."

"Yeah, hi." Daniel stood in front of her, his tall figure blocking the sunshine Ava had been enjoying.

"Can I help you, Daniel?"

"Where's your mistress?"

"The Palisades." Ava raised her brows. He seemed even bitchier than usual. "The Hedy Lamarr biopic?" Gwen was meeting with the director of the film. She had taken the part, much to Ava's excitement.

"Shit," Daniel snapped his fingers. "That was this morning." He typed something on his phone. "I'll meet her at my office."

"Whatever works." Ava was annoyed that he'd interrupted her little morning work session. She expected him to leave, but he stood there, watching her with a curious expression.

"I didn't believe it at first, you know. I thought she was doing it for the publicity. Engaged to Gooding one moment, shacking up with her assistant the next."

Ava was about to protest that they were not "shacking up," when Daniel continued, "But at that meeting the other day, the way she looks at you. I should have seen it earlier."

Ava leaned forward, suddenly very interested. "What do you mean?"

"Oh, the secret glances and lingering looks. If I didn't know you were already banging, I'd tell you both to get a room. It's insufferable, really."

Ava laughed. She couldn't help it. The idea that it was Gwen's actions and not her own puppy-dog eyes that had convinced Daniel was ridiculous.

"What can I say?" Ava threw her hands up. "We're just crazy about each other."

Daniel pulled a face of distaste. "Let her know I came by. I want her to understand that I braved the traffic for her."

"Will do."

"By the way," Daniel began as he turned to leave, "congrats on taking the plunge. To be honest, I thought you'd have quit long before this. Time for someone else to fetch those lattes, huh?"

"What are you talking about?" Ava frowned, and tried to ignore the way her stomach dropped. "Why would somebody else be—" Ava cut herself off, remembering Gwen saying that they would talk, and her face the night before when Ava had all but confessed her undying love.

"Oh, honey." Daniel looked awkward. "I thought you knew. You didn't really think you'd be her assistant forever, did you?"

Ava opened her mouth to speak, but no sound came out.

"Well." He winked at her. "Gotta run. See ya, Sunshine."

Ava slumped down in her seat, confused and hurt. She picked up her tablet again, but the screen was blurry and she couldn't focus. Gwen had said they would talk. She hadn't realized it at the time, but what Gwen had most likely meant was, "We need to talk." The four words that spelled the end of a relationship.

So, Ava thought, this was where honesty got her.

It was more than an hour later when she heard Gwen's car pull up, and then the click of her heels as she walked out to the garden.

"Oh, good. You're here." If Ava hadn't been so angry, she would have noticed how Gwen's expression softened.

But all Ava felt was betrayal. "Is it true?"

"What?" Gwen asked, distracted by a text that had just come in. "Oh, damn. I just saw Danny's message." She dropped her phone back into her purse and strolled towards Ava, all flushed and excited. "He can wait. I almost called you from the car. The meeting went terrifically. I—"

"Am I fired?"

Gwen stopped, looking startled. "What on earth are you talking about?"

"Daniel was here. He said—"

"Oh." Gwen crossed her arms over her chest. "Oh, *Daniel* said…"

"Is it true?" Ava stood, trembling with self-righteous anger and hurt. "Am I fired? Is…is this about last night?"

"You have no idea what you're talking about." Gwen turned and walked into the house forcing Ava to jog to catch up with her.

"Then tell me," Ava responded, louder than she knew Gwen would like.

"I'm not going to talk to you like this." Gwen was still walking away.

"You barely talk to me at all. I have no idea what you're thinking or feeling! So, excuse me, Gwen, for trying to make sense of—"

Gwen whirled around, her eyes sharp and focused, poised for a fight. "First of all, I do not appreciate being yelled at in my own home, by an *employee* no less," she said with emphasis, and Ava deflated. "There are rules about this. We do *not* blur the line between business and personal."

Ava exhaled a humorless chuckle. "Seriously?"

Gwen closed her eyes for a moment and pinched the bridge of her nose, as if unable to contain the weight of her exasperation. "Secondly," she began, her voice measured now, as if she was talking to a child, "I had hoped that you would wait to hear my intentions before listening to hearsay from Daniel Cho. Clearly, your little speech last night about trusting me was premature, because here you are, assuming that I would….what? Fire you?" Gwen's expression turned incredulous. "After everything that you've…" She bit down on her lip for a moment, as if to physically stop herself from continuing. "After you've proven yourself over and over to be invaluable?"

"It wasn't premature," Ava argued. "You *know* everything I said was true. And that's why I…" She crossed her arms over her chest defensively, feeling as petulant as she sounded. "I thought that maybe you were freaked out."

"I was not…" Gwen's eyes went skyward in an impressive eye roll, *"freaked out."*

"So, I'm not fired?" Ava asked in a small voice.

"No, you dimwit. You're being promoted. I've set up a meeting for you with Third Planet."

"I'm—" The apology was replaced by confusion. "You're getting me a job?"

"I was," Gwen said with a sigh as if Ava had tired her. "Until you decided to throw a tantrum and make me reconsider."

"Where?"

"Jackson Alvarez is moving to the company. He's on the lookout for writers. His new pilot just got picked up at Showtime. I suggested he speak to you. I also took the liberty of giving him the screenplay you foisted off on me when you first started. It was good."

Ava blinked in disbelief, trying to ignore the smile tugging at the corners of her mouth. "So, Jackson Alvarez, creator of one of my all-time favorite shows, wants to meet with me?"

"If that's something you want." Gwen sniffed. "You know, there are procedures for this. A proper meeting with the company."

"Gwen." Ava sighed and gave of feeble sort of shrug. "I don't know what to say."

"You could start with 'thank you' and go from—"

"Mom!" They turned to see Luke, tossing his backpack on the ground and running towards them.

Gwen bent to sweep him into a hug. "Sweetheart! How was school?"

"I got an A+ on my science test! Mrs. O'Neal said it's the biggest improvement she's seen from anyone all semester. And I—"

"Luke! That's wonderful!" Gwen hugged him again, holding on until he got restless and tried to shrug her off.

"Hey, Ava," he said, his cheek still half-squished against Gwen's shoulder.

"Hey!" She laughed as Gwen finally let him go. "Congratulations on your test!" She gave him a quick half-hug. "That's really awesome."

"Thanks!" He grinned, looking between them. "I thought..." He hooked his thumbs into his belt loops and rocked back on his heels. "Um, Ava and I were talking about ice cream, and I thought maybe we could go? There's this new place downtown that makes milkshakes with pop rocks, and when you drink it, your mouth explodes. It's pretty awesome."

"That doesn't sound very safe," Gwen said, reaching out and brushing curls off Luke's forehead. "But we should absolutely celebrate." She smiled at him, her face softening in a way that had started to become familiar to Ava, a way that made her heart hurt.

Luke's eyebrows shot up excitedly. "Can we go when you're done with work? I think they're open late. And I'll do my homework until—"

"No." Gwen glanced at Ava and then back to Luke. "We'll go now."

"Really?" Luke was practically bouncing on his heels beside her.

"Really," she said, smiling so hard that the little dimple in her chin became visible, and Ava thought she might swoon.

The ice cream parlor was called The Cosmic Creamery and looked like a bad episode of *The X-Files* had hit a *Roswell* merch stall. They were met with a buzzing neon sign that said, "Try All 50 Flavors. We Dairy Ya," below which was a very comprehensive statement explaining that not all the ice cream contained dairy, and that customers were welcome to explore the non-lactose options.

Ava had been worried that they'd be recognized, but the clientele consisted mostly of preteens giggling over milkshakes.

Luke ran to the *Star Wars* pinball machine in the corner, leaving Gwen and Ava to find a table. There was a silver spaceship hanging from the ceiling, and Gwen glanced up, made a little hum of amusement, but didn't say anything.

"This is...interesting." Gwen eyed the turquoise pleather booth, and Ava could see her barely resist the urge to wipe it down with her antibacterial spray.

There was an antique refrigerator in one corner—its metallic door heavy with fridge magnets and bumper stickers. Right next to a faded "The Truth is Out There" sticker was a large Swiftwing crest.

Ava scrunched up her face. "I'm not sure if I should be offended or flattered. The honorable House Vala, reduced to a fridge magnet at The Cosmic Creamery."

"That's your family crest?"

"Yeah." It was strange and wonderful, being able to talk to Gwen about her origins.

"They had birds on your planet?"

"Afyah," Ava answered, conjuring the word as if from a dream. "That's 'bird' in my language."

"Afyah," Gwen echoed, almost reverently. "It's beautiful."

"I know what I want," Luke came barreling back, sliding into Ava's side of the booth with a distinct lack of finesse.

"Does this place have a menu or—"

"It's on the wall, Mom," Luke said, pointing to the huge chalkboard behind the serving counter. "And we go up to place our order. It's totally cool."

"Totally," Gwen replied dryly, and Ava laughed.

"Come on, I'll go with you." Ava scooted out. "Can I get you anything, Miss Knight?" she asked, with deliberate facetiousness.

"You choose," Gwen waved her hand dismissively. "You know what I like."

"I, uh…" Ava could feel herself blushing.

"My beverage preference," Gwen clarified pointedly.

"Yes. Got it." Ava put her hands on Luke's shoulders and steered him in the direction of the counter. "Come on. Let's see how many flavors they'll let us try before we have to order."

In the end, they got through eleven samples before the pimply-faced teen at the counter asked if they'd made a decision. Luke went for a sticky-fudge-cookie-dough whirlwind (with sprinkles). Ava got a cone with chocolate chips and a simple vanilla milkshake for Gwen (almond milk, with a butterscotch drizzle and a few chocolate sprinkles).

"I thought you'd been abducted by a tin spaceship," Gwen said, tucking her phone away as they came back to the booth.

"We were very busy deliberating on very important matters," Ava stated, forced to move over as Luke clambered in beside her.

"Like what kind of syrup to get."

Gwen's eyebrows rose at Luke's huge glass bowl of swirled ice cream. "I see you went with tummy ache."

"This is awesome. Jacob is gonna be so jealous." Luke gleefully stuck his spoon into the dish, and Gwen smiled at him, wide and indulgent.

"Well, an A+ is awesome."

"Thanks," Luke replied, his mouth full of ice cream.

Gwen sniffed the drink in front of her. "Vanilla and...butterscotch?" She sipped from a bright blue, oversized straw and closed her eyes with a hum. "I don't think I've had a milkshake in years."

"Yeah, it looks good on you," Ava said, biting on her cheek to keep from laughing.

Luke giggled.

"What?" Gwen looked between them, perplexed, completely unaware of the froth on the tip of her nose.

"You've uh," Ava wrinkled her own nose. "There's..." She wiggled her finger in front of Gwen's face. "A little..."

"Oh for goodness sake." In a surprisingly indelicate move, Gwen wiped her nose with the back of her hand, getting most of it, but leaving a single chocolate sprinkle behind.

At this point, Luke was laughing so hard that he was wheezing.

Ava's shoulders began to shake with the effort it took to not follow suit. Instead, she reached out and swiped her thumb gently across the tip of Gwen's nose, watching Gwen go cross-eyed in her efforts to watch Ava's actions.

"There," Ava said softly.

Gwen rolled her eyes, but her lips were pursed in that way that they sometimes were when she was trying not to smile. "You're both ridiculous," she said, losing the battle and smiling. There was that dimple again.

"We weren't the ones wearing our ice cream," Luke laughed.

Gwen leaned forward to dip her finger in his chocolate sauce before smudging it down his cheek.

"Oh, really?"

"Mom!" Luke scooped up a dollop of ice cream and aimed his finger at Gwen, who held her hands up, obviously regretting what she'd provoked.

"Truce," she said. "Truce."

Luke narrowed his eyes at her, western showdown style, and lowered his finger slowly before licking the ice cream off.

Ava watched the interaction with a mild sort of wonder. She'd seen Gwen and Luke interact before, of course—their easy domestic exchanges, the way Gwen completely lowered her guard around him, the way he doted on her. But this was new—this playful, sweet, utterly engaging tableau. She felt a little like she was intruding, like this was a moment not meant for her.

But then Luke said, "Hey Ava, did you know that grasshoppers can jump twenty times their own body length?"

Ava licked her way around her own ice cream. "I did not."

Gwen's phone vibrated in her purse, and her fingers twitched around her milkshake glass.

"How high can you jump?" Luke asked.

"I, um..." Ava glanced at Gwen, who suddenly seemed very interested in her answer. "Pretty high," she answered, eyes still on Gwen, who smirked at her.

"Tree frogs can jump 150 times their own body length. Aaron Lewis got a frog for his birthday and taught it to sit on command."

"What?" Ava exclaimed, teasing. "That's not true."

"It totally is," Luke replied seriously. "He's teaching it to respond to simple commands."

The phone vibrated again, and Luke said, "It's okay, Mom. You can take it."

Gwen looked almost grateful as she reached for her phone. "I'll just be a minute." She hurried out of the booth, phone in hand, leaving Ava at the mercy of Luke's infinite "did you knows."

By the time Gwen returned, Luke was licking his spoon, having only finished half of his bowl. "Can I get this to go?" He hopped out of the booth, flitting around his mom.

"Not unless you want it to melt and make a mess in the car," Gwen replied distractedly, sliding in next to Ava.

Luke sighed, looking wistfully at the ice cream he was too full to appreciate. He pulled his phone out of his back pocket and aimed it over the remains. "To show Jacob," he explained when Gwen made a remark about the compulsive need to take pictures of everything.

With a cheeky smile, Luke flipped his wrist and snapped a picture of Gwen.

"Luke!"

"What? It's a good one!" He turned the screen around to show them. The picture had caught Gwen mid-frown, with one finger up in emphasis. Ava was next to her, chin resting on her palm, watching Gwen with a dreamy, faraway look.

"That's, uh…" Ava winced at how obvious she was. "You should delete that."

"'Kay," Luke half-heartedly promised, shoving his phone back into his pocket. "Can I go and play on the pinball machine?"

"Two games," Gwen said. "Do you need quarters?"

"Nah. Dad gave me some money."

Gwen's smile didn't waver, but Ava could see the sudden tenseness in her face. "Okay. Good."

"Are you okay?" Ava asked, after Luke went running off.

"Fine," Gwen pushed her glass away.

"Was the shake not—"

"Did you really think that I'd fired you?" Gwen turned to her, and Ava wanted to scoot closer. She didn't move.

"I…" Ava looked down. There was a pink drop of melted ice cream on the table. "I told you. I thought you were upset. And when you're upset you can get…"

Gwen raised an eyebrow, as if daring her to continue.

"…irrational."

Gwen pursed her lips and shrugged, almost proud. "I suppose I've had my moments."

"I panicked." Ava continued. "I-I didn't want to leave."

"And now?"

"Now?"

"Do you want this opportunity?" She watched Ava carefully. "Are you ready to start being seen as more than just an assistant?" It was a throwback to Ava's comments from the night before, and it made her feel strangely vulnerable, sitting there, knowing that Gwen knew everything that she knew, knowing that all of her cards were laid out. Vulnerable, but also relieved. It was all out there.

"I-I think so."

Gwen's expression was intense. "I want you to want this, Ava. For yourself." It felt like the most honest conversation they'd had since Gwen had sat her down and drunkenly proposed.

"I do," Ava replied emphatically, and then, with a little less confidence, "I guess I'm still wondering if you're pushing me away because of everything that… I mean, I get it. It's a lot. These last few weeks. The Swiftwing thing and the…the other stuff. I wouldn't blame you if you wanted some distance." She said it in a rush, because she wouldn't say it at all if she thought about it too much.

Gwen's voice was uncharacteristically patient when she said, "I knew that I wanted to present you to Jackson the moment I met him. Long before anything came of this." She motioned to the space between them. "You're a good writer, Eisenberg. You could even be great. Your stories deserve to be told. And I want you attached to the company." Gwen looked across the restaurant, toward where Luke was slamming into the pinball machine. "It's a business move, nothing more."

Ava's heart beat heavy in her chest. "You read my screenplay?"

Gwen hummed in acknowledgement. "The first week I hired you. It's beautiful. The descriptions in the beginning, you were writing about your home." It wasn't a question.

"Of what I remember," Ava said quietly.

Gwen looked back to her. "How much do you remember?"

"Everything," Ava said in a whisper; it was a secret she'd never shared before. "All the time."

Gwen blinked slowly, and the change in her face was almost imperceptible. But Ava saw it. Gwen looked at her the way Rachel had looked at her when she'd first arrived, the way Nic used to when Ava slept over and would wake up in the middle of the night, chased by nightmares. It was a look that said, *I'm sorry. I will never understand, but I'm sorry.*

Gwen didn't say any of that, though. She didn't force Ava to play the poor orphan alien. She moved right on, pushing past the pity, making it okay.

She said, "There's another reason I promoted you."

"Besides my amazing creative talent and being an asset to the company?"

"Yes. Besides that." Gwen deadpanned. "It, well, it occurred to me that it makes this whole thing a little less scurrilous if you're not dating your direct superior. I assume you agree."

Ava nodded her head quickly. "I do."

"Good." Gwen sat back, seemingly satisfied.

"So, when do I start?"

"As soon as you can find a suitably competent replacement." Gwen inclined her head toward Ava. "Superpowers optional."

"Oh, well, no pressure there."

"I'm starting to regret this already. This has obviously gone to your head."

Ava laughed. "I *am* dating Hollywood royalty."

Gwen hummed, amused. "And how is that going for you?"

"Harder than you'd think." Ava waited a beat, considering, evaluating, before she finally said, "She's, uh...difficult to read."

"Really?" Gwen's amusement shifted to curiosity. She turned in the booth, facing Ava completely. "How so?"

"I don't know." Ava felt her bravado failing her and she shrugged. "Sometimes, I think that maybe she..."

"What?" Gwen pressed, scooting closer until their knees touched under the table.

"I sometimes imagine that she wants the same things I do."

"She doesn't?" Gwen asked, her voice low, searching.

"No."

"Has she said as much?"

"She doesn't have to." Ava's lips quirked up wryly. "She's pretty consistent about going after what she wants."

"What if what she wants..." Gwen leaned in closer—she smelled sweet, vanilla and butterscotch, "is so extraordinary, so absolutely inconceivable, that she's scared?"

"I don't think she gets scared," Ava whispered.

"Oh, she does." Gwen's gaze flickered between Ava's mouth and her eyes. "When it counts."

Ava swallowed. Her heart began an erratic rhythm against her ribcage, fighting to be heard over the voice in her head that screamed at her to not get her hopes up. Ava leaned in closer. She was struck by the vivid memory of what kissing Gwen felt like. The stuttered breath, soft skin, the way Gwen's fingers curled around her neck, always so insistent.

"Does this count?" she asked on a breath. She could've leaned in a little further, just to test, just to *see*…

Ava's phone rang, obnoxiously loud amid the din of the diner, and she jumped back. Their bubble was instantly burst, and Ava clumsily scrambled for the phone.

"H-hello?" she answered, eyes still on Gwen, who cleared her throat and looked down. Ava was met with the monotone of a telemarketer asking if she was happy with her current phone service.

She allowed him to drone on for a full ten seconds before saying, "Okay. No thank you, bye."

By the time she was done, Gwen had moved to the far end of the booth and was gesturing at Luke.

"I, uh…"

"We should probably head out," Gwen began before Ava had a chance to say anything. "Luke has homework." Her mouth flickered up into a quick smile, but that tenseness was back.

Ava glanced down at Gwen's hand, resting on the table. For a moment, she was tempted to cover it with her own. She missed the contact. To have this emotional intensity without touch. It was like an ache, a loss. "I never actually thanked you."

"It was a business move." Gwen waved it off. "I told you."

"No, not just for the job. But for everything. For being such an amazing mentor and…" it took her a second to decide on the word. "…friend."

"Well, you're not gone yet." Gwen stood and inclined her head, motioning for Ava to come along. "So, don't think you can renege on your duties. I expect my latte hot and punctual tomorrow."

"Of course." Ava stood, smiling.

"Do you want to ride back with us?" Gwen asked, and Ava shook her head.

"I'll fly." It was mind-boggling that she could say these things to Gwen.

Ava looked across the floor to where Luke was furiously jabbing his finger against the side of the pinball machine.

"Bye, Luke!" she called.

He gave her a distracted wave before turning his attention back to the machine.

Gwen shook her head at her son. "So fickle."

"I should probably—" Ava inclined her head toward the door, and Gwen reached out, just brushing Ava's elbow.

"Thank you. For coming along. I know Luke appreciated it, though he may be too sugar riddled to show it."

"It was my pleasure. Besides, free ice cream, right?"

Gwen watched her closely and then seemed to come to some sort of decision.

"What you asked before, if this counts." Gwen sighed, looked down. "It does. It counts for a lot." When she looked back up, her expression was alarmingly vulnerable, and Ava fought the urge to apologize.

All she managed was, "Oh."

They said nothing then, as a million things fluttered around in Ava's head. But nothing seemed quite right, nothing seemed significant or profound enough to capture the fragility of what was happening.

In the end, Gwen clapped her hands together. "Well…" She exhaled, and all trace of vulnerability was gone. "You need to go. And I have to get my son home."

"I…yeah." But Ava didn't move, not for a long time, not until she was almost sure of what Gwen was trying to say. And Gwen stood with her, in the middle of a kitschy, alien-themed ice cream parlor, while Britney Spears blasted out of the speakers, and someone yelled for a mop.

It was a perfect moment.

CHAPTER 15

THERE WAS A THUNDERSTORM THE day of the BAFTA LA Gala. Ava woke that Friday to gray skies and rain that didn't seem like it would ever stop—an anomaly for Los Angeles. She took it as a good omen.

She talked to Gwen exactly twice that day.

Once, in the morning as Gwen left the house, looking over her shoulder to say, "I'll see you this afternoon." After that, Gwen was held hostage at the production office, but managed to get away for long enough to call Ava and tell her that she was running late.

"I'm going to leave as soon as I can. You should go home. God knows how long it's going to take you to get ready."

"Ha, ha," Ava replied dryly.

"How's the search for the new PA going?" Gwen asked.

"Great. I put feelers out this morning and already received a few calls from recruitment agencies. I'm working out interview times, since mornings are probably best for—"

"You'll be doing them."

"Me?"

"Who better than you to find me a competent replacement? You're the one leaving me." She said it as if she was not the architect of this move.

"What if you don't like who I choose?" Ava asked.

"Then I fire them."

"Oh. Okay then."

Gwen stayed on the line, as if waiting for Ava to say more. Ava couldn't quite define what exactly it was that had changed between them, but there was definitely something there—an almost tangible feeling of newness, possibility. Ava still felt a little high off Gwen's esoteric confession in the ice cream parlor.

She didn't know exactly what Gwen wanted to achieve by telling her that she mattered. She didn't know how Gwen actually felt, or even what she wanted. All Ava knew was that she went to bed each night feeling more hopeful than she had in weeks.

"I really wish you'd let Paulo do your make-up." Gwen sighed on the other end of the call. "I don't trust you with an eyelash curler."

"I have it covered. I told you."

Gwen huffed her skepticism, but conceded. "All right, fine. I'll see you this evening then."

"Okay." Ava smiled against her phone. "See you later."

The plan, as Ava had conceived it, involved Nic ditching work and playing fairy godmother. It was safer than having strangers scrutinize her with her hair down. The blue dress was already a risk. *A worthwhile risk*, she thought, remembering how Gwen had looked at her first time she'd tried it on.

Nic arrived on time, pizza box in hand. She angled it out of Ava's reach. "Not for you, you'll get pizza sauce on your face. Besides, I'm starving."

"Fine," Ava grumbled. "I just stress-ate a bag of Cheetos anyway."

Nic wrinkled her nose. "Curse your alien metabolism." She motioned to the little chair in front of Ava's dresser. "Hair first and then make-up?"

"I think so."

"All right," Nic rubbed her hands together dramatically. "Let's do this."

The process was less painful than Ava had anticipated, and she only flinched once when Nic came at her with the mascara brush.

"You know I can't actually hurt you, right?"

"That's not the point." She scowled when Nic tugged a comb through her hair. "How are you so good at this anyway?"

"Oh my God," Nic pulled off a perfect valley girl accent. "I was totes down with the party squad in college."

Ava smirked. "I remember."

"Not my proudest moments."

"What? You don't miss being constantly hungover?"

"Not even a little."

"Hey." Ava looked up at Nic, who was currently armed with liquid liner. "Thanks for doing this."

Nic shrugged. "Bestie code dictates that I do your make-up for all major events. I don't make the rules."

Ava smiled, about to reply when her phone buzzed. She read the email that had come in while Nic went to work on her hair.

"It's from Captain Fernandez."

Nic paused mid-curl. "Yeah?"

"They've confirmed that Norman is a Mantipodis in larvae stage."

"Cool." Nic resumed her twirling of Ava's hair.

Ava sighed.

Nic paused again. "Not cool?"

"We're keeping a mother from her baby."

"Ava, there's nothing you can do right now."

"What if I find the mother? I can talk to her," Ava argued. "I can explain—"

"You tried that," Nic pointed out. "And she stabbed you in cave. And then she tried to stab you in a tunnel."

"You're not wrong," Ava said, defeated.

"It'll work out." Nic's voice softened. "Tonight, your only job is to survive the red carpet."

"I think I'd rather fight a giant bug," Ava mumbled, causing Nic to chuckle.

Ava made Nic wait while she tried on the dress in the bathroom. She was walking out, barefoot and adjusting her earrings, when Nic gasped.

"What?" Already self-conscious about her fancy hair and layers of make-up, Ava fiddled with the dress strap. "The earrings are a bit much, aren't they? I should take them—"

Nic stood staring, and Ava watched her warily, trying to assess her expression.

"Are you sure about this?" Nic sounded tentative. "Because if you go out looking like that, no one's going to be able to tear their eyes from you."

Ava looked down at herself. She felt like a kid playing dress-up. Like when she was little and used to put on her mother's star suit, pretending she was about to go on an intergalactic mission. "Is it…too much?"

"It's a lot." Nic bit down on her bottom lip and raised a shoulder. "But, good." She exhaled. "Wow."

"Oh my God." Ava snorted as she struggled into her heels. "Are you tearing up?"

"No." Nic wiped at her eyes. "Shut up."

Ava turned to the full-length mirror and smoothed down the front of the dress. "Think Gwen will like it?"

"The woman has eyes, doesn't she?"

"Okay." Ava let out a little "Phew," and her phone buzzed as if on cue. "That's Jonah," she said, texting back to let him know that she was on her way down. "Wish me luck," she said, with her arms crossed over her chest.

"Don't flex your superhero arms like that! God, the dress is bad enough."

"But…good-bad?"

"Yes!" Nic laughed. "Now go. You don't want to keep her royal highness waiting."

Ava grinned and gave a dramatic curtsy.

The drive to Gwen's was slow through late evening traffic, and Ava wished she could have flown instead, but she doubted that she'd be able to explain Swiftwing flying through the sky in a Tom Ford evening gown.

So she sighed, leaned back against the plush leather seat, and thought about Gwen.

The light outside changed from pale ash to ominous gray. The rain had calmed down, but everything was still covered with a light sheen of drizzle. She imagined that the air might be a bit chilly for someone with human thermoreceptors, and wondered if Gwen would be wearing a coat or a shawl. She remembered the little red dress Gwen had worn two months prior at a DNC fundraiser. She remembered scrolling through the photographs and feeling a knot in her stomach every time she came across a picture of Gwen in that dress, talking or dancing with some penguin-suited politician.

Ava almost laughed. How had it taken her fake-dating Gwen to realize that she'd rather be real-dating Gwen? Of course, she still didn't know if

Gwen wanted to be real-dating her. There was a big difference between "it counts" and "I want to be in a relationship with my super-powered, twenty-seven-year-old employee."

There was so much she wanted to ask Gwen directly, without the subterfuge and mixed messages. At the same time, just the fact that this might be real, that Gwen might be interested, was heart-in-your-throat kind of scary. Having feelings, telling Gwen about those feelings was one thing, but navigating an actual relationship? Realistically, being Gwen Knight's significant other wasn't something that Ava knew she'd be good at.

By the time they reached the house, Ava had worked herself into a state of nerves and tangled emotions.

Jonah smiled at her when she exited the car. "Have fun, Miss Eisenberg."

"You're not driving us?" Ava asked, ducking down to look at him through the open window.

Jonah shook his head. "You're taking the limo."

"Oh," Ava blanched. "The, uh, limo. Great." It struck her suddenly that this was a big deal. Her first official public appearance with Gwen. Her first public appearance as Ava Eisenberg. It was more than a little daunting.

Ava fidgeted nervously as she rang the doorbell. She had to ring a second time before she heard Gwen's faraway, "Come in."

"Gwen?" Ava called out, hanging her coat up on the rack before wandering in. She was balancing better on her heels than she had the last time.

"This humidity is going to wreak havoc with my hair," Gwen groused, walking into the corridor from her room, still barefoot, but otherwise entirely dressed.

Ava found herself frozen for a moment, actually overwhelmed at the sight of her. Gwen in her green and ivory Valentino tea-length gown, soft and lush. Gwen with her thick, dark hair all tousled around her face. Gwen with her feet bare, toes painted a matte cranberry.

"Wow," Ava's breath caught. She was unable to keep the reverence from her voice.

Gwen only really looked up then, as if forgetting that she had just told Ava to come in. She looked startled as her eyes trailed across Ava's figure in one slow, languorous sweep.

"You..." Gwen licked her lips, and Ava frowned.

"Is it…okay?"

"It's…" Gwen swallowed, just loud enough for Ava's hearing to catch. She cleared her throat and took a step forward. "I see you mastered the eyelash curler."

Ava smiled. "My roommate did it."

"Ah. Could you—" Gwen turned, exposing the smooth expanse of her back where the dress dipped low. The zipper was even lower, and the material gaped open, revealing just a hint of lace.

Ava nodded fast. "Yeah, of course."

Ava closed her fingers around Gwen's waist, aware of her warm body beneath layers of silk, and pulled the zipper up slowly, then trailed her fingers down to smooth out the crease of fabric at the base of Gwen's spine. Her fingers traced their way up, brushing soft skin, and for a second, she lost herself, until Gwen straightened.

"Ava," Gwen breathed out in soft reproach, jolting her back.

"Sorry." She let her hands fall to her sides. "It's, uh, you're all set."

"Thank you." Gwen turned to face her, a small smirk pulling at her lips, and Ava flushed in mild embarrassment. "The limo should be here. I'll just get my shoes."

"'Kay."

Gwen disappeared into the corridor and turned left into her bedroom, leaving Ava to wait. When she returned, she was a few inches taller and clutching a black velvet box.

"Here." Gwen held it out casually, as if she was offering a pen or a candy bar.

"What's this?" It was heavier than Ava expected.

"Hmm." Gwen shrugged and stepped a little closer. Ava's nostrils flared as she caught the sharp, spicy scent of perfume. "A little gift."

Ava opened the rectangular box to find a pendant embedded in a cushion of velvet. The thin chain was delicate white gold, Ava guessed. It was connected to a deep blue sapphire—small and bold, the exact color of Swiftwing's suit. It looked like it cost as much as Ava made in a year.

"It's ethically sourced," Gwen murmured, watching Ava closely.

"Gwen, I-I can't…"

"Oh, calm down." Gwen took the pendant out of the box and dangled it from her fingertips. "Consider it an early apology for the madness you'll endure tonight."

"It's beautiful."

"Yes, well." Gwen took a breath and allowed herself a small smile. "So are you." She twirled her finger. "Turn around."

Ava obeyed. "I…um. I mean, it's just the make-up. It's not…"

"Hair up."

Ava swept her hair to one side. "I mean, you're the one who's…"

"Beautiful and babbling. Be still my heart." The jewel fell just low enough to draw attention to the swell of Ava's chest. "There."

She looked down, trying to imagine an occasion where she'd ever wear it again. "Wow."

"Indeed." Gwen smiled, satisfied. "Right. Shall we?"

"You're fidgeting," Gwen said without looking in Ava's direction, and Ava clasped her hands together in her lap.

"Sorry. I'm nervous."

Gwen reached out and put a hand on Ava's thigh, effectively stilling her. "You'll be fine. If you remember that most of those people are slaves to a vacuous industry that promotes self-loathing and narcissism. You're better than all of them."

Gwen said it so matter-of-factly, so simply that Ava struggled to disbelieve her. They were a block away from the venue, and Ava could already hear the roaring pandemonium of snapping cameras and screeching fans. Gwen's hand hadn't left Ava's thigh, and as they pulled up, she gave it a comforting squeeze.

Ava's senses were immediately overwhelmed. The flashes were blinding, the screams were deafening, and it felt all at once as though everyone was looking at her, seeing through the layers. She expected someone to point and yell, "Look! It's Swiftwing!" She felt herself tense up as her mind screamed to retreat. And then, Gwen's hand slipped into hers, solid and firm.

"Ready?" she asked, leaning in close, warming Ava's neck with her breath.

Ava looked at Gwen, not seeing the flashes, or hearing the crowd. There was only Gwen, in an ocean of chaos. Ava gripped Gwen's hand as tightly as she could without hurting her. "Let's do this."

They walked onto the red carpet, hand in hand, past rows of cheering fans and screaming photographers.

Gwen leaned in again, pressing up against Ava to whisper. "Smile a little. Relax. You look like you're being led to get a colonoscopy."

Ava laughed at that, and Gwen smiled at her, that cheek-dimpling smile that made Ava's heart skip a few beats.

"Gwen!" One of the lenses yelled out. "Gwen over here!"

"Who are you wearing?" another asked, and Gwen stopped walking for a moment to face the cameras. Ava wanted to ask her what was the matter before she realized that Gwen was striking a pose, allowing the photographers to get their fill. She was alarmingly good at pouting at the camera. Ava stood beside her helplessly, having no idea how to navigate the situation, until Gwen tugged on her hand and drew her close.

"What are you—"

"Something for the front page," Gwen whispered, before pressing her lips against Ava's cheek. She lingered long enough for a few good shots, but it was all too brief for Ava, who would have held her there all evening if she could.

The first drop of rain hit her forehead, and then the tip of her nose, and then Gwen was pushing her forward toward the enclosed pavilion they had to pass in order to get into the venue. In the center, a smarmy blond host was interviewing celebrities. Behind them, hundreds of assistants were producing umbrellas and holding them over stars to protect hair and make-up, and the red carpet suddenly became a sea of black.

Ava found the whole thing utterly bizarre.

"Oh my goodness, Gwendolyn Knight. Folks, we're in the presence of media royalty. Bow down." The smarmy blond man waved them over.

"Hello, Dylan." Gwen smiled that perfect, fake smile, reserved primarily for photo shoots and reporters.

"Step up to the podium! Let's have a little chat!"

"We should get inside," Gwen replied.

"Now, I might get into trouble for saying this, but I do think you get tonight's loveliest date award."

Gwen turned to Ava with a hint of a smirk. "I suppose I can't fault you there."

Ava recoiled slightly when a microphone was pushed in front of her. "Hi, and how are you doing tonight?"

"Good," Ava smiled graciously. "Excited to be here." She looked at Gwen, and her smile widened. "It's going better than expected."

"You were a little nervous?" Smarmy Blond asked.

"A little," Ava answered.

"Well, it helps that you're on the arm of entertainment royalty."

Ava laughed a little. "It does."

He turned his attention to Gwen. "Two films and a producing credit. And now, a new relationship?" He managed to look even smarmier than before. "It has been a busy year for Gwendolyn Knight." He was daring her to deny it, but Gwen only smiled placidly.

"Oh, you know me. Work, work, work."

"Not too hard, I hope." Smarmy Blond laughed. "Okay. You lovebirds enjoy yourselves."

Gwen moved past the cameras, still clutching Ava's hand. From behind her, Ava heard the host addressing the camera. "As far as coming-out parties go, this is pretty dramatic, but I guess we can't expect any less from the most powerful woman in Hollywood."

Once they were in the plush theatre lobby, surrounded by more celebrities than Ava could count, Gwen let go of her hand. "I'm sorry, I should have prepared you for the insipid questions."

Ava shrugged, her fingers still tingling. "It's no big deal." But then she paused. "But, uh... We won't have to do these often, will we? I mean, in the future?"

Gwen looked at her curiously, and it took Ava a moment to realize that she was implying that there would be a future. Before she could backtrack, Gwen said, "No, we won't."

"Gwen?"

They both turned at the sound of the voice, and Ava felt Gwen stiffen beside her as Ron Gooding approached.

"Ronald."

Gooding smiled that dazzling toothpaste smile for which he was famous. His arm was in a sling and he walked with a slight limp, but he was still inexplicably handsome. Ava wrinkled her nose. Beside him was a skinny young woman Ava remembered from the BET Awards, the one beside him the night he'd bailed on Gwen.

"How are you, Gwen?" Gooding leaned in to peck both of Gwen's cheeks as if they had not seen each other just a few days prior. The woman beside him made no move to introduce herself.

"Oh, this is Tamika." He motioned to his date.

Gwen only inclined her head. "Yes, I know."

Gooding looked between Gwen and Tamika with a tense expression, and finally turned his attention to Ava.

"Ava, isn't it?"

"Yes." Ava took his hand and shook it firmly. "We've met on set... numerous times."

"Well, there's nothing like a formal introduction."

Tamika stepped forward with a sour expression. "Are you fucking kidding me?"

"Mika, please," Gooding muttered and looked at Gwen with an apologetic expression. "We were just coming over to say hello."

"You wanted to assuage your guilty conscience," Tamika muttered.

"Well, I can't imagine why," retorted Gwen, who, for her part, had crossed her arms over her chest and was staring Tamika down with a raised eyebrow. Ava was familiar with this stance. She was in fight mode.

"So, we're just going to stand here and pretend we're all friends?" Tamika asked, sounding incredulous.

Gooding visibly winced. "She's had too much champagne."

"Clearly."

"You know, what you did with Ron was bad enough," Tamika continued, undeterred. "But now you've roped your assistant into your little game?"

"Former assistant," Ava mumbled.

But Gwen's voice was low and deadly. "Excuse me?"

Behind them, some up-and-coming popstar whose name escaped Ava turned his head at the sound of scandal, and Tamika was prudent enough to lower her voice.

"She's what? Half your age? Thank God I talked some sense into Ron before you ruined his reputation. Encouraging him to cheat just so you could use him? Do you think about anyone but yourself?"

Ava's heart dropped to her stomach. She glanced at Gwen, whose face had flushed red with rage and embarrassment.

"I encouraged no such thing. My arrangement with Ronald was entirely mutual." Gwen shot Gooding a furious glare, and he lowered his gaze. "He made no mention of his relationship at the time, and seemed very happy to play pretend. And I will not stand here and justify my choices to an idiotic cheerleader.

"You have no idea what you're talking about," Tamika bristled.

"Neither do you, but you seem to think you have the right to say it anyway."

"At least I'm not a desperate old woman who needs to coerce people into fake relationships."

"I—"

Ava watched Gwen struggle for words. No witty comeback, no scathing remark on the tip of her tongue. She'd touched a nerve, Ava realized.

Without any thought, Ava stepped forward, almost in front of Gwen, shielding her, protecting her.

"My relationship with Gwen is none of your business." There was a prickle of heat behind her eyes. A spark of anger at the thought of anyone causing Gwen discomfort or guilt. Ava wouldn't do anything, of course, but that didn't mean she didn't want to hurl Tamika into the sun.

Gwen closed her hand around Ava's elbow. "Ava—"

"No." Ava clenched her hands into fists at her sides. "No, she doesn't get to talk to you like that, or make assumptions about us."

Gooding cleared his throat and put his hand over Tamika's shoulder. "I'm sorry. We should go. Come on, babe."

Tamika squared her shoulders and glared at Gwen before turning.

Ava was compelled to call out, "Mr. Gooding?"

He turned back to her, and Ava took another step forward.

"I just wanted to thank you."

"Thank me?"

Ava nodded earnestly. "Yes. I mean, if you hadn't pulled out of your agreement and left Gwen in such an awkward predicament, well, we'd never have engaged in…in any of this. And I wouldn't have gotten to spend the most amazing few weeks as Gwen's partner. I wouldn't have realized how completely in love with her I am—always have been, really." She looked directly at Tamika. "And the sex. Wow. It's been…" Ava glanced back at Gwen, who looked a little pale. "A revelation. So while I appreciate your attempt to save my virtue from the big, bad boss, I assure you I am in very, very good hands."

"Whatever," Tamika huffed and stalked off.

As they left, Ava could hear Gooding's feeble, "Baby, we weren't even exclusive then…"

Ava's heart pounded the entire time. "I shouldn't have said that," she muttered. "I'm sorry, I don't know what…"

"Ava—"

"No. You know what, Gwen?" She spun around to face Gwen. "I don't regret it. I don't take it back. Because I wasn't going to stand here and let him accuse you of awful things when I—"

It took Ava a moment to realize that she wasn't talking anymore and another to realize that it was because Gwen was kissing her. Her hands fluttered around Gwen feebly, before settling on her shoulders. The buzz of the crowd outside, the hum of people inside, all of it disappeared as Gwen smiled against Ava's mouth, before pulling away, leaving her breathless and startled.

"I…you…"

"Breathe, Ava."

Ava inhaled dramatically and smiled as she exhaled, feeling warmth radiate out of her.

"Good." Gwen's smile became more of a smirk. "Now come on."

"Where are we going?"

"Home."

"But…" Ava looked up the stairs, to the auditorium, where music had begun to play. "The show…"

"Screw the show. You hate it here, and I'm beginning to see your point. Besides, I'm confident that the gossip about the Evil Queen and her hot young date has made its way through the appropriate media channels. Our work here is done." Gwen watched her expectantly.

Ava knew this wasn't the plan. She knew that the show was important, and that they should probably stay. But right now, Gwen was looking at her with a glint of reckless excitement, and the adventure of ditching the evening became all too tempting. "You mean it?"

"I do." Gwen offered her hand and Ava took it. "Let's go home."

CHAPTER 16

THE RIDE HOME WAS FILLED with a sort of giddy anticipation. They didn't speak about what Ava had said to Gooding or about the kiss. They didn't speak about leaving early or what was going to happen once they got back to the house.

Home, Gwen had called it.

Somewhere between walking out of the auditorium and getting into the car, they had let go of each other's hands. Now Ava sat with hers in her lap, fingers neatly interlocked. She stared out at the passing vista, not daring to make contact with Gwen. The night sky was a gurgling blanket of gray storm clouds. The air crackled with electricity. Ava felt it against her skin. Or maybe it was just the air inside the car.

They were in the town car, not the limo. Her breath misted the window, and she was tempted to draw a heart with her fingertip but didn't think Jonah would appreciate it.

Gwen had somehow summoned him within minutes, and Ava wondered if he was just circling the block, waiting for them to finish. He didn't seem particularly surprised when she and Gwen climbed into the car only half an hour after arriving. Then again, Ava guessed that he was paid to not be surprised about anything Gwen did.

They were both silent until Ava asked, "What are you going to tell Luke about why we're back early?"

"Nothing," Gwen replied, still facing the window. "He's at the Levinsons' for the evening. The boys are working on a science project."

"Oh." Ava didn't state the obvious. She didn't say that they'd be alone. That they'd be alone after she'd basically confessed her undying love, and Gwen had kissed her for it.

They stopped at the house, and Gwen was out first without waiting for Jonah to open the door for her. Ava followed as best she could in her heels. They didn't talk as they entered. There was no eye contact, no frenzied making out against the door as Ava might have possibly fantasized about once or twice. There was only Gwen, striding in ahead, leaving Ava trailing behind in a cloud of perfume and uncertainty.

By the time Ava caught up, Gwen had discarded her coat and shoes, and was already on her way to the kitchen.

"Are you thirsty?" Gwen didn't wait for an answer before reaching for glasses. "I'm parched."

"I'm okay." Ava walked toward her cautiously. Something was wrong. She saw it in Gwen's too-quick gestures, the stiffness in her frame, the almost indecipherable warble in her voice.

Gwen poured two glasses of wine anyway and gulped down almost half of hers. Ava narrowed her eyes, trying to figure it out. And then it dawned on her. It was preposterous and implausible, but there was no better explanation.

Gwen was nervous.

"Gwen?" Ava advanced slowly. "Are you okay?"

Gwen lowered her glass and blinked at Ava. "Of course. Why wouldn't I be?"

"Because you've barely glanced at me since we left the show and you're all…" Ava ignored Gwen's warning look and continued, "wound up."

Gwen made a little noise of offense. "I am not wound up."

Ava pointed to the glass in Gwen's hand. "You just finished a glass of wine in under five seconds."

"I was—"

"Thirsty," Ava found that she quite enjoyed Gwen like this. "Yeah." She approached the kitchen as Gwen stepped out from behind the island counter. Ava was nervous too. Of course she was. But somehow knowing Gwen was equally affected comforted her.

She wanted to say something smooth, wanted to sound more confident than she felt. But Ava found her courage waning now that the moment was here, now that the only thing separating her from Gwen was a couple of footsteps.

Gwen watched her with caution, as if she wasn't quite sure what Ava was going to do or say next. "You're staring."

Ava knew she was. She was staring and considering and risking it all as she said, "You know, you didn't have to bring me back here."

Gwen stepped toward her, short in her bare feet, forced to tilt her head up. "Don't be ridiculous. Where else would you go?"

Ava knew she was playing with fire. "I have an apartment."

"Yes, I'm aware," Gwen replied dryly. "I've been there."

What they'd done there was left unspoken, but hung heavy in the air between them.

"I didn't think you were that impatient to get back," Gwen added. "Unless you have something super on the agenda."

Ava thought about the Mantipodis. She thought a moment too long, because Gwen shrugged, as if indifferent, and Ava forgot about being smooth and confident. She didn't want Gwen to retreat, didn't want to lose whatever was burgeoning between them.

"I...no. Nothing on the agenda, super or otherwise. I'm all yours. I mean, not, not all yours as in I belong to you. Although I mean, I could if that was something you..." she trailed off with a helpless shrug.

Gwen smirked.

Gwen—1, Ava—0.

"Ava," Gwen said with that specific combination of amusement and exasperation that Ava seemed to arouse. "We don't have to do anything tonight. As I said, what happened before was just—"

"Physical?"

Gwen pursed her lips. "Exactly."

"No," Ava blurted out.

"Excuse me?" That familiar frown. Ava wanted to smooth it away with her lips. *Now or never*, Ava thought, and "never" seemed impossible at this point.

"What I said...to Ron..."

"*Oh.* Hmm. I see." Gwen tilted her head knowingly. "You're embarrassed." It was said fondly. "Relax. You get a free pass on things said in the heat of the moment. Believe me, I've had my fair share of outbursts."

"I don't want a pass," Ava protested, making sure she had Gwen's full attention before she continued. "I meant it all. Everything I said." She exhaled shakily. "I meant it."

Gwen's amusement fell away. She was startled—all rabbit-eyed and skittish. "Ava..."

"No, please just...let me say this." Her heart climbed up to her throat and settled there. "You said you were scared."

"You might be taking me out of context." Gwen's voice was quiet now.

"And you're right," Ava continued as if Gwen hadn't spoken. "It *does* count. And that is..." she searched for the word, "it's terrifying. But I'm not going to run from this because it's scary. What kind of superhero would that make me?"

"A smart one," Gwen quipped.

"I mean it."

"So do I." Gwen's eyes intently searched Ava's face for...what? Doubt? Hesitance? "This isn't going to be the fairytale you imagine. These last few weeks—the press, the judgment, the exes and aliens—that's the tip of the iceberg. You are..." Gwen inhaled and paused dramatically, "Swiftwing. And, while some might call me a legend in my own right, I'm also challenging and contrary and *older* and..."

"Worth it," Ava announced, effectively stopping Gwen mid-lecture. And she meant it. She was done apologizing for how she felt, done tip-toeing around whether Gwen may or may not reciprocate. This was happening, and she could either run from it or fight for it. "I know you, Gwen. Better than I know myself sometimes. And you? You don't scare me."

Gwen raised her eyebrows skeptically, and Ava huffed out a laugh.

"Okay, maybe a little. Before you're sufficiently caffeinated."

Gwen searched her face with an intense look. "So, this is what I get for bumping you up from assistant?"

"This is what you get for making me fall in love with you."

The change in Gwen's face was subtle. Her eyes widened just a little, her cheeks flushed only barely, but her breath hitched, her heart raced.

Gwen bit the inside of her cheek and looked as if she was trying her hardest not to be charmed. "Did you practice that line?"

Ava managed a sheepish smile. "Did it work?"

In response, Gwen trailed her fingers around Ava's neck and pulled her down for a kiss. Ava almost lost herself against Gwen's lips before she forced herself to pull back, holding Gwen at arm's length, careful to be gentle.

"Wait, wait." Ava was already breathless with anticipation. But she needed to say it, to be sure. "This isn't going to be some desperate hookup, or something we can blame on a spur of the moment decision, right? I… want this. I really, really want this and everything this means. And I need to know if you want this too." And then softer, in almost a whisper, "If you want me."

"I—" Gwen was speechless for a moment. The longest moment of Ava's life, punctuated by the erratic beat of her heart. "Of course." Gwen's voice was quiet. "Of course I do."

"Okay, because the last time—"

Gwen pressed her finger against Ava's lips, silencing her. "The last time I was angry, and you were acting like an imbecile."

"And now?" Ava asked, resisting the urge to draw Gwen's finger into her mouth.

"Now…" Gwen trailed that finger down Ava's chin, down her throat, and hooked it into her neckline of her dress. Then she yanked Ava forward, against her. "Now I really want to find the zipper to this dress."

Gwen leaned up and kissed her then, and it wasn't exactly what Ava had wanted, but she wasn't going to push Gwen to say something she wasn't ready to say, despite how much she needed to hear it.

Gwen's eyes fluttered shut as she exhaled through pursed lips, grounding herself. "Come on."

She took Ava's hand, linking their fingers as if it was the most natural thing in the world. Ava was led down the hallway, past a wall full of photographs that she might have spent some time analyzing if she wasn't completely distracted by the realization that she was being led to Gwen's bedroom.

Somewhere between the living room and the bedroom, Ava lost her shoes, and her feet sank into the soft rug covering the hardwood floors.

Gwen's bedroom was exactly as Ava had imagined it. And she had imagined it more often than she'd ever admit. Gwen turned on the lights, then dimmed them, just enough for them to still see each other, and Ava wished she'd left it a little brighter.

When Gwen turned to her now, they were more equally matched in height, so it would have been easy for Ava to just lean forward and continue what was started in the living room. But Gwen was watching her with earnest eyes—a foreign expression that Ava couldn't quite place.

"I do want this," Gwen said slowly, solemnly, watching Ava the entire time. "I want you. *All* of you." She emphasized it with a quirk of her brow. "All of this clumsy, fashion disaster, selfless, Zrix'dhorian you. Is that enough? Are you satisfied? Would you like me to write it down on the company letterhead?"

"No, I think it'll do." Ava swallowed, completely embarrassed by the fact that she felt like she might cry. *This is it*, she thought. This was a defining moment, like flying for the first time, putting on that suit, going in for that job interview. "I, um…" Ava smiled widely, all fluttery. "I want you too."

"I'm delighted," Gwen deadpanned, but she was pleased; Ava could hear it in the warm timbre of her voice.

Their kisses became more desperate, and it began to feel like they were building up to something rather than just kissing for the pleasure of it. Gwen eventually pulled back, pressing her hands up against Ava's chest as she gasped for air.

Ava trailed her finger along the sleeve of Gwen's dress and gently took the material between her thumb and forefinger. "Can I…take this off?"

Gwen turned around without saying anything, and Ava lowered the zipper slowly—a feat for someone who was prone to ripping the paper off her Christmas and birthday presents.

Once it was open, and that hint of lace peeked out from the V of the open zipper, Ava reached up and slid the top off of Gwen's shoulders. It fell to the ground like liquid, and Ava had the sudden image of champagne dripping off Gwen's body. It was an image to explore another time. Right now, she was more than a little distracted by the sight of Gwen, still turned away from her, in expensive lingerie. Her naked back—narrow and smooth—was a canvas that Ava thought she might want to paint with her tongue and her fingers. Then she stopped thinking altogether, because Gwen was almost naked, and she was right there, and Ava could feel every cell in her body responding.

Part of her was almost hoping Gwen wouldn't turn around. She wanted to ask Gwen to just give her this moment, to revel in, to appreciate what was about to happen. But then Gwen was facing her, and Ava forgot to breathe, let alone revel.

She allowed herself a lingering gaze, struck, suddenly, by the difference between Gwen standing in front of those cameras at the show, proud and unflinching, and Gwen standing before her now.

"You are," her eyes were hungry as they raked over Gwen, but her voice was filled with reverence, "so beautiful."

Gwen smiled a slightly cocky, amused smile that made Ava's insides swirl with anticipation. "Your turn."

Gwen was *not* as tentative as Ava. She wasted no time in getting the dress down Ava's shoulders and finally pulling the zipper down. It pooled around Ava's feet, and she stepped out of it, towards Gwen, vaguely self-conscious in her black lingerie. She'd only worn it because Nic had told her that wearing her preferred underwear featuring T-rexes vomiting rainbows would be entirely inappropriate. Ava wondered how disturbed Nic would be if she thanked her for her foresight.

Gwen seemed more interested in what was under the fancy material, so Ava reached back to unsnap the clasp of her bra. It joined the dress on the floor.

Gwen's sharp inhale was insanely gratifying. It wasn't that Ava didn't like her body—she'd always been more or less comfortable with herself—but seeing Gwen's blatant appreciation made her feel bold, made her feel desirable in a way she'd never experienced before.

When she moved in to kiss Gwen, it was with a delirious, trembling kind of urgency. Ava was filled with the need to whisper all sorts of things that she wanted to do, things she could hardly even think without blushing. Instead, she showed Gwen with her actions. Gwen moaned when Ava sucked on her tongue. She whimpered when Ava reached up to cup her breasts, nipples hardening against Ava's palms. It suddenly became very important that Ava find out just how many different kinds of sounds she could provoke from Gwen.

Ava walked backwards as Gwen pressed up against her, impatient, demanding. The backs of her calves hit the bed, and then Gwen was pushing her down. Ava fell with a gasp and bounce.

"I imagine it grows tiring," Gwen stood before her, above her, and reached around to unhook her own bra, "having to be in control all the time." The bra fell away, leaving Gwen in only her lace panties. "Having to limit your abilities." Gwen hooked her thumbs into the sides of her underwear. "The overwhelming burden of responsibility."

Gwen pulled them down and shimmied out, and Ava thought she might faint with the sheer intensity of her desire.

"I…" She almost swallowed her own tongue. "Sometimes."

"Lie back," Gwen instructed, watching Ava carefully.

Ava scrambled back, quick to try and please. She propped her head up on pillows that smelled like Gwen's shampoo.

Gwen waited until Ava was settled before murmuring, "Tell me what you want."

Ava's brain short-circuited. "I…anything."

Gwen crawled onto the bed with sleek, feline-like movements. "Tell me what you want."

"You." Ava's breath came out in short, shallow bursts as she watched Gwen advance. She flashed back to that night in her apartment, and thought about everything they could have, should have done. "Your mouth."

"Do you trust me?" Gwen was almost upon her, still on all fours, still watching Ava with that predatory intensity.

"I…yes."

"Yes?" Gwen trailed her index finger under the frilly waistband of Ava's underwear.

"I just…" Ava's hips jutted up reflexively, impatiently. "This is new. Letting go like this."

"Ava."

"Yes," Ava said with certainty. "Yes. I do."

"Good girl." Gwen bowed down and grazed her lips over the space just below Ava's belly button; her stomach muscles quivered in response.

Ava felt a rush of warmth between her thighs. She'd be embarrassed about her body's very enthusiastic response if it weren't for the little whimper Gwen made as she lowered her head.

Ava strained her neck, peering down as Gwen nuzzled against her soaked underwear.

"God, Gwen." Her voice quivered. Gwen had barely touched her, and already Ava was utterly out of control. "I don't know if I can—"

"Shhh," Gwen murmured, her breath hot against Ava's inner thigh. "You're all right." She nipped at the soft skin there before tugging on Ava's underwear and pulling them off completely.

Ava arched up with a rasped cry as Gwen swiped her tongue up the length of her. And *of course* Gwen would be as good at that as she was at everything else. Ava flung an arm over her eyes; it was *too much.*

All the while Ava thought, *this is Gwen. Gwen* emitting those contented little noises. Gwen with her palm flat against the expanse of Ava's stomach, anticipating Ava's movements as she slid two fingers inside.

Gwen moved at a torturously slow pace, provoking a choked Zrix'dhorian curse word from Ava—one she'd never said out loud before. Now she repeated it like a mantra, between stuttered bursts of "God. Gwen. Please. Yes. *Gwen. Gwen. Gwen.*"

Gwen kissed her thoroughly, lovingly, before lifting her head up and proceeding to fuck Ava until her vision went blurry.

The world narrowed to a maelstrom of contact, and Ava was only tangentially aware of the creak of springs as she clutched the edge of the mattress. She was very aware of Gwen's body sliding up hers, the way Gwen's fingers curled forward, the way Gwen lowered her head to press her lips against Ava's temple, and the low, raspy way she whispered, "Come for me, Ava."

Ava saw the stars as she'd never seen them before—color and light and the overwhelming, spiraling sensation of losing herself and being put back together.

When she opened her eyes, Gwen was there, watching her with a warm, tender expression that made Ava smile in return.

"Hi," she murmured, suddenly shy, despite the fact that Gwen's fingers were still inside her.

"Hmm," Gwen hummed and kissed Ava tenderly. "Hi."

"Are you okay?" Ava asked, watching Gwen, trying to read every miniscule change in her face.

"I should be asking you that."

"I'm...so much better than okay. Except there better not be any sort of disaster in the next little while, because I'm pretty sure my body has turned into jelly."

"Well, that's no good." Gwen reached up and pushed Ava's hair, damp with perspiration, off her forehead. "Considering the things I still have planned."

Ava laughed and then almost choked when Gwen teased a fingertip around her nipple, just enough to tickle. "I, uh…" Her eyes rolled back when Gwen ducked her head and took that nipple between her teeth, biting down, hard enough to make Ava gasp and reach around to tangle her fingers in Gwen's hair. Ava felt the tightening in her abdomen, and the quickening of her pulse, and she gently tugged on Gwen's hair, urging her up.

Gwen looked confused for a moment—her pupils blown wide, her mouth swollen and moist, her cheeks flushed pink. Ava thought that the sight alone might be enough to induce a second orgasm. But she was impatient now that she had Gwen here, on top of her.

"What?" Gwen asked with a hint of annoyance that she'd been interrupted.

"Your turn," Ava said in a rush.

Gwen's throat bobbed and her eyes fluttered. "In a minute."

"Can't wait." Ava reached down and gently gripped Gwen by her upper arms before pulling her up effortlessly, evoking a startled, somewhat indignant cry.

"What are you—" Whatever protest Gwen was about to launch became a broken moan that seemed to reverberate through her entire body. She settled down, her knees causing the mattress to dip on either side of Ava's head, and once Ava was sure she was comfortable, she rubbed her palms up Gwen's thighs and drew her nearer.

Ava dissolved into the feeling of Gwen completely surrounding her.

Gwen pushed her palms against the wall above the headboard, stuttering out a litany of things that would have made Ava blush had they been more coherent.

Ava looked up, at Gwen above her, utterly undone and disheveled. Gwen's eyelashes fluttered and she opened her eyes, searching Ava's face with an expression of awe, as if she, like Ava, was amazed to have made it here. Their gazes locked, and the air seemed to crackle with this intangible thing—more intense than any power Ava had experienced before. For the first time, maybe ever, she was seeing Gwen, all of Gwen—no acting, no masks, nothing but the truth of who they were. Her heart felt full and heavy.

Gwen came against Ava's mouth with a strangled cry, and still, Ava didn't stop until Gwen shuddered and pushed herself off with a half-laugh, half-sigh. "God, you're insatiable."

Ava wiped the back of her hand against her mouth and turned on her side to face Gwen, who had splayed out on her side, looking like some elemental goddess—the night sky in her hair and stardust on her skin. "You're wonderful."

Gwen smiled a lazy, post-orgasmic smile and still managed to roll her eyes. "You know…"

Ava scooted closer, warm and content in their little intimacy bubble. "What?"

"You continue to surprise me, in all these unexpected ways."

"You didn't expect me to be good at that, huh?"

"Honestly?" Gwen smirked at her. "Not that good."

Ava pressed her lips together to keep from grinning like an idiot. "I was well motivated."

Ava wondered if it was too soon to start kissing Gwen again. She was still sort of in awe that this was happening at all, especially when Gwen's humor faded and she blinked, surprisingly vulnerable.

"What am I doing with you?" She asked it as if she wasn't really looking for an answer, more to herself than anyone else.

Everything, hopefully, Ava was tempted to say, but instead she shrugged. "I don't know." Her gaze flickered across Gwen's face. "But I don't want to pretend anymore."

Gwen rolled onto her back with a huff, and something inside Ava withered a little. But then Gwen reached over, and her hand rested on Ava's hip, casually possessive.

"This isn't going to be easy."

"I know." Ava's breath hitched when Gwen's fingers drummed lightly against her skin.

"There's a difference between what we've been doing, and really…" She trailed off and Ava leaned up on her elbow, gazing down at Gwen's conflicted face.

"Not for me," Ava admitted. "Everything I said today, every time we're out with Luke, when I touch you in front of those cameras." Ava swallowed, terrified, but forcing herself to maintain eye-contact. "It's always been real. And I know that for you it's new, but—"

Gwen's expression shifted to surprise and then confusion. "You think this is new for me?" She reached up and twirled a lock of Ava's hair around her finger. "Why on earth do you think I asked you to partake in this charade in the first place?

"I was...convenient?" It was Ava's turn to look confused. "You *were* a little drunk when you proposed. I mean, in those first few days, I kept waiting for you to admit that you'd made a mistake."

Gwen's eyes flitted to the ceiling incredulously. "How can someone with enhanced senses be so blind?"

Ava shifted closer. "So, why then?"

Gwen was quiet for a long time, and then she said, "Partly because I knew I could trust you. Partly because...I was...alone and you..." She glanced at Ava briefly and then turned back to analyze the ceiling. "It's easier when you're around, Ava. It always has been. And I've long since realized that I'd rather have you near to me than...not."

Ava's heart thudded so hard against her chest that she was sure Gwen must have noticed it. "So this is your roundabout way of saying..."

Gwen sighed, turned to face Ava, and shot her the equivalent of a "duh" look. "I need water. You've exhausted me."

"Oh." Ava couldn't deny that Gwen's reticence to actually *say* it was a little disappointing, but they had moved fast tonight, faster than Ava could ever have hoped. And so she smiled and leaned down to press a quick kiss against Gwen's cheek. It was absurdly polite considering they were both naked.

"I'll be right back." Gwen stood and reached for her robe. It was black and silky, and so very Gwen. "And then...we'll talk." The look she gave Ava was comforting, reassuring. "All right?"

"Yeah." Ava smiled. "Okay."

Ava fell back against that big springy mattress that creaked a bit more than it had when she'd first hopped on it, and she thought they might have twisted a spring or two. She wondered how expensive the bed was, and then marveled at the fact that she was naked on Gwen's expensive bed.

She smiled to herself, wondering if she'd ever stop smiling now that she'd started. A lot of it was endorphins. After what was very possibly the best orgasm of her life, she imagined that her body must be flooded with them. But it was more than that. It was the way Gwen looked at her now, all soft and tender. It was the—

Ava heard the scream before the crash of glass, but it happened almost simultaneously.

It took almost 0.7 seconds for her to get to the living room, to orientate herself and fully absorb the situation. But by then, the Mantipodis already had an unconscious, slime-covered Gwen in its pincers and was hovering by the broken window on the balcony, a dark silhouette against the stormy night sky.

"Please—" was all Ava got out before the Mantipodis used her camouflage and disappeared, leaving Ava naked and alone, surrounded by broken glass and the memory of Gwen's scream.

CHAPTER 17

"It's been forty minutes." Ava walked to the round table in the operations room and laid her palms down on the flat surface. It shuddered under her weight. "Where are we on this?"

The surrounding officers didn't flinch at the clipped tone of her voice. They had been with her for the past half hour, since she'd shot in like a bullet in a blur of blue and yellow. Now they stood at command, ready to move at a moment's notice.

"Still no signal, but we're working on luring it out," reported one of the more senior officers—Bromwell, Ava thought his name was. "It seems the camouflage masks the creature's bioreceptors, and if it somehow managed to camouflage the civilian as well…"

Gwen, Ava wanted to say. Her name was Gwen.

"…and so our best bet is to lure it out using ultrasonic sound waves recorded from the young Mantipodis."

Ava frowned. "We can assume the mother wants to trade. That's why she took G—the civilian. She wants to trade the thing most precious to her for…" Ava cleared her throat, cutting herself off. Gwen Knight was dating Ava Eisenberg, not Swiftwing. "If the Mantipodis realizes that we don't actually have her baby, she could become unstable, volatile."

"We won't let that happen." Captain Fernandez walked in. "Protecting the civilian is our first priority."

"Then we do the trade," Ava pushed back. "Properly."

"At the risk of endangering the public?" One of the younger, female officers spoke up. "If we release the junior Mantipodis and we're unable to secure a capture of the mother, then we have two class-five AOs loose in LA."

"So we'll make sure that we capture them," Ava said. "After we make sure that Miss Knight is safe. What we're doing is wrong. We're keeping a mother from her child, and we're facing the consequences of our choices. We need to make better choices. We need—"

"Swiftwing." Captain Fernandez crossed her arms over her chest. "Could you come to the armory for a moment?"

Ava sighed. She didn't need the captain's placating, or her assurances that they knew what they were doing. What she needed was Gwen safe and with her. Ava couldn't forget how small Gwen had looked, slung over the Mantipodis's shoulder. She couldn't shake the feeling that if she had responded faster, if she hadn't been so caught up in her head and her heart, she might have been able to stop the abduction. She couldn't shake the guilt that she had brought this terrible thing on Gwen.

She followed Captain Fernandez through the exit and into the armory. "With all due respect, Captain, I know you need to think of the greater good, but I—"

"I'm not going to argue with you."

Ava stopped in mid-rant. "You're not?"

"No."

"Oh," Ava deflated. "Oh. So, why…"

"Because you looked like you needed a breather."

Ava nodded, not trusting herself to say anything.

"You know, if any of my officers had this level of emotional involvement, I'd keep them off the mission." Ava started to argue, but Captain Fernandez held up her hand. "I'm not going to stop you from helping, but I need you to know that you're here because I say so. I need you to follow orders. No going rogue because you think you know better. Understood?"

Ava swallowed and exhaled deeply. "Understood."

"Swiftwing, Captain." They both looked to the door as a uniformed officer announced herself tentatively. "We're ready."

Ava shared a last determined look with Captain Fernandez and steeled herself. She would get Gwen back. There was no alternative.

By the time they reached the cold, sterile basement corridor, officers had secured Norman and placed a hood over his head—presumably to discourage any further secretion. He struggled initially, and then calmed once they cleared the perimeter.

They took an ops van and a medical van, and it took more than an hour for the vehicles to reach the desert. Ava flew above, ears attuned to every sound. She heard the grainy rustle of a sidewinder snake against the cold night sand, and the low hoot of an owl as it watched a mouse scurry under a rock, searching for cover. Still there was no Gwen. Not a breath, not a heartbeat. Ava willed herself to be calm, to focus. But then, a sudden, high-pitched whine from the baby Mantipodis in the black ops van stopped her in mid-air.

The van swerved and Ava squinted, finally making out the shape of a cave in the distance.

"Are you seeing that?" Officer Bromwell's voice came through her earpiece, and Ava nodded to no one before answering.

"Yeah, but I swear it wasn't there before. I would have noticed it."

"The camouflage isn't physical, it's psychic. That's how the Mantipodis manages to conceal things around her. She's not the one altered—"

"Our minds are," Ava surmised.

"Neat trick," the captain came through the walkie-talkie. "Come down here and we'll discuss how to proceed."

Ava shot down with a whoosh, and landed in a billow of sand and dust beside the two vehicles, which had stopped a fair distance away from the newly revealed cave.

"Why now?" Officer Bromwell hopped out of the van. "Why reveal herself?"

"I think she can hear him." Ava squinted into the distance. "She wants us to know where she is."

Bromwell brought his walkie-talkie up to his mouth and waited for the scratchy static to quiet before he said, "We're go for the trade." He waited for a response, and then nodded at Ava. "We're all set. The snipers will be ready to—"

"Wait." Ava blinked. "Snipers?"

"Armed with tranq darts," Bromwell explained. "We'll take Norman to the cave, lure the mother out, and then you'll go in and get the civilian."

They walked the Mantipodis baby toward the mouth of the cave, two agents at each side, helping its fat body amble along. By now, his cries were loud enough for everyone to hear. To Ava, they were almost deafening.

They took his hood off, and a screech echoed from inside the cave.

The rest happened almost too fast even for Ava to keep up with. The mother Mantipodis was barely at the cave entrance before she was hit with tranquilizer darts from two sides. The cave seemed to flicker for a moment, as if threatening to disappear right before their eyes, and Norman pierced the still night air with a cry so poignant that Ava felt her heart clench in a weird sort of pain.

The mother staggered for a few steps as the drugs kicked in, and then fell with a heavy thump that shifted the sands. She hadn't even hit the ground before Ava scooped up a blanket from one of the medical personnel and zoomed past the sedated alien into the cave. She followed the sound of Gwen's breathing, moving through tunnels and archways.

Ava stopped just short of her destination to gather herself, to take a breath. Gwen was slumped against a wall, her arms wrapped around her knees, thin satin robe skimming her thighs, and Ava was grateful for the blanket.

"Gwen?" she asked softly. Gwen's head snapped up at the sound, and the change in her face was immediate and unmistakable, eyes brimming with tears that she blinked away. Ava approached slowly, tamping down the urge to run and scoop Gwen into her arms.

Gwen shook her head and bit down on her lips. Her voice, thin and raspy, asked, "Is it gone?"

"She's gone. You're safe now."

Gwen attempted to stand, and then Ava was by her side, helping her up, throwing the blanket around her shoulders. Gwen was cold and trembling, all thin human limbs and goose-pimpled skin. "Is that oka—"

She was cut off by the fierceness of Gwen's arms around her neck. Ava swallowed back a sob of relief and buried her hands in Gwen's tangled hair, sticky with alien goo. "I'm here," she breathed into Gwen's neck. "I'm here."

"Took you long enough," Gwen replied, and Ava could hear the hint of a humor in her voice.

"I'm sorry." Ava pulled back, her eyes flickering over Gwen's face, taking in the mascara tracks down her cheeks, the crystallizing alien extract in her hair. There was a purplish bruise on her collar bone that, Ava realized with a stomach flip, was the result of her own fervent ministrations hours earlier. "Are you okay? Did it—?"

"I'm fine," Gwen answered quickly. "A little underdressed for an abduction, but—"

"I'm sorry," Ava said again. "I should have—"

"Don't." Gwen was stern. "There was nothing you could have…you're here. I knew you would be." Gwen reached out to brush the hair from Ava's forehead, causing Ava's eyelashes to flutter. "Now…" Ava looked at Gwen expectantly. "Take me the hell out of this—oh."

For a split second, Gwen looked almost as confused as Ava, but then her eyes rolled back in her head until they were just a gruesome sheen of white. Ava caught Gwen before she fell, almost weightless in Ava's arms. The panic choked her. It swelled up in her stomach and made her dizzy.

"I've got you." Ava's voice cracked as she held Gwen close, flying out of the dark cave as fast as she dared.

"Help!" Ava yelled the second she was out, going straight for the medical van.

The med staff extricated an unconscious Gwen from Ava's grip, and she watched them cover her face with an oxygen mask, feeling her throat close up in fear.

"The toxins are moving fast. Her body is mimicking organophosphate poisoning."

"What can I do? Can I fly her to the hospital?"

"No. Get her to the helicopter," an officer yelled out, and the med team was quick to move. "There's a team waiting at Clinton."

Ava took a breath and attempted to swallow down her panic, hazarding one last look at Gwen before the helicopter took off.

CHAPTER 18

Ava yawned.

Her eyelids felt as heavy as the weight in the pit of her stomach. It was strange to realize that it had been only a few hours since she had been nervously following Gwen into the bedroom, a mess of hormones and disbelief. That felt like days ago, like a dream that she remembered but knew couldn't be real. Except it was real, it had happened—the feverish touches, the whispered intimacy, the incredible look on Gwen's face when she'd come undone under Ava's touch.

Ava had reached the hospital before the helicopter, but had changed out of her suit and pretended she'd been called in as Gwen's significant other. It wouldn't do to have Swiftwing hanging about.

Eventually, one of the younger doctors had come out to ask Ava a series of questions that she'd rattled off as easily as breathing.

Name: Gwendolyn Jane Knight
Date of birth: November 11, 1973
Blood type: A-
Medications: Zoloft, occasional Excedrin for migraines
Allergies: The dioxide in certain laundry detergents

After that, Ava had hung around outside of the room, pacing until she almost created a ditch in front of the door.

A brutally long twenty minutes later, Dr. Shepard came out to tell her that Gwen was fine, but sleeping. The toxin had left her dehydrated and slightly delirious, but there would be no lasting effects.

"So...she'll be all right?" Ava asked.

"After some sleep." Dr. Shepard smiled at her. "She'll be fine, Miss Eisenberg."

"When will she be awake?"

"Tomorrow morning is a good bet."

Ava sighed and slumped into a chair. "Thanks."

"Get some sleep," Dr. Shepard said kindly. "You look like you've had a rough night."

When she woke, it was late evening, and Gwen was still sleeping. Her breaths were shallow and her brow furrowed, even in sleep.

After watching her for a while, Ava changed back into her suit and flew to the holding cells, where the Mantipodii, newly reunited, were getting acquainted with their glass cell. She had expected some sort of hostility, or at the very least a screech, but the mother Mantipodis seemed entirely preoccupied with her young, who was nuzzling its head against hers. In the weeks that he'd been detained, Norman had gone from a pale, translucent color to greenish, and his skin was scalier. He was maturing.

The wall behind her was hard, the floor beneath her cold. Ava sat with her chin resting on her knees and her cape splayed out around her. The lights in the holding facility were dimmed and comforting. She watched the mother Mantipodis coo and hum as the younger one slept. Ava was not sure she'd ever seen him sleep before this.

"You'll be taken to a better home soon," Ava said in Zrix'dhorian, not knowing if they understood her or not. It was strangely comforting seeing them together, despite the circumstances. "There's a place," she continued. "A sanctuary with all sorts of creatures...alien species. They made it for survivors of the *Andromeda* who couldn't function in human society. I think you'll be happy there."

The mother looked up at her sharply then, and Ava was quick to add, "Both of you."

Ava was quiet for a long time, watching as the young Mantipodis settled down against his mother.

"I'm sorry," she said, redirecting the mother's attention toward her. "About what we had to do. We didn't understand at first."

Unexpectedly, the older Mantipodis stepped toward the glass wall and cocked her head, as if listening intently.

"I know you didn't mean to hurt Gwen. She's a mom too. She has a son. And she's great at it."

The Mantipodis made a cooing sound.

Ava smiled. "It's sort of the reason we're together at all. So she could keep Luke. It's about more than that now. I mean, I think that's what tonight meant. I just..." She swallowed back a stinging bubble of tears that seemed to come from nowhere. "I wish she'd wake up."

An age of silence then, with the Mantipodis retreating back to her young and Ava resting her cheek on her knees, wondering if perhaps Gwen was right, that the situation was more complicated than Ava was willing to admit.

She sat there while both Mantipodis mother and young slept, until the sun peeked through the high basement windows, and Ava's body ached from sitting in the same position for so many hours.

She was so wrapped up in her thoughts that the sound of someone clearing their throat startled her. Ava looked up to see Captain Fernandez in the doorway, watching her with a thoughtful expression.

"Is it okay that I'm here?" Ava asked, already making to get up. But the captain waved her back down and, surprisingly, came to sit beside her.

"You know I've been doing this for fifteen years," Captain Fernandez began. "Almost right from the beginning. Right from when we realized that we needed to protect ourselves from the creatures that fell from the sky." Ava stiffened, but Captain Fernandez continued, "Before that, I thought only humans were capable of such violence and atrocities." She paused and looked at Ava. "As it turns out, we're not the only ones capable of love and compassion either." The captain nodded towards the cell. "You did a good thing here. Bringing them together."

Ava blinked, surprised and touched. "I—thank you."

"Take a few days off. We'll look after the city for you. When you come back, we'll discuss how you can be more of an integral part of the team."

"Does this mean I finally get a badge?"

"Don't push it." Captain Fernandez stood, putting an end to their little moment. "By the way, when this is done, do you think you could ask you girlfriend to sign something for me?" She looked sheepish. "My husband's a fan."

Ava's eyes went wide. "You know?"

"I'm a detective, Miss Eisenberg." She raised her eyebrows. "Give me a little credit."

Ava watched the captain disappear around the corner, and smiled for the first time in hours.

When she got back to the hospital, she was more than a little surprised to find Nic sitting on one of the chairs in the waiting area, looking half-asleep.

She looked up as Ava walked down the corridor. "Hey."

"Um. Hey," Ava replied, as if this was totally normal. "What are you doing here?"

"I got your message about Gwen. I'm sorry."

"Yeah." Ava slumped into a chair next to her. "How did you know I'd be here?"

"Where else would you be?"

Ava exhaled and laid her head on Nic's shoulder, feeling exhaustion creep through her limbs and settle over her bones. "You're here," she said, in a soft, sleepy voice, and Nic twisted to get an arm around Ava's shoulders.

"Figured you might need someone."

"You figured right."

They were quiet for a while, until Nic said, "Stupid question, but, how are you doing?"

"I'm fine."

"Once more with honesty."

"I'm..." Ava straightened. "I will be fine. As soon as she wakes up and I can..." she trailed off with a helpless shrug.

"It's okay." Nic's voice was quiet. "I get it."

Ava sighed and let her head fall back on Nic's shoulder. "I love her, Nic. Like...in a forever kind of way."

Ava could feel Nic's deep inhale, and she was quiet for a long time before asking, "Does she feel the same way?"

"I think so. I... it's harder for Gwen. There's a lot more...yes." Ava nodded, allowing herself to trust. "I think she does."

"Wow," Nic breathed, and then chuckled softly.

Ava lifted her head. "What?"

"I'm just thinking… Our game nights are going to be pretty interesting from now on."

Ava laughed for the first time in hours. "Oh my God. Can you imagine?"

"Eisenberg!" Nic did a terrible impression of Gwen. "This is Pictionary, not Charades! Why are you flailing your arms around?"

Ava snorted and shoved Nic hard enough almost to make her fall off her chair. "Shut up. She calls me Ava now."

"Oh, well then, it must be love."

Ava's laughter died down and her face softened. "Must be."

Nic straightened and bumped her shoulder against Ava's. "If you're happy, then I'm happy."

"Yeah?"

"Yeah."

They both jumped a little at the sound of footsteps coming down the corridor.

"Miss Eisenberg, she's awake."

Gwen was sitting up in bed, but with her eyes closed, as if she were still sleeping. Her black robe had been traded in for a standard-issue hospital gown. The image was jarring, incongruous; Ava couldn't quite reconcile the vision of Gwen Knight, strutting around set, all sound and fury, with the defenseless-looking woman in the bed. And while she knew that Gwen would throttle her for thinking it, Ava's heart broke just a little as she was faced with the stark reality of loving a human.

She tapped her knuckles on the doorframe, suddenly hesitant. "Hi."

Gwen opened reluctant eyelids and blinked. She frowned for a moment and then rasped, "Water."

Ava was quick to pour some into a glass from the jug at the base of her bed. She practically bounced on her heels, eager to help in any way she could. "Anything else?"

"No. I'm…" Gwen cleared her throat. "This is fine."

Ava couldn't help herself. She reached out and tucked some of Gwen's hair behind her ear. It was a simple, casual gesture that made her feel grounded somehow, especially when Gwen leaned into her touch.

"How are you feeling?" Ava asked.

Gwen offered her a wan smile. "Like I was kidnapped and poisoned by something out of a B-grade horror movie. What was that thing?" And after a moment's consideration, "And where the hell am I?"

"The species name is *Mantipodii dictyoptera*. She's from a planet not far from Zrix'dhor actually."

"And are all your neighbors that prone to violence?"

"She was sort of…provoked. It happened so fast."

Gwen's face went impassive. "I can't imagine it was a particularly pleasant experience for you either."

"I'm sorry," Ava felt guilt swirl in her stomach. "It was my fault."

"Ava—"

"If I had been faster, then maybe—"

Gwen clasped her fingers around Ava's wrist and gently swiped her thumb against Ava's pulse point. "And if I had been less distracted by the thought of hurrying back to bed with you, I might have seen it sooner. It's not your fault."

"I just…" Ava sighed and dropped her head, feeling suddenly so tired.

"Out with it."

Ava found Gwen's expectant glare and shrugged. "I guess I can't help thinking that maybe you were right. That this isn't going to be as easy as I thought it could be. Not because my feelings have changed, but because I'm Swiftwing. I'm always going to come with a danger sign. And asking you to be part of that? It's not fair."

Gwen's thumb stilled and her grip tightened as Ava continued. "You were taken tonight because of your association with me. Because the Mantipodis knew what you meant to me and—"

"Oh please," Gwen cut her off. "As if this was my first brush with danger. I've survived MET Gala after-parties. I'll survive this. And if you think I haven't weighed the pros and cons of dating a superhero, then you don't know me as well as you claim. I've made my decision." Gwen's eyes were fierce, intent.

There's that sound and fury, Ava thought. She tried one last time, partly to hear Gwen's resolve, partly just to quell that last, lingering scrap of doubt. "That was before—"

"Have you ever known me to back down on a decision?" Gwen raised her eyebrows.

"No." Ava shook her head, fighting back a smile. "You're frustratingly stubborn."

"Well," Gwen's expression was smug. She knew she'd won, but in some ways, so had Ava. "Then you know there's no point in arguing." She trailed her fingers up Ava's arm. "I choose you, Ava. You and everything you come with." Her gaze was steady, deliberate. "That's how this works."

Ava bit down on her bottom lip as a plethora of emotions welled up inside her, making her chest feel tight and warm. "I was really scared today," she whispered.

Gwen's face softened, and there was a tenderness there that Ava had rarely glimpsed. "I wasn't. Not really." Gwen took the loose material of Ava's shirt between her fingers and held on. "I knew you'd find me, Swiftwing."

"Really?"

Gwen nodded and tugged her forward. "Come here." She scooted over, and Ava toed off her sneakers before climbing in. The bed was narrow, and she curled herself against Gwen's body, resting her head on Gwen's chest, soothed by the strong, steady sound of her heart.

Gwen's fingers combed through her hair and Ava was lulled into a sleepy state. She almost missed the way Gwen's heart rate picked up just a moment before she murmured, "I love you, Ava."

Ava smiled sleepily and tilted her head up, so close that their noses were almost touching. She felt warm, safe, cared for. "I love you too."

Gwen pressed her lips against Ava's brow and pushed her hair back. "Shh. Sleep now."

And they did.

CHAPTER 19

Ava didn't like change. Change meant leaving home and crashing ships. Change meant a new language, a new culture, a new family. Change meant that things that were once easy became difficult; people who were once close drifted away. On principle, Ava did not like change.

But sometimes, change was good.

The way they interacted changed. They talked now. About everything and nothing. No mixed signals, no coy confessions or veiled compliments. They spent a night sitting on opposite couches debating ethics and politics, the best shows on Netflix, and why German words didn't count when playing Scrabble (even if they had been absorbed by the English language) until Gwen was yawning and the sun was threatening to break through pink clouds.

Gwen listened when Ava ranted on about global warming and how the ice caps around the north were smaller than they'd ever been, or about Nic's recent obsession with nanobots, which had led to a Horatio upgrade and subsequently a black eye for Ava.

Gwen shared stories of her early life, trying to make it in LA. Waiting tables and waiting for callbacks.

It was mundane and insignificant and normal.

It was exhilarating.

There was an ease to this, a naturalness that Ava couldn't have anticipated. They fit. It worked. And Ava could hardly remember a time when this wasn't the norm. She didn't want to.

The constant fear of disappointing Gwen was replaced with the constant fear of losing Gwen.

A week after Gwen came home from the hospital, they argued about whether she was ready to go back to work or not. Ava left in the middle of the fight to deal with a chemical fire, and when she came back, Gwen Knight, who never apologized, told Ava that she was sorry, that she might have been suffering from a touch of cabin fever but that she'd meant what she'd said about not being some wilting flower, restricted to her bed by some hack alien doctor.

Ava learned to read Gwen all over again. Nuances and gestures that were hidden from Ava the Assistant were revealed to Ava the Girlfriend. Smiles, frowns, gasps.

These were the realities of being in a relationship.

By day ten, Gwen was able to go to set for a few hours, Ron being recovered enough by this point to resume filming. Ava hadn't seen her own apartment since going over to get the necessities. Nic had called it U-Haul syndrome and told Ava that she never thought she'd see her so stupidly in love.

Ava had raised an imaginary glass and grinned. "To being stupidly in love."

The sun filtered in, making Ava hum in sleepy contentment as lucidity crept over her. She thought she might have been dreaming about the stars. She turned toward the light, and immediately wrinkled her nose as she was tickled by a dark cloud of hair, splayed out on the pillow beside her. Automatically, she wiggled closer, bringing her arms around the sleeping body.

Gwen mumbled something unintelligible and scooted back against Ava, fitting their bodies together intimately.

"Morning," Ava whispered into Gwen's neck as she settled her open palm against the flat space between Gwen's breasts, fingers twitching against skin, warm under silk pajamas.

"Hmm," Gwen hummed. "Good morning."

They lay there for a while, breathing in sync, bathed in diluted sunlight. Ava traced idle patterns down Gwen's ribcage, spelling out Zrix'dhorian symbols that had no equivalent English translation.

"What time is it?" Gwen finally asked.

Ava wiggled even closer. "Too early to be awake."

Gwen made a little scoffing sound. "There's no such thing."

"Fine, then too early to get out of bed."

Gwen disentangled herself and turned to face Ava. Ava loved her like this—slow-blinking eyes and sleep-flushed cheeks, messy hair and all the telltale signs of age that she'd expertly cover with make-up later. Ava loved seeing her like this because Gwen *allowed* Ava to see her like this. This version was exceeded only by Gwen all tingly and hot, all racing pulse and damp skin.

"And what, pray tell," Gwen trailed a fingertip along Ava's lower lip, "do you propose we do instead?"

Ava wiggled her eyebrows. "I have a few ideas."

"You can't be late," Gwen cautioned, pressing a warning finger against Ava's parted lips. "Sleeping with the boss does not excuse tardiness."

"Well, there have to be some perks." Ava opened her mouth and gently bit down on Gwen's finger, prompting Gwen to roll her eyes and exhale an amused breath. Ava's tactile sentimentality still embarrassed her sometimes. "Besides, I can be done in like three seconds."

"Not something I would brag about, darling." Gwen didn't do endearments unless she was teasing.

Ava didn't mind. She liked the way Gwen said her name—the way she dragged it out when she was impatient, the offhand way she said it after a sentence, the way she whispered it when Ava's mouth was between her legs.

"I meant done, as in ready for work."

"Good. Because I'd prefer you took your time."

Ava leaned in and nuzzled her nose in the space just under Gwen's jaw. "Glad we're in agreement," she murmured as Gwen threaded her fingers through Ava's hair.

She was so immersed in the little sighs Gwen was making that it took Ava a split second to hear the deep buzz of Gwen's phone vibrating against the nightstand.

Gwen emitted a growl of frustration and splayed her arm out, reaching blindly for the phone as Ava closed her lips around the shell of her ear. "Too early for phone calls," Ava whispered.

Gwen squinted at the screen and then frowned. Ava pulled back immediately. The lit-up name on the screen read Alfonso Moretti. Gwen swiped her thumb to accept the call and sat up.

"Alfonso." She cleared her throat and started again. "It's early."

Ava moved back and watched the slow change in Gwen's face, the way she closed her eyes and pinched the bridge of her nose. Ava's stomach dropped. Something was wrong.

Her suspicions were confirmed when Gwen said, "What do you mean he's there?"

Gwen tossed the duvet off and walked out of the room. "No, of course I didn't know."

Ava focused, following the conversation as Gwen made her way to Luke's room.

"Well, has he explained? Do you need me to—" Gwen sighed. "Yes, I think that's best. I'll be here."

Ava listened to erratic sound of Gwen's heart and the creak of springs as she sat down. Two minutes went by, then five. Ava waited for Gwen to come back. Eventually, when it felt as though Gwen had been gone forever, Ava climbed out of bed and made her way down the hall.

Gwen was sitting at the edge of Luke's rumpled bed, staring down at her hands.

"Hey," Ava started softly, unsure.

Gwen looked up at her. "My son apparently decided to sneak out of the house at God knows what hour and get a bus to his father's place." She emphasized the word bus, as if this was the worst element of the situation.

Ava hunched her shoulders up and went to sit beside Gwen. "He's safe though, right?"

Gwen made a vague sound of assent.

"Do you want me to…I mean, I could go and get him."

"And have me explain why I was using Swiftwing as my personal collection service?" Gwen shook her head. "No. Alfonso's bringing him back. They'll be here in a couple hours."

"Oh." Ava felt helpless. This wasn't really a job for Swiftwing.

"Well, it doesn't help for both of us to sit here and pace the halls." Gwen absently patted her knee. "You should get ready for work."

"You don't want me to stay?" Ava tried her best to keep the hurt from her voice.

"You're already doing so much reshuffling, and you're getting your portfolio—"

"I want to stay," Ava interrupted. "If…I mean, if that's okay. I want to be here."

Gwen looked at her with some surprise, the way she sometimes did when Ava caught her off-guard. "All right. Call the office."

Ava smiled softly and exhaled.

"He's not a reckless boy," Gwen muttered, looking a little lost. "I can't imagine why he… He's always asked to see his father. It's never been a problem. But to sneak out…"

"We can't know until they get here," Ava replied, trying her best to say the right thing. "I mean, I'm sure he had a good reason."

"I doubt it'll be good enough to get him out of a lifetime of solitary confinement."

Ava rested head on Gwen's shoulder and closed her hand over the palm on her knee. "He's so much like you."

She said it offhandedly. And because it was true. Ava didn't expect Gwen to tense up and exhale on a shudder.

"Hey," Ava sat up immediately. "What's wrong?"

Gwen sighed, and her gaze swept around Luke's room. "He's half-Yanagharian."

It took a while for the words to sink in, but when they did, Ava gasped in surprise. "He is?"

Gwen nodded slowly. "His mother…his biological mother worked as my housekeeper for half a decade." She smiled. "Her name was Lali."

"Did you know?" Ava asked.

"She told me. She…had an accent that I couldn't place. I asked her where she was from and it never occurred to her to lie. This was before the protection act. She was still seen as an illegal immigrant. But she told me the truth."

"What happened to her?"

"She…fell in love. She didn't know she could get pregnant. I don't think the boyfriend did either. Even after he left her, she was so excited." Gwen's voice turned soft and wistful. "We spoke about adding a nursery to the guesthouse, where she lived." Gwen cleared her throat and continued. "Anyway. There were complications with the pregnancy. Luke was born almost two months early, but he was healthy, so strong."

"Is he?" Ava searched for the word and remembered Rachel's phrase. "Is he extraordinary?"

Gwen's smile was slow and soft. "He is. We were worried for a long time that his ability would make him a target. But he hides it well. He's an empath." Gwen stated before Ava could ask.

"He absorbs others' emotions?"

"In a sense. It's more that he feels them acutely. He can tell me what I'm feeling before I know I'm feeling it. He knew at four that Alfonso and I were breaking up. He apologizes before I've yelled at him. It's why he's so sensitive."

"And Lali?" Ava asked, although she guessed the answer.

"Died in childbirth. She never even saw him. But Alfonso and I wanted Luke to grow up knowing about his other mom, and about why he's so special."

"And that's when you started the foundation."

"I wish I could say that I was doing it because I was altruistic at heart. I wish I'd been more sensitive to AO rights earlier, but we started it for Luke, so that he, and children like him, could grow up in a better world."

Ava took this in. She had no idea what to feel. Luke's mother had been on the ship with her. He was, in some strange way, a connection to her own mother. A connection to the ship and everything she'd thought was lost.

"I think," Ava began slowly, "that I'm going to get us some breakfast."

Gwen looked at her gratefully, understanding that Ava was giving her some space, and perhaps, getting some space herself.

"Donuts," Gwen stated. "A whole box of them."

Ava pressed a kiss to Gwen's cheek. "As my lady commands."

Ava returned a good fifty minutes later. Super speed wasn't particularly useful when armed with two cups of coffee and a box of donuts.

She found Gwen in her study, staring at her laptop screen. She wasn't really reading; Ava knew this because her glasses were dangling between her fingers.

"Penny for your thoughts?"

"They're worth far more than that." Gwen accepted a coffee and hummed into her cup at the first sip.

"Any word from Alfonso?" Ava sat cross-legged on the opposite couch.

"Only to say that he's on his way."

"Have you spoken to Luke?"

"No." Gwen's reply was sharp, almost impatient. "No, he refuses to speak to me on the phone."

Ava drank slowly, unsure how to proceed. She wanted to comfort Gwen, say it'd be okay, but she had no idea why Luke would have left and didn't know for sure that it was going to be all right.

"The deposition is tomorrow." Gwen said the one thing that Ava had been very careful to avoid. "This is…" Gwen tossed a file onto the coffee table and leaned back with a sigh. "Not going to go well."

"You can't know that," Ava said.

"Yes, Ava. A runaway child is a great tick in my favor."

Ava winced at her tone. "I just meant—"

Gwen sighed again and held up a hand. "I know. I know that you're just… But that eternal optimism of yours isn't going to fix anything right now."

"Then how can I help?"

Gwen watched her for a moment and her features relaxed, her face softened. "Tell me what you're currently working on. Which meeting has Jackson set you up for?"

Ava leaned forward and proceeded to tell Gwen about the pilot she was starting. She told her about meetings that week, and how she was nervous about the one at Showtime. And in the end, it helped, even if Gwen already knew most of what Ava was relaying.

Half an hour later, they had moved to the same couch, and Ava was reading some of her script out loud, while Gwen gave her very honest commentary.

The knock jarred them both.

"Should I…wait here?" Ava asked as Gwen stood and straightened her top over her pants.

Gwen shook her head and offered her hand to Ava, who took it with a firm little squeeze.

Ava hung back when Gwen opened the door to Alfonso and a sheepish-looking Luke, who stared at his feet, biting his lip nervously, one backpack strap slung over his shoulder.

"Alfonso." Gwen stepped back to let her son and ex-husband in. She didn't acknowledge Luke, but Ava watched her assess him carefully, almost desperately.

"Gwennie." Gwen's eyes narrowed for a second at Alfonso's use of the pet name, but she didn't otherwise react. "I come bearing our outlaw son."

It occurred to Ava that this was the first time she had seen all of them in a room together. She tried to imagine them as a family. Gwen, bouncing a young Luke on her hip, Alfonso pulling faces to make him laugh. The image made her feel strange, almost lonely.

Gwen's eyes went skyward. "This isn't funny."

Luke shifted, but he still refused to look at Gwen.

"Didn't say it was," Alfonso replied. "And he's not saying much of anything."

No one acknowledged Ava, who stood at the end of the hallway, feeling more like a guest than a participant in this scene.

"I wanted to wait for Mom," Luke mumbled to the ground.

Ava wondered if only she heard it, but then Gwen sighed and bent down to look at Luke.

"Luke, what the hell were you thinking? Running off alone? In the dark? Why didn't you ask to see your father? You know it's never a problem."

"Cause you just would have dropped me off," Luke answered, softly, but with an edge of petulance. "Or you would have asked Jonah to do it. You never stay to talk to Dad."

Gwen tilted her head up to look at Alfonso with surprise. "Your father and I have said all we really need to say to each other."

"No, you haven't." Luke's voice warbled, but he didn't cry. "You just yell over the phone. And you never really listen."

"Well, we're listening now, buster." Alfonso crossed his arms over his chest.

Luke finally looked up, between his parents. "I went to Dad because of Ava."

Gwen stood and swallowed whatever she was going to say. She glanced back at Ava, who decided that she would very much enjoy if a pit opened up below her and swallowed her up.

"What did you say to him?" There was an edge to Alfonso's voice, and Ava shook her head.

"I...didn't."

Gwen said, "Alfonso, please," just as Luke said, "It's okay, Dad. It's nothing bad."

Luke looked at Ava and she gave him an encouraging nod, despite being completely terrified that she'd somehow messed up.

"She told me to, um, tell you guys how I feel." Luke turned to Gwen. "I know that Dad wants me to come and live with him."

"Buster," Alfonso stepped forward and placed his hand on Luke's shoulder. "This is really something between your mom and me."

"No, it isn't!" Luke shrugged out of his father's grasp and turned to face him. "Cause you wanna take me away from my school and my friends. Me and Jacob—"

"Jacob and I," Gwen and Alfonso corrected simultaneously, and the moment would have been amusing if it wasn't so tense.

"Jacob and I are planning our science fair experiment for next year, and if I'm not there, he's going to be partnered up with Ernie Miller. Ernie Miller still eats glue, you guys!"

"Kid, there are other schools," Alfonso tried.

"Not like this one. And I really like staying over with you and Stephanie. But I don't wanna move."

Gwen's breathing picked up, her eyes flicking between Luke and Alfonso.

Alfonso sounded frustrated when he said, "There are so many other factors..."

"Mom doesn't work that much anymore!" Luke interrupted, anticipating Alfonso's argument.

He really was perceptive, Ava thought.

"We—we went for ice cream last month. In the middle of the day! And she's been home all week with Ava."

Ava felt a slight blush creep up her neck.

"And it's good here, Dad. We laugh a lot, and Ava's teaching me to draw. She says I could be a comic book artist if I wanted."

"If you live with me, you'll still see your mom and Ava all the time."

"It's not the same. I don't want it to change."

Alfonso exhaled and ran his fingers through his hair with some exasperation before looking at Gwen. "What do you have to say to this?"

"Nothing." Gwen shrugged. She didn't sound smug or superior, only relieved. "He's said it all."

Alfonso appraised Gwen with an expression somewhere between furious and defeated.

"Hey." He looked down at Luke. "Give your mom and me a minute, okay?"

"But—"

"You wanted your father and I to talk," Gwen interrupted his protest. "So let us talk." She turned. "Ava, would you—"

"Of course." Ava practically ran toward Luke. "Come on, you." She took his backpack from him and steered him down the corridor. "Let's go be elsewhere."

They walked to Luke's room, where he slumped into his desk chair with a sigh. "Think they're super mad at me?"

Ava sat on the edge of his bed, in almost exactly the same spot she'd occupied earlier with Gwen. "For running away? Definitely. For telling the truth?" Ava shook her head. "No way. You know your mom's always been a big fan of the truth."

Luke reached for a small *Adventure Time* figurine on his desk and twirled it in his fingers. "Yeah."

Ava watched him for a moment. "Can I ask you a question?"

He looked hesitant, but nodded.

"Why didn't you just ask your mom to take you? Why'd you sneak out?"

Luke shrugged and said nothing for a long while.

Ava waited.

"I guess I wanted to talk to my dad first. Like, without her knowing, you know?" Luke looked down. "I wanted to fix things for her."

Ava's heart suddenly felt too big in her chest, and she wanted nothing more than to reach out and hug Luke, who suddenly looked so young and unsure.

"But then I got there, and Dad sort of freaked out and called Mom, and then she freaked out at him and I got sort of scared."

"Oh, buddy." Ava moved forward and knelt on the floor in front of him. "It's okay to be scared. And it's okay to want to fix things, but it's good to ask for help too. There are so many people who care about you and want what's best for you."

"But what Mom wants and what my dad wants is different. What about what I want?"

"What do you want?" Ava asked.

"To stay here," Luke whispered. "With Mom and…and you. And to finish my science project with Jacob. Is that…will that make my dad mad?"

Ava sighed and thought for a moment before sitting back and crossing her legs, so that she was looking up at Luke, slumped in his chair.

"You know," she began, "when I was younger, just a little younger than you are now, I remember overhearing an argument between my mom and some other really important people. They were arguing over something my mother had decided. My mom," Ava's lips pulled up into an involuntary smile, "was really important. She sort of made the decisions for everyone, and they trusted her."

"Like, a president?" Luke asked, leaning forward now, looking genuinely intrigued.

"More like a captain," Ava answered. "I remember being really confused about why everyone was so upset, because my mom was always right. She always knew what was best." Ava's voice faltered and she cleared her throat. "It took me a long time to realize that sometimes our parents aren't right, and they don't always know what's best. But they try because they love us. Your dad believes that living with him is what's right for you. You've told him differently, and I think that's really brave. I think he'll think so too."

Luke thought about it, and Ava pushed down the well of emotion bubbling up inside of her. It happened sometimes when she talked about her mother.

"You loved her lots, huh?"

Ava looked at Luke, seeing, for the first time, the little differences that made him alien. The flecks of gold in his irises, the slight, almost imperceptible pointed tip of his ear.

"I did."

"Ava," he finally started. "I'm really glad you're here."

She smiled then, widely and without reservation. "Me too."

A light tap against the door caused Ava to turn around, and there was Gwen, leaning against the doorframe, watching them with an unreadable expression.

"Five minutes to pack your school things," Gwen addressed Luke. "You're going to your father's for a few days."

"Am I going to have to live with him?" Luke asked in a small voice.

Ava's heart seized up for a moment, waiting for Gwen to answer, but she shook her head. "Nothing is going to change unless you want it to. But he does want some time to talk to you."

"Am I in trouble?" Luke asked, sinking back into his chair, in a way that reminded Ava of a scolded puppy.

"I wouldn't get attached to any of your new Xbox games for a while," Gwen looked at him pointedly. Luke opened his mouth to protest, but then wisely thought better of it.

"That said," Gwen walked in and stood beside the chair. "I am proud of you for being honest. You will never be in trouble for sharing your feelings. Do you understand?"

Luke nodded slowly and looked at his hands. "I'm sorry I just took off."

"And?"

"And I'm sorry I lied and made you worry."

"And for putting yourself in needless danger—"

"I wasn't—"

"Luke."

"Yeah, okay. I'm sorry. I really am, Mom."

Gwen looked at him with an indulgent expression. "I know."

"So," Luke looked hopeful. "Can I take my Nintendo Switch with me?"

Gwen's mouth pulled into a small, barely-there smile before she reached out tapped him on the nose. "Not a chance."

Ava missed saying goodbye to Luke. Some idiot decided that 1 p.m. on a Thursday was a good time to provoke a high-speed chase. She mumbled some excuse about forgetting something at her apartment before sprinting down the hallway of the building and flying out a window on the floor below.

The chase itself was over the moment she landed on the hood of the car and forced the driver to stop. The part that came after took a bit longer. Being mobbed by adoring fans came with the job, but it was exhausting. And so, Ava posed and smiled and did her heroic duty, all the while thinking about Gwen, alone after Luke left with his father, pacing around an empty house.

Ava made it back within the hour, and returned to find Gwen in the garden, back against the lemon tree, her phone to her ear. Gwen wiggled two fingers at her, summoning her close, and Ava took about eight seconds to rush to the bedroom, change into plainclothes, and come back.

By the time she returned, Gwen was hanging up with an "Okay, Georgia. Thank you. I'll come by sometime next week."

"Everything okay?" Ava asked, leaning next to Gwen so that they were shoulder to shoulder.

Gwen clucked her tongue and picked paint chips out of Ava's hair. "Fine. That was the lawyer."

Ava leaned into Gwen's touch, almost unconsciously. "I thought you guys worked it out."

"We did." Gwen dropped her hand and fell back against the gnarled tree trunk.

The afternoon was warm and sunny—a typical Los Angeles day. Gwen looked beautiful in the dappled sunshine. There was something different about her—a lightness.

"Alfonso has agreed to drop the petition," Gwen murmured, breaking Ava from her reverie. "We'll have to work out new visitation terms, in which Luke spends more holidays with him, but for the most part, nothing is changing."

"And the deposition?"

Gwen shrugged. "Called off."

"That's...wow," Ava breathed out. "So...that's it?"

"It would seem so."

"What now?"

"Hmm." Gwen tilted her head thoughtfully. "I propose a celebration."

Ava looked at her with excited curiosity, and Gwen smiled.

"Dinner. Tonight. At Abortorium. No aliens, no exes, no custody petitions. Just you," Gwen trailed a finger along the collar of Ava's light summer dress. "And me."

"Golly, Miss Knight." Ava pressed her lips together to keep from grinning. She was unsuccessful. "Are you asking me out on a date?"

"Play your cards right, Eisenberg, and you may even get lucky." Gwen winked.

"You don't think that's moving a bit too fast?"

"Says the girl who plays tag with the sound barrier."

Their interplay was like gravity, a universal constant.

"It's funny," Ava stated, staring up at the sky through leaves. A flock of birds flew overhead in perfect formation.

"What is?"

"I guess you didn't need me in the end." Ava looked back to Gwen, suddenly a little shy, a little insecure.

"Oh, I wouldn't say that." Gwen said nothing for a long while, and Ava thought that might be the end of the conversation, until, "Without you, my lion-hearted son might not have found his courage. You inspire people, Ava." Gwen's voice was filled with warmth that Ava was only beginning to understand was because of her. "You always have."

"Did you practice that line?" Ava asked, not even trying to hide her smile now.

Gwen raised an eyebrow and mimicked Ava's earlier retort. "Did it work?"

"Oh, yeah."

Ava leaned closer, giving in to that ever-present magnetic pull. Gwen sighed against her, no hesitation, no walls. Everything they had ever been to each other—assistant, boss, mentor, student, lover, equal—all seemed to lead to this place. She tried to articulate this with a kiss, tried to tell Gwen everything she felt, everything that seemed too big, too complex to vocalize. She kissed Gwen and thought of words like "belonging" and "home."

She kissed Gwen and felt as if things lost had been found.

"Come on," Gwen breathed, pulling away just slightly before linking her fingers through Ava's and leading the way inside. Ava didn't ask where they were going.

In truth, it didn't matter. Anywhere with Gwen was exactly where she needed to be.

ABOUT ALEX K. THORNE

Alex K. Thorne graduated from university in Cape Town, South Africa with a healthy love of the classics and a degree in English Literature.

She assumed that this entitled her to a future of pretentious garden parties, while drinking fancy tea and debating which Brontë sister was the wackiest (Emily, obvs).

Instead, she spent the next few years, teaching across the globe, from Serbia to South Korea, where she spent her days writing fanfiction and developing a kimchi addiction.

When she's not picking away at her latest writing project, she's immersing herself in geek culture, taking too many pictures of the cats and dreaming about where next to travel.

CONNECT WITH ALEX
Website: www.alexkthorne.com
Facebook: www.facebook.com/AlexKThorneAuthor
E-Mail: alexandra.k.thorne@gmail.com

OTHER BOOKS FROM
YLVA PUBLISHING

www.ylva-publishing.com

SHATTERED

(The Superheroine Collection)

Lee Winter

ISBN: 978-3-95533-563-2
Length: 194 pages (69,000 words)

Shattergirl, Earth's first lesbian guardian is refusing to save people and has gone off the grid. Lena Martin, the street-smart tracker with a silver tongue and a disdain for the rogue guardians she chases, has only days to bring her home. As the pair clash heatedly, masks begin to crack and brutal secrets are exposed that could shatter them both.

THE POWER OF MERCY

(The Superheroine Collection)

Fiona Zedde

ISBN: 978-3-95533-854-1
Length: 113 pages (37,000 words)

To her family, Mai Redstone is weak. When she becomes Mercy, a rooftop-climbing chameleon with at least nine lives, she finds her power. But when Mercy is called in by police to a murder case, her whole world threatens to crumble. The dead man made her childhood a hell. She is torn between giving the murderer a medal and finding the killer for her family. Mercy is a blade that can cut both ways.

THE LILY AND THE CROWN

Roslyn Sinclair

ISBN: 978-3-95533-942-5
Length: 263 pages (87,000 words)

Young botanist Ari lives an isolated life on a space station, tending a lush garden in her quarters. When an imperious woman is captured from a pirate ship and given to her as a slave, Ari's ordered life shatters. Her slave is watchful, smart, and sexy, and seems to know an awful lot about tactics, star charts, and the dread pirate queen, Mir.

A lesbian romance about daring to risk your heart.

SURVIAL INSTINCTS

May Dawney

ISBN: 978-3-95533-934-0
Length: 358 pages (133,000 words)

Civilization has fallen. Lynn, alone in the debris of a world reclaimed by nature and hiding from the threat of man, is forced to go on a dangerous journey through decaying New York City. As Lynn's feelings for her guard, Dani, grow, she's forced to face her belief that staying alone is the only way to survive.

A fast-paced dystopian adventure where love trumps instinct.

Chasing Stars
© 2018 by Alex K. Thorne

ISBN: 978-3-95533-992-0

Also available as e-book.

Published by Ylva Publishing, legal entity of Ylva Verlag, e.Kfr.
Ylva Verlag, e.Kfr.
Owner: Astrid Ohletz
Am Kirschgarten 2
65830 Kriftel
Germany

www.ylva-publishing.com

First edition: 2018

Credits
Edited by Lee Winter and Alissa McGown
Cover Design and Print Layout by Streetlight Graphics